Lucky Star

By Allie Everhart

Lucky Star
By Allie Everhart

CHAPTER ONE

Star

Luck. You either have it or you don't.

I don't. But that might be starting to change, with the exception of my car which completely died this morning.

But I'm trying to look on the bright side. And on the bright side I'm starting a job today. A real job where I'll finally make decent money. And I have my own apartment now. Well, it's not mine. I live there with some guy and his girlfriend but at least I'm no longer living in my parents' basement. I'm finally on my own, in a new city, with a new job.

So yeah, things are going well, except for the fact that I have to bike to work today. But hey, it's good exercise, right? I've heard positive thinking leads to positive results so I figure if I keep looking on the bright side, my luck will keep changing for the better.

Something wet hits my face. I ignore it and keep riding my bike, a hand-me-down from my brother. It's a blue ten speed that's rusted because he always left it outside. I wasn't going to move it here but at the last minute I decided to take it just in case my car gave out. Good thing I did or I might've missed my first day on the job, which could've meant losing the job, which can't happen. I really need this job.

Another drop of wetness hits my face, then another. I glance up at the sky. It's clouding over and getting dark. It better not rain. I'm wearing brand new black dress pants that ate up a good chunk of my pitiful savings.

A drop hits me right in the eye. It burns and stings and blurs my vision.

1

"Shit," I mutter, blinking repeatedly as I pedal faster.

Thunder booms from above and the few drops of rain become a steady downpour.

"Seriously?" I yell at the sky as the thunder booms again. "You couldn't give me a break today? Just one lousy break?"

I'm almost at work. If I'd left just a few minutes earlier I would've beat the storm but how was I to know it was going to rain? I don't watch the weather.

My new pants are getting soaked and sticking to my legs. At least my blouse is covered by my jacket, but the sleeves are riding up as I grip the handlebars. I can already feel the water seeping up my arms. Damn! Why didn't I leave earlier?

I'm approaching a stoplight and see the countdown on the walk button. It has eight seconds left. If I hurry I can make it across the street. The office is just a block away. I'm ten minutes early. I'll get there, run to the restroom and use the hand dryer to dry my clothes.

I hunch down and pedal faster, my eyes focused on the countdown timer, which is now at five seconds. As I enter the intersection I'm hit by a force so strong it launches me from my bike. Thunder claps, and for a moment I think I might've been struck by lightning.

My body lands in the street with a thud, my head hitting hard against the wet pavement. I see stars, then my vision fades in and out. I hear yelling but it sounds distant, like an echo.

Cars start honking and I hear a man's voice.

"Miss, are you okay?" he asks.

I feel him next to me but can't see him. My eyes are closed. I feel like I'm falling asleep.

"Talk to me," he says. "Tell me where it hurts."

Pain shoots through my head and remains there, throbbing, getting worse by the second.

Cars start honking and someone yells, "Get out of the damn street!"

It's followed by more honking and then someone yells, "She's been hit!"

Voices start chattering all around me. I feel people there but can't see them. My eyelids are heavy. Too heavy to open.

"Stay back," the man beside me yells. I feel him covering me with something. Maybe a jacket?

It all seems to be happening in slow motion. It feels like I'm not really here. Like I'm just watching from afar. Am I dead?

"Miss, can you tell me where it hurts?" the man next to me asks, but I'm unable to answer. Instead I moan a little as my head falls to the side.

Warm strong hands slip under my neck and I hear the man again. "Don't move. You don't want to damage your spine."

His hands move to the side of my head, holding it in place.

"I'm so sorry." His voice is soft and steady but I can hear his concern. Why is he worried? What's wrong with me? Am I dying?

"You're going to be okay," he says, which makes me wonder if I asked the question out loud. I don't think I did. I can barely open my eyes so I doubt I was able to talk. "The ambulance is on its way."

The man's hand continues to hold my head in place while his other hand reaches down and wraps around mine. "I know you're scared but I'm right here. I won't leave you. I promise." He lightly squeezes my hand. "Just stay with me, okay?"

My eyes try to flutter open but can't. It's like they've been weighted down.

"Stay with me," I hear the man say as he clutches my hand. "They're almost here." I hear him exhale a long heavy breath. "God, I'm so sorry. I'm so, so sorry."

CHAPTER TWO

Earlier that Morning

Corbin

Lauren comes out of the bathroom wrapped in a towel, using another one to blot the water from her long blond hair.

"We need to be at my parents' house by six on Saturday," she says. "We can't be late. They want to leave at seven to beat the traffic."

"There's no traffic on a Saturday morning," I say, going past her to the bathroom. I shut the door but she continues to talk.

"It doesn't matter if there's traffic or not," I hear her say from the bedroom. "You know how my father is. He'll be very upset if we don't stick to the plan."

Lauren's the same way. She has a plan for everything and trying to veer from that plan just leads to arguments, which is one of the many reasons we argue so much.

Not responding to her comment, I pick up my razor and run it along the side of my face, then rinse it in the sink, turning the water on all the way.

"I'll pack your bag when I get home tomorrow," she says. "I'll be packing your navy suit for dinner and I'm going shopping to get you a new tie."

4

She's bought me at least twenty ties. I have so many I can't even wear them all. I don't even like ties. Even when I wear them loose I still feel like I'm being choked. Lauren knows this and yet she still buys me ties, then tries to make me feel guilty if I don't wear them.

"On the way there you should wear the khakis and your green polo shirt," she says. "Oh, and wear those new loafers Mother got you. You know the ones that match Father's?"

Lauren's mother bought me shoes. Stuffy old man loafers that are the same kind her father wears. As if it's not bad enough my girlfriend tries to dress me, now her mother's doing it too.

"And don't think for one second you're bringing those sneakers you love so much," she says, raising her voice to make sure I can hear her over the running water. "I can't believe you tried to wear those to dinner last week with John and Liz. Honestly, Corbin, sometimes I just don't understand you."

It isn't just sometimes. She *never* understands me. Never has. Because she doesn't listen. When I try to tell her what I think or how I feel, she interrupts and talks about something else. She doesn't want to know the real me. If she did, she wouldn't be with me. The Corbin she knows is the one she wants me to be. The one who likes wearing ties, and shoes that match her father's. The one who likes taking weekend trips with her parents and putting on a suit for what's supposed to be a casual dinner with friends.

None of those things are me. They should be, given my upbringing, but they're not. And nobody, not even my own family, accepts that, which is why Lauren and I started dating in the first place. I did what was expected of me. I chose a rich, intelligent, career-driven woman who comes from a good family.

Given that criteria, I could've picked someone else. There are plenty of other women in the Boston area who have those characteristics. But I chose Lauren because I already knew her. Our families have been friends for as long as I can remember.

Lauren was my first kiss. I was fifteen. She was fourteen. Our families took us on a summer trip to Nantucket and one night we were alone on the beach and I kissed her. It wasn't great but it made me feel closer to her. We'd shared something special that no one else knew about, and although we didn't date after that, we kept in touch. She went to a different school but we'd meet up now and then, just to hang out.

We started dating in med school. Back then I didn't see her as my parents' choice. I knew they'd approve of her but that wasn't the reason I asked her out. I did it because she's beautiful, extremely smart, and I admired her ambition. And we had similar goals, or at least I thought we did. In reality, the only thing we had in common is that we both wanted to be doctors. Our differences didn't start to show up until we'd dated a few months but I ignored them because I wanted it to work between Lauren and me. It made sense for us to be together, and our families loved that we were a couple. They've been talking about us getting married for years. We're not even engaged and her mother is already buying bridal magazines.

Lauren's mother will be furious when she finds out about the breakup. My father will be too. But I can't do this anymore. I can't keep pretending everything's great between Lauren and me when it's not. I can't keep telling myself I love her when I don't.

Our relationship's been over for a long time but I haven't been able to end it. Every time I try, I tell myself I need to give it more time. Or I make excuses for why we're not getting along, like the fact that we both work a lot and never see each other.

Work definitely puts a strain on our relationship but even if that wasn't an issue, we still wouldn't get along. We're too different. We want different things. And at this point, neither of us is invested enough in this relationship to keep it going. It's not that I haven't tried. I've read books. Read relationship advice online. I've even asked Lauren to go to couple's counseling, which caused a huge fight because she assumed I was trying to tell her there's something wrong with her.

That wasn't it at all. I suggested counseling because I thought it would help us communicate better. Figure out how to talk to each other so we could stop arguing so much. But Lauren refused, and now, whenever we start to argue, she changes the subject or leaves the room. She's decided to deal with conflict by avoiding it, which has only made things worse.

The bathroom door swings open and Lauren appears, now dressed in a black skirt and beige blouse, her hand on her hip. "Corbin, are you even listening to me?"

"I have to get ready," I tell her as I slide the razor over my chin.

She huffs. "Like I don't? I still have to do my hair and you won't even let me use the bathroom."

"There's another bathroom down the hall."

"Then YOU use it. I need this one. All my products are in here." She pushes past me to open a cabinet.

This is my apartment, not hers. I never asked her to move in. She just did it, gradually bringing her things over and leaving them here, hoping I wouldn't notice. When I called her on it, she said it made more sense for her to live here because it's closer to the hospital where we work. I didn't argue with her because I thought living together could be our final test to see if this relationship could be salvaged. Unfortunately, it just proved once again how incompatible we are and confirmed my decision to end things.

"We need a new place," Lauren says as she runs a glossy liquid through her hair. My bathroom cabinets are overflowing with her hair products and make-up. I barely have room for my stuff.

"This is my grandfather's place." I tap the water off my razor and place it in the one drawer I have left since Lauren took all the others. "I'm not moving."

"Your grandfather could rent it to someone else," she says, leaning forward to inspect her eyebrows in the mirror. She's obsessed with her eyebrows. She's always plucking them, combing them, then plucking them again. "We need a place that's ours. A place we both pick out."

Both? I almost laugh. If we were choosing a new place I'd have no say in it.

"I have to get dressed." I walk out of the bathroom to the bedroom and go to the closet. I hear the blowdryer turn on as I change into my pants and dress shirt.

Just as I'm about to leave, the blowdryer shuts off and Lauren storms into the room, her hands on her hips.

"I'm so sick of you not listening to my concerns."

"Lauren, I—"

"Don't you even CONSIDER how I feel living in a place that's not mine?" She steps closer to me, her eyes narrowed. "I'm not even going to ask you anymore, Corbin. I'm just going to do it. I'm going to go out next week and find us a new place."

"Good idea," I say, folding my arms over my chest. "But I'm not going with you."

I hadn't planned to do this today, and definitely not now, when I need to be heading to work, but it can't wait. I can't take another day of this.

"Of course you're going," she says. "And you're going to like whatever I pick out."

"I'm not going." I look her in the eye. "Lauren, I'm sorry but I can't do this anymore."

"Do what?" she snaps.

"This. The constant arguing. Being told what to do. What to wear. I can't do it anymore."

"What the hell are you talking about?"

"I'm done. This relationship is over. It has been for a long time but neither one of us wanted to admit it."

"You can't be serious," she says with a laugh. "We're getting married, Corbin. My mother's already looking at wedding invitations."

"Which she shouldn't be doing. We've never even talked about marriage."

"Because we don't need to. We've been dating for years. We live together. The next step is to get married. It doesn't need to be said."

"I'm sorry but it's not going to happen. It's not what I want. And I don't think you do either."

She shakes her head really fast. "I don't have time for this. Go to work and we'll talk about this later." She storms off to the bathroom and slams the door.

"Lauren." I walk across the room and knock on the bathroom door. "Lauren, I'm serious. I've thought about this a lot. I've tried to make it work with us but it's just not. We need to end this." I try the door handle but it's locked. "Lauren, open the door."

The hair dryer turns on. She's tuning me out. Giving me the silent treatment because she refuses to talk about this or even acknowledge what I said. Once again, it's all about her. She doesn't care what I want.

There's no use trying to talk to her now. I'll have to try again tonight. Knowing Lauren, it'll take several tries before she finally listens to me and moves out.

I walk over to the nightstand, grab my phone and leave. On my way to the hospital, I hit traffic that's worse than usual. It's raining and traffic always gets worse when it rains.

My phone rings and I see it's my father calling. I answer it. "Hey, I'm on my way into work."

"Yes, this won't take long. I was just calling to ask what time you and Lauren will be back on Sunday. Helen wants us all to go out for dinner. We haven't seen you two in almost three weeks now."

"Sorry, work's been crazy. More for Lauren than for me. She's had to work double shifts."

I finished my residency last year and now work at the urgent care clinic that's connected to the hospital. The job has regular hours so I can actually have a life as opposed to all those years of med school when I never had free time. Lauren's in the last year of her residency so she works constantly.

"I'm sure you'll both be glad when she's done," my father says. "I assume that's when you'll propose?" His voice lifts slightly, which indicates he's telling me what he expects me to do. He always phrases it like a question but his tone implies the answer is already decided for me. But what he wants isn't going to happen.

I can't get into this now. I need to tell him about Lauren and me but I'll do it later. And in person.

"Dad, let's talk tomorrow. I need to get to work."

"Son, I need to know a timeline here. Helen and Eve are planning a summer gathering to celebrate your engagement and they need to book a venue soon."

Helen is my stepmother. She's almost as bad as Eve, Lauren's mom, when it comes to making plans for me without asking. For the most part, we get along, except for when she does stuff like go behind my back and plan an engagement party when I'm not even engaged.

"Tell them to hold off," I say, turning my wipers on as the rain comes down harder.

"Why? Are you and Lauren fighting again?"

Even my father knows how much we fight. Lauren and I used to reserve our fights for when we were alone but they became such a regular part of our relationship that we started arguing in front of our parents. Now we argue more than we don't, and yet our parents still think we should get married.

"Let's talk about it later," I say, trying to merge into the other lane.

"You didn't break up, did you?"

I might as well tell him. Then he can tell Helen, who will tell Eve, and by the time I get home tonight the whole family will know.

"Yes. Lauren and I broke up."

"Well, obviously, you'll get over it. You always do."

"Not this time. We're done for good. I told her this morning."

"So this was YOUR decision, not hers?"

"Yes, but neither one of us is happy. All we do is fight. It needed to end."

"Corbin, you're being rash. You had a fight and you're angry. Give yourself time to cool off and you'll feel differently."

"We didn't fight. That's not what this is about. I've given this a lot of thought and I just can't see us together in the future."

"Of course you can. You and Lauren will get married, have successful careers, a couple children. Perhaps buy a house near your father. I can see it plain as day. And if I can see it, you can as well."

"You don't understand. I don't want that with Lauren. Marriage? Children? A house? I don't want it."

"You don't want children?" He huffs. "I expect grandchildren, Corbin. More than one."

"It's not that I don't want a family someday. I just don't want it with Lauren."

"You're clearly angry with her but you'll get over it. You just need to give it time."

"I've already given it time. I've given it years and my feelings haven't changed. I don't love her. And I'm not staying with someone I don't love." I turn into the other lane. "Dad, I really have to go. Traffic's bad and I'm late to work."

"This isn't over. We'll discuss this later," he says in a harsh tone, then hangs up.

The phone rings again and I answer it, thinking it's the office calling.

"I'm almost there," I say.

"Corbin!" I hear her shrill voice and realize it's Lauren. Shit. I shouldn't have answered.

"Lauren, I can't talk now. I'm in heavy traffic and trying to get to work."

11

"How DARE you try to break up with me!" she yells. "Do you have any idea how lucky you are to be with a woman like me?"

"We're not talking about this now. I—"

"You are NOT ending this, Corbin. We are getting married and you will propose to me this weekend at a dinner hosted by YOUR mother on Sunday night. I've already told her we'll be there."

"You what?" I slam on the brakes, almost hitting the car in front of me. "Lauren, this is one of the many reasons this has to end. You do things without even asking me."

"I don't have to ASK your permission to do things."

"You do when it's planning a dinner in which I'm supposed to propose!" I say, raising my voice. "You can't seriously tell me you don't see what's wrong with that?"

"We can't keep waiting on our engagement. Mother needs to reserve a room for our party, which we've tentatively decided will be in June."

"Tell your mother there isn't going to be a party," I say, clenching the steering wheel. "We are NOT getting engaged. It's over, Lauren. I'm not going to change my mind about this. It's not working and I don't want to do this anymore."

She's quiet, then says, "Who is she?"

"What? Who?"

"The woman you're seeing," she snaps. "Who is she?"

"I'm not seeing another woman. I'm not cheating on you. This isn't about that. It's about our relationship needing to end. Lauren, I don't want to keep talking about this. There's nothing more to say. You can take your time moving out but we're not going to be together. I'll sleep in the guest room until you find a new place."

"You're not doing this," she snaps. "I'm NOT moving out."

"I have to go." I end the call, too angry to keep talking to her. She really thinks I'd cheat on her? I'm not that type of guy. Never have been, which she would know if she actually took time to get to know me in all the years we've dated.

My phone dings with a reminder to call and check about a patient's test results. Working in urgent care, I usually only see patients once for whatever they came in for, then refer them to their regular doctor to handle any follow-up care. But in this case I wanted to follow up myself.

I call the radiology department.

"Hey, Jim," I say when he answers. "It's Corbin. Just checking in on the Raynor girl. You get a chance to review the scans yet?"

"Yeah," he says with a sigh, "and it doesn't look good."

I rub my jaw, which is still tight from talking to Lauren. "I was afraid you were going to say that. How bad is it?"

"There's definitely a mass in her lungs. And there's more, farther down in her abdomen."

I blow out a breath. "Have you told her pediatrician?"

"Not yet. I will when he gets in. Sorry I couldn't give you better news."

"It's part of the job. I just wish I'd been wrong about it. She's so young."

The patient is a five-year-old girl that came in last week with what her mom thought was bronchitis. I could tell when I examined her it was more than that. I told her mom I wanted to run some tests, trying not to alarm her, but when I mentioned a CT scan I saw the fear in her eyes. She knew what I was looking for and now I've confirmed it. Her daughter has cancer.

"Corbin, I need to go," Jim says. "I've got another doctor on the other line."

"Yeah, go ahead. And thanks for the fast turnaround."

"You bet." He ends the call.

Cancer. The little girl with the pink dress and blond hair, smiling and showing me her stuffed unicorn, has cancer. Her mother will find out today, and from that moment on, everything will change. Their lives will never be the same.

It's frightening how life can change that quickly and yet, as a doctor, it's a reality I live with every day. It's why I can't stay in a relationship with someone I don't love. And why I can't keep

13

pretending to be someone I'm not. I wish my family understood that but they don't and never will so I need to stop waiting for that to happen and just live my life.

I haven't even considered what that life will be. For so many years I pictured the life my father wanted for me. The one Lauren had planned for me. As for what I wanted myself, I'm still figuring that out.

The rain continues to pour and the traffic isn't moving. I'm already ten minutes late to work and I'm guessing it'll be another ten minutes before I get there. I text the nurse to let her know.

Someone honks and I look up and see a car turning down a side street with less traffic. I decide to do the same. I turn on my signal and as soon as the car in front of me inches forward, I sneak around him to the other lane.

Just as I'm about to turn, I see something in front of me. Before I can hit the brakes, my front bumper slams into a bike and I watch in horror as a small body is thrown up in the air, then back down, landing on the street in front of my car.

"Oh God!" I shut off the car and jump out.

My heart pounding, I race in front of my car and see her on the ground. A young woman dressed in black pants and a black jacket. She's on her back, her legs twisted, her arms extended out, her head on the wet pavement.

"Miss!" I kneel down beside her as I get my phone out to call for an ambulance. "Miss, are you okay?" I take her wrist and check her pulse. It's strong but she doesn't seem to be conscious.

The emergency operator answers and I tell her where to send the ambulance. Then I tell her I'm a doctor and give her my initial assessment of the girl, although without running tests, it's hard to be sure of her injuries.

As I end the call people gather around me, all shouting questions.

"What happened?"

"Is she dead?"

14

"Did you call an ambulance?"

I keep my focus on the girl, checking her head and neck for injuries that could lead to paralysis.

I can't believe this is happening. I can't believe I did this! I'm always such a careful driver. I always check before I turn, but I didn't this time. I didn't even look. My mind was still on that little girl, and I was angry about Lauren, and frustrated with my father. And then the rain. It was fogging up my windows.

I didn't see her. I should have, but I didn't.

She's hurt. I don't know how much yet but she's definitely hurt. She could be paralyzed. She could be paralyzed and it'd be all my fault.

What the hell have I done?

CHAPTER THREE

Star

"I don't know," a man says in a hushed voice. "I'll call you later."

I hear him getting up, followed by the sound of footsteps as he walks away.

Where am I? Last I remember I was lying on the ground. There were people all around me, yelling, asking questions. Cars were honking. And there was a man beside me. He wrapped his hand around my mine and held it in a strong yet gentle way that, along with his deep soothing voice, calmed me as I laid there, scared and confused, having no clue what was going on. He asked me to stay with him. I wasn't sure what he meant.

My eyelids feel weighted down and I struggle to open them. After several tries I manage to pry them apart enough to see myself lying in a bed, covered in a sheet.

I'm covered in a sheet? Am I dead?

When I try to sit up, pain shoots through shoulder, my arm, my back, down to my leg.

"Ugh," I moan as I lie back down.

"Star?" a man rushes up beside me. He has his phone to his ear and says, "She just woke up. I have to go."

I open my eyes wider to see him. He looks like he hasn't slept in a while. Or shaved. Or combed his hair.

He sits beside me on the bed. "How are you feeling?"

My foggy brain struggles to figure out how I got here. Why can't I remember?

"What happened?" I ask but it doesn't sound like me. My voice is low and hoarse, like when I have a bad cold. Actually, I kind of feel like I have a cold. My head's congested and I have a sore throat.

"You were hit while riding your bike," the guy says. "It was pretty bad but considering what could've happened...well, you were lucky."

Who is this guy? Do I know him? I can't know him. I've lived in Boston for less than a week. I don't know anyone but my roommates, who I've only seen a few times since moving in.

"I got hit on my bike?" I try to sit up but pain shoots from my ribs, making me wince.

"Don't get up." He gently places his hands on my shoulders and coaxes me back down on the pillow. "You need to rest. "

"What's going on? What's wrong with me?"

He sits back, folding his arms over his chest. "You have a concussion, stitches near your eye and on your knee, swelling and bruising along your shoulder, arm and back and swelling around your ribcage. As I said, it could've been much worse but even so, it's too soon for you to be getting up. We need to run some more tests and then—"

"*We?* Who's *we?* Are you the—"

Before I can finish, the door swings open and a nurse walks in. "Dr. Sterling, Dr. Miller will be here shortly."

The guy next to me stands up as the nurse walks over and checks the beeping machine next to my bed.

"She woke up a few minutes ago," the guy says to the nurse. "She doesn't seem to remember what happened but that's to be expected."

So this guy's my doctor? He looks too young to be doctor. I'm 23 and he looks like he's only a few years older than me.

He's wearing black pants and a white dress shirt with the sleeves rolled up. Both the shirt and the pants are really wrinkled. Shouldn't a doctor be in scrubs or a lab coat or at least be wearing clothes that aren't so wrinkled?

The nurse, a young petite blonde wearing pink scrubs with hearts all over them, records something in her tablet, then looks at me with a sad smile. "How are you feeling?"

"Not great," I mutter.

Her smile brightens. "We'll have you feeling better in no time." She winks at the guy next to me. "Dr. Sterling will make sure of it."

"Thanks, Shannon." He gives her a smile as she leaves.

He has a nice smile. It goes well with his face, which is very symmetrical. I took an art class a few years ago where we learned how to draw faces and the teacher said a truly symmetrical face is very rare. Most people have uneven eyes or a nose that's a little off or a crooked mouth, but this guy has everything aligned perfectly. And he has beautiful eyes; a deep rich brown that match his thick, dark brown hair. He's really hot for a doctor. Not that doctors can't be good looking. I've just never seen one this good looking in real life.

"So you're my doctor?" I ask.

Before he can answer, a man walks in. It's an older man with gray hair, wearing a lab coat.

"How's our patient?" the man asks Dr. Sterling. It feels weird to call him that. He doesn't seem old enough for that title.

"She's experiencing some discomfort," Sterling says to the man in a very formal, professional tone. "And she's having trouble remembering what happened."

"That's to be expected," the other doctor says. He's beside me now and asks, "Do you know your name?"

"Yes. It's Star."

His brows rise. "Last name?"

"Jenkins. Star Jenkins."

He smiles. "Interesting name. One you don't hear very often."

"Actually Jenkins is pretty common," I kid, knowing he's referring to my first name. "Like Jones or Smith."

He laughs a little and looks over at Dr. Sterling. "Her sense of humor is intact. That's a good sign." He looks back at me. "I'm Dr. Miller. I'll be taking care of you until you're released. Now that you're awake and alert, we'll need to collect some information about you, such as the name of your personal physician."

"I don't have one," I say. "I just moved here."

"Well, we'll at least need your insurance information but we can worry about that later."

Insurance. I don't have insurance. How am I going to pay for this?

And then I remember, I *do* have insurance. It's through my new job. That's where I was going when I was hit. I have a job. It was my first day. Shit! I missed my first day!

"I need my phone," I say, frantically searching the room for it.

"Relax," Sterling says, coming around beside me and putting his hand on my arm. "Getting agitated will just make your head hurt more."

"But I need to call my boss!" I say, coughing through the words. "I missed work!"

"You won't be going to work for a while," Dr. Miller says. "You need to recover from your injuries and get over that cold."

So it IS a cold. How did this happen? Everything was going great. I was finally living on my own with a real job. And now I'm in a hospital bed with a broken body and a cold.

Maybe if I call and explain to my boss what happened, she'd be okay that I missed a day.

"How long have I been here?" I ask.

"They brought you in yesterday morning," Sterling says. "So about a day."

It's a whole new day? I'm missing another day of work! I'm going to get fired!

"I've ordered some more tests to be run later this morning," Dr. Miller says. "Until then, try to eat something and get some rest."

He leaves the room but Sterling remains.

"I need my phone," I say, making grabby hands at him as though he's hiding it somewhere on him.

"I don't have it," he says. "It's at the nurses' station. They're keeping it in case someone calls."

"In case? You mean no one's called?"

"Uh, no, not yet," he says as if not wanting to imply I'm a loser that nobody noticed was missing even though that's probably what he's thinking. Whatever. I don't care. I just need my phone.

"Could you go tell the nurse I need it back?"

"Let's wait until we get your tests run. It'll only take an hour or so."

"You don't understand. Yesterday was my first day on the job and I didn't show up. If I don't tell my boss what happened I'll be fired and I really need this job."

"I'm sure he'll understand." Sterling sits beside me. "I'll talk to him myself if it helps."

"It's not a him, it's a her, and she's very strict about being on time. My friend, Haley, showed up two minutes late one time and almost got fired. And that was after she'd worked there a year. This lady doesn't tolerate people not showing up. I have to call her. It can't wait."

"Star, I really don't think—"

"Please." I put my hand on his arm and look him in the eye. "I'm begging you. Let me call her. I can't afford to lose this job."

He looks at me a moment, then nods. "Okay, but keep it short." He stands up. "While you're at it, you should call your parents and anyone else who needs to know what happened. They'll want to know you're okay."

"My parents don't need to know. But I'll call Haley and tell her what happened. I'm surprised she hasn't called yet but she did just start a new job so she's really busy."

Sterling's brows draw together. "You're not going to tell your parents?"

"Why would I? I'm 23. I'm an adult. I don't tell my parents everything."

"Maybe not, but this is something they should know."

"Trust me, it wouldn't make a difference. It's not like they're going to drive all the way to Boston to check on me."

"Where do they live?"

"Worcester."

"That's not that far. I'm sure they'd make the drive."

"You don't know my parents. Now could you get me the phone, please?"

He leaves the room and returns with my phone. He hands it to me and I see the screen is cracked. It must've happened during the accident. It'll have to stay that way. I don't have money for a new one.

"I'll get that fixed," Sterling says, noticing my concern over the cracked screen. "Or I'll just get you a new phone."

"Why would you get me a phone?" I ask, giving him a confused look.

My phone rings. It's Haley.

"Haley, I was just about to call you."

"Star, what the hell happened? Sandra just called and said you didn't show up to work yesterday. She said you didn't even call. She gave the job to someone else."

"What? No!" I sit up, cringing from the pain. "She can't give the job away! I need that job! It's the only reason I moved here."

"Star, you can't not show up to work and expect to keep the job. What happened? Why didn't you go?"

"It's a long story but basically my car died and I had to take my bike to work and I was almost there but then a car hit me and I ended up in the hospital."

"Oh my God, are you okay?"

21

"Yes. I mean, kind of. I have a concussion and some stitches and bruises and stuff but otherwise I'm okay. I need to call Sandra and explain. I'll call her right now and then call you back."

"It's too late. She gave the job to someone else."

"But if I explained what happened, maybe she'd reconsider. I at least need to try. I'll call you later, okay?"

"Yeah. And hey, I hope you feel better. Sorry I can't be there with you."

"Just send me one of your e-cards. That'll cheer me up."

Haley sends e-cards for any occasion, or no occasion at all. She just likes sending cards, especially animated ones with dogs or cats doing funny things.

"Let me know how it goes," she says. "Love you! Bye!"

I immediately find Sandra's number in my phone and call her.

"Sandra Caldwell's office," a guy says. "How can I assist you?"

That's the guy who got my job! I should be the one answering the phone, not him.

"Could I speak with Sandra, please?"

"Who may I ask is calling?"

"It's Star." I glance over at Dr. Sterling, who's standing at the window looking at his phone. Why is he still here? Doesn't he have other patients to see?

"Star who?" the guy on the phone asks.

"Star Jenkins."

He sighs. "I'll put you through but make it quick. She has a meeting in five minutes."

He's not very friendly. I'd make a much better assistant.

"This is Sandra," she says in a curt tone.

"Sandra, hi." I race the words out before she hangs up. "I just wanted to explain what happened yesterday. My car broke down and I had to bike to work and when I went to cross the street, someone hit me and I had to go to the hospital. I wasn't able to call until—"

"Who is this?" she snaps.

"It's Star, your new assistant?" I shouldn't have said it like a question. I should've just acted like the job is mine. Haley said Sandra likes confident, assertive people. "I missed work because I'm in the hospital but I'll be there tomorrow. I promise."

Sterling appears beside me, a stern look on his face as he shakes his head. I ignore him. I'm injured and sick, but not enough to keep me from working. I just have to sit at a desk and answer phones. I can handle that.

"The job has been given to someone else," Sandra says.

"But I didn't do this on purpose. I swear! I was almost there. I was even early and then—"

"I don't have time for this. The job belongs to someone else. Goodbye, Star." She hangs up.

I sigh as I lie back on the pillow. "She gave someone else the job."

Sterling takes the phone from me. "Let me call her. I'll explain your condition and why you couldn't be there."

"I already told her all that and she didn't care. She's not going to give me the job. It's someone else's now."

"If I tell her it was impossible for you to be there, I'm sure she'll understand. She can't be that unreasonable."

"Believe me, she is. Ask Haley. She hated working for Sandra but the job pays really well so she put up with her." I cough, wincing from the pain it's causing my ribs. "I really needed that job. I'm out of money, my car is broke and—" I cough again and sit up. "I have to get out of here." I shove the sheet back.

Sterling yanks it back over me. "You're not going anywhere until you've been cleared to leave."

"I can't. I don't..." I look away, tears threatening to fall. I don't usually cry so maybe it's the meds. Or maybe it's because I feel so hopeless right now.

I feel Sterling's hand on my arm as he softly asks, "You don't what?"

"I don't um..." I look down. "I don't have insurance. And I don't have money. I can't pay for this. I'm sure I've already racked up thousands of dollars in bills and I can't pay for it. I can't stay here."

"Don't worry about it." He sits next to me. "It's all taken care of."

My eyes goes to his. "What do you mean?"

"Insurance will cover it."

"But I just told you, I don't have insurance."

"There's coverage under the car insurance. Coverage for medical costs."

"Oh." I pause a moment, thinking back to the accident. "I don't even know who hit me. It happened so fast I didn't have a chance to look at the car or see who was driving it."

He looks down. "About that."

"About what? Do you know who it was?"

His eyes go back to mine. "It was me. I was the one who hit you."

CHAPTER FOUR

Star

"You're the one who hit me?" I ask. "Why didn't you tell me?"

"I did, but then you acted like I didn't so—

"When did you tell me?"

"When you were awake earlier."

"I was awake?"

"You woke up several times but not for long. The pain meds made you drowsy and really out of it. I'm not surprised you don't remember us talking."

"I don't even remember waking up." I pause to see if I can recall anything from the past twenty-four hours, but the last thing I remember is lying on the ground with some guy holding my hand.

"Was that you?" I ask.

His brows furrow. "What do you mean?"

"On the street. The guy sitting beside me, holding my hand. That was you, right?"

He nods. "As soon as I realized what happened, I raced out of my car to see if you were okay. I called for help and stayed with you until the ambulance arrived. I would've gone with you to the hospital but the police had me stay and fill out an accident report. They'll want to talk to you as well, when you're able to."

"Why?"

"In case you want to...you know." He hesitates. "Press charges."

"Press charges?"

"I understand if you do."

"I don't want to press charges. I mean, it was an accident, right? It's not like you hit me on purpose."

"Yes, but still. I should've been more cautious. It's just that I was running late and had a lot on my mind and—" He stops suddenly and shakes his head. "Forget all that. It's no excuse for what I did. I should've been more careful."

"So what exactly happened? Because all I remember is seeing the walk signal counting down, then next thing I know I'm being thrown off my bike."

He sighs. "I'm so sorry. I didn't even see you. I was turning right on a red and looked left but you were coming from the right. I didn't look in time to see you. Plus it was raining and my window was fogged up and—" He sighs again. "I can't tell you enough how sorry I am." He puts his hand over mine. He does that a lot. I wonder if it's something he does with everyone or just with patients. Maybe it's something they teach you in medical school. I don't mind that he does it. Actually, I like it. It's comforting and makes me feel better.

"So are you my doctor?"

"No." He takes his hand off mine and sits back a little. "I *am* a physician but you're not my patient."

"Then why are you here?"

"To make sure you're okay."

I check my phone for the time. "It's ten-fifteen. Don't you need to be at work?"

"I'm taking time off. I took yesterday off as well."

"Because of the accident? Did you get hurt too?"

"No, I'm fine. But I couldn't leave you, knowing what had happened. I had to know you're okay."

I look him over; his wrinkled clothes, messy hair, unshaven face. "Have you been here this whole time?"

"I have. I hope that doesn't make you uncomfortable. I just needed to know you're okay, and being a physician myself, I wanted to make sure you were getting the best care possible. Which you are, by the way. This hospital and its staff are excellent." He grins slightly. "Of course, I could be a little biased given that I work here, but that aside, you really are getting the best possible care. And don't worry about any expenses outside of what my insurance covers. I'll take care of any and all bills."

How would he have the money for that? Med school costs a fortune and there's no way he's paid off his loans already.

I look at him, my head cocked. "How old are you?"

"Let me guess...you think I'm too young to be a doctor," he says with a smile.

I really like his smile. It's sexy. Confident. The rest of him is sexy too. I wonder if he's married. I glance down at his hand. No ring.

"How old do you *think* I am?" he asks.

"I don't know. Maybe 27? 28?"

"Good guess. I'm 28."

"And you're already a doctor? I thought doctors were still in school at your age. Don't you have to do like ten years of school?"

"It's four years of college, three years of med school and a residency. Most people finish their residency at 29 but I started college a year early so I finished my residency last year."

"And you work here at the hospital?"

"Not actually in the hospital but at the clinic that's attached to it. It's the urgent care clinic. We see broken bones, sore throats, and everything in between."

"Huh." I stare at him and he stares back, that slight grin still on his face. I almost feel like he's flirting with me but I'm sure it's just the meds messing with my brain. Why would he flirt with me? He doesn't even know me. I'm just some random girl he hit with his car.

"You're a mess," I blurt out, then realize I said what I was thinking out loud.

Sterling laughs, a deep sexy laugh that matches his sexy smile. "Is it the hair or the clothes? Or am I just a mess in general?"

"Sorry. I didn't mean to say that. I just noticed your wrinkled clothes and blurted it out without thinking. I don't do well with meds. I say stuff I shouldn't."

"I noticed."

"What do you mean?"

He chuckles. "You were pretty talkative earlier."

"I thought I was asleep."

"You've been in and out of sleep, but in the few times you were awake, you were quite talkative."

"I was? What did I say?" I feel my face warming, worried I said something embarrassing.

"It doesn't matter. Like you said, it didn't mean anything. It was the meds talking."

I squeeze my eyes shut. "Oh God, it was bad, wasn't it? Just tell me. I need to know."

He gets up and moves the chair that's next to my bed so that it's facing me. He sits down and rubs his hand over his chin, his eyes on the ceiling. "Well, let's see."

He's purposely drawing this out, making me more and more nervous about what he's going to say.

"Just spit it out, Sterling. I don't have time for this."

"Actually, you have nowhere else to be right now," he says with that perfect smile.

"Just tell me."

He cocks his head. "Why'd you call me Sterling?"

"Because it's your name."

"It's my LAST name."

"Yeah? So? You didn't tell me your first name. Would you rather I call you Doc? Or *Dr.* Sterling?"

"I'd rather have you call me by my name."

"Which is what?"

"Corbin. Corbin Sterling the third."

"The third? Huh. Your family really likes that name."

"It's a legacy thing. I come from a long line of physicians. My father's a heart surgeon, and my grandfather, the first Corbin Sterling, was a brain surgeon."

"Impressive. So why aren't you a surgeon?"

He holds his hand out. "Not steady enough. I played basketball as a kid and broke a finger. It damaged the nerves and it's never quite been the same. If I try to do something that requires a steady hand, this finger starts to shake." He wiggles his index finger.

"That's too bad. I bet the other Corbins were pissed you ruined your chance to continue the legacy," I joke.

He doesn't laugh and I notice his jaw stiffen. "Pissed doesn't even come close to describing how angry they were. After it happened, I never touched a basketball again. My father took it away and banned all sports from then on. He and my grandfather won't even watch basketball on TV. It makes them too angry."

"You're still a doctor. They've gotta be happy about that. It's every parent's dream to have their kid grow up to be a doctor."

"For them, that's not enough. I was supposed to be a heart surgeon like my dad." He shrugs it off. "Enough about me. Tell me about you. You said you're from Worcester?"

"Yeah. Been there my whole life. I moved here for that assistant job but I guess that's not happening now."

"Let me talk to her. She can't be that unreasonable. What happened wasn't your fault. I'm sure I could get her to change her mind."

"You won't change her mind. Besides, she already has someone else, and honestly, I really didn't want to work for her. Haley used to go home crying from that job. She was so stressed her hair was falling out."

29

"And this girl got you the job? Doesn't sound like much of a friend."

"She warned me it'd be bad but I really needed the money so I was willing to put up with Sandra."

"Can I at least try talking to her? That is, if you still want the job. Personally I don't think you should work for someone like that. There's gotta be other jobs out there. Ones without an abusive boss."

"Maybe but they won't pay as well."

"It's not always about money."

"Says the rich doctor. Actually, you're probably poor until you pay off your student loans."

"Don't have any."

"Really?"

"My parents paid for school. So yes, you're correct. I am comfortable financially."

Why can't rich people just say they're rich? Instead they avoid it like it's a dirty word and use phrases like 'comfortable financially'.

"Maybe I could help you get a job," he says. "Is there anything in particular you're interested in?"

"I don't want to talk about that right now. I want to know what I said earlier. Stop changing the subject and just tell me."

A slight smile crosses his face. "I don't think I should."

"Why? Was it that bad? Was I being inappropriate? Using curse words? I'm telling you, it's because of the drugs. It's why I avoid meds of any kind." I sneeze. "Even cold meds." I sniffle.

He hands me a tissue. "You have a cold by the way."

"Yeah, I noticed that." I roll my eyes. "As if getting hit by a car and losing my job wasn't enough. Anyway, going back to what I said, just spit it out."

"Okay, well, when you first woke up you said—"

He stops as the door swings open. A nurse walks in with a wheelchair. "They're ready for you downstairs."

Corbin gets up from his chair.

I point at him. "Don't think this means we won't be finishing this."

He just smiles as he takes the wheelchair from the nurse and moves it beside my bed.

"I'm serious," I tell him. "We're continuing this when I get back."

He helps me stand up. "How do you feel? Dizzy? Lightheaded?"

"I'm fine." I look at him as he helps me in the chair. "You'll still be here, right? When I'm back from the tests?" I hear the desperation in my tone.

I don't even know the guy but I don't want him to leave. If he leaves I'll be alone. I usually don't mind being alone but being alone in the hospital really sucks. And Corbin, because of his training in bedside manner, or just his general personality, makes me feel more relaxed.

"I'll be right here." He gives my hand a squeeze.

"You might want to use this break to take a shower," the nurse says, smiling at Corbin.

"Is it that bad?" he asks, sniffing his shirt.

She laughs. "No, but you've been here since she arrived. And you haven't slept. The shower might at least help wake you up. Why don't you use one of the showers here? There's plenty of extra scrubs to change into."

"That's a good idea." He leans down to me. "I'll clean up and meet you back here."

"Thanks." I feel bad making him stay but I really don't want him to leave.

The nurse starts wheeling me toward the door.

"Wait." I grab Corbin's arm.

He turns back to me. "What is it?"

"What's happening? Where are they taking me? What are they going to do?"

"They'll test your vision. Ask you some questions. They're just trying to assess the severity of your concussion."

"So no needles?"

He smiles. "No needles. And no scary machines. They did all those tests yesterday."

"They did?"

"Yes. You were awake but out of it. That's why you don't remember."

I feel the area next to my eye where he said I got stitches. "Was I asleep when they did this?"

He chuckles. "You were but then you woke up."

"Why are you laughing?"

"Because you smacked the doctor in the head. Actually, you hit him with your fist, right in the eye."

"Oh my God, is he okay?"

"He's fine. Your punch didn't have much strength behind it."

"Still, I feel bad that I hit someone."

Corbin leans down by my ear so the nurse can't hear. "Don't worry about it. You hit Dukin. We went to med school together. I never liked the guy so I'm actually glad you punched him. It made me instantly like you."

I smile. "Okay, well, that makes me feel a little better."

"We need to go," the nurse says.

Corbin looks at me with those deep brown eyes. "Relax. You're going to be fine."

Oddly, I believe him. I don't know why I trust this guy so much and believe what he tells me but for some reason I do.

The nurse whisks me away and we go down a floor to a small exam room. A doctor shows up and takes me through a series of tests to assess my brain health. When I'm done I wait in the room for the nurse to come back and take me upstairs.

She finally arrives and when I get back to my room, it's empty. Corbin isn't there. What if he decided not to come back? What if he got in trouble for missing work and had to leave? Or maybe he just got tired of sitting here with me. I can't believe he's been here since I arrived. And that he hasn't slept.

"You okay?" the nurse asks, probably noticing the slump in my shoulders when I saw Corbin wasn't here.

"I'm just tired."

"Let's get you back into bed so you can rest."

She positions the wheelchair next to the bed and just as she's about to help me, I hear Corbin's voice.

"I've got her," he says.

I look up and see Corbin beside me, that gorgeous smile on his freshly-washed face. He didn't have time to shave but I like his five o'clock shadow. It's hot. And that smile. Damn sexy.

He's changed into scrubs, which I've always thought were ugly but on him? Not ugly. At all. They're short sleeve so his arms are exposed and damn, this guy works out.

"Star?"

My eyes were stuck on his biceps but I quickly revert them back to his face. "Yeah?"

"Let's get you in bed."

I immediately imagine his words meaning something totally different than he intended.

"You okay?" he asks, bending down in front of me.

"Yeah. Why?"

"You got all flushed. Your cheeks are red."

"Really? Huh, that's strange. I feel okay."

My face is red because I was fantasizing about being with him. Why was I thinking about him that way? He's my doctor, or *a* doctor. And he hit me with his car! The last thing I should be thinking about is having sex with the guy who hit me with his car.

"You're starting to worry me." He shoves the sheet back, then picks me up from the wheelchair and carefully lays me in bed and pulls the covers over me.

"I could've done that myself," I tell him. "It's not like my legs are broken."

"Your knee had a deep cut, which is why you needed stitches. Keeping weight off it will keep the swelling down as it heals which is why they'll be sending you home with crutches. And they want you using the wheelchair until the dizziness subsides."

33

"How long am I going to be here?"

"Probably another day. Depends on how you're doing."

I look around and see the nurse is gone. I didn't even hear her leave.

"You really should call your parents," Corbin says as he sits down in the chair. "They should be here."

"You need to finish what you were saying before. About what I said when I was out of it."

"I told you about punching Dukin."

I laugh. "I can't believe I did that. Did he get a black eye?"

"Not really. Just a little bruising."

"Why do you hate the guy so much?"

"I don't hate him. I just don't respect him. He uses the doctor thing to get women. Even wears his scrubs to the bars."

"I'm sure a lot of doctors do that."

"I don't. I don't want a woman dating me just because I'm a doctor." He smiles. "At least you asked me out before you knew."

"Wait—what?" I ask, my face heating up. "I asked you out?"

"Twice. But you had no idea I was a doctor so I'm taking that to mean that my career choice doesn't matter to you, which is refreshing actually. It's hard to find—"

"Okay, stop. When did this happen? When did I ask you out?"

"When you first woke up and then again in the middle of the night."

"You're lying."

"Why would I lie about that?"

"Fine. Whatever. So what did I say?"

"You called me ruggedly handsome," he says with a laugh, "then asked if I'd be your cowboy."

My jaw drops, then snaps shut. "I did not say that. I can't even imagine those words coming out of my mouth."

"Then last night, you asked me to get into bed with you. You said we could skip the date and get right to the good stuff.

Those were your exact words." He cracks up laughing. "And you kept calling me Hot Stuff."

I cover my face. "Please tell me you're making this up."

"Sorry, but it's all true. I wasn't going to tell you but you made me." He pauses. "Do girls your age really call guys Hot Stuff? That sounds like something an old lady would say to a male stripper."

"It is." I pull the sheet over my head. "My aunt goes to those male strip shows in Vegas and calls all the guys Hot Stuff. I must've been thinking of her."

"Hey." He takes the sheet off my head. "Don't worry about it. People say strange things when they're taking meds. The drugs affect everyone differently. And apparently, they make you a little flirty."

"A little?" I pull the sheet over my head again. "It sounds like I was trying to rip your clothes off last night."

"You tried but I didn't let you."

I lower the sheet enough to peek at him. "You're lying. I didn't have the strength to rip your clothes off."

"True, but you did try to unbutton my shirt."

"Ugh," I moan. "Please tell me that's it. I didn't do anything else, did I?"

"No, that was it."

I turn away from him on my side. "Sorry about that. I honestly had no clue what I was doing or saying. I don't know what it is with me and meds but we just don't get along." I sneeze, which is followed by another.

"Here." Corbin sets the box of tissues beside me. "The nurse left some cold meds over there on the table. Would you like them?"

"Are you kidding?" I turn back to him. "You want me to act even crazier? No more meds."

"I'm just saying, if you need them, they're right here." He points to the table next to the bed. "Why don't you get some rest?"

"Are you going home now?"

"No. I'll be here when you wake up."

"Corbin, you really don't have to stay. You've been here long enough. Maybe you could just stop by and check on me during your lunch break tomorrow. Or actually, forget it. You don't need to check on me. I'll be fine. Like you said, the hospital staff will take care of me."

"I'm staying. Now go to sleep." He gets up and pulls the blanket over me. It's sweet and reminds me of when I was a kid and wished someone would tuck me into bed at night. My parents never did. They were either at work or out with their friends or watching TV in the living room. I had to put myself to bed.

I close my eyes and try to sleep but I keep thinking about what I said. Did I really ask Corbin out? Twice?

"What did you say?" I ask, keeping my eyes closed.

"About what?"

"When I asked you out, what did you say?"

"I respectfully turned you down."

"Yeah. Obviously." A nervous laugh follows as I adjust my pillow.

I keep quiet after that and try to sleep but I keep wondering if he would've said yes if I'd asked him when I wasn't under the influence of pain meds. I doubt he would. He's a rich doctor. He wouldn't date someone like me. And I wouldn't date someone like him. Well, I might, but still, I'm sure I'm not his type.

CHAPTER FIVE

Corbin

Star's been asleep for an hour. I haven't left her side. I've just sat here, watching her, making sure she's okay. Having reviewed her charts, I know she'll be fine but I can't make myself leave her. I feel so much guilt for what I've done. How could I be so careless? I'm never careless. I wasn't allowed to be. My father expected better, and so I've always been cautious. But yesterday I wasn't and that one slip-up could've caused Star her life.

She turns on her side, still asleep, and I notice the bruise on the side of her face. The one caused by me being careless. But even with the bruise, her face is still strikingly beautiful. Flawless skin. Golden brown hair. Those deep chestnut eyes.

She's such a stark contrast from Lauren with her porcelain white skin and pale blue eyes, her face long and thin with bony cheeks. Lauren is constantly complemented for her appearance. People tell her she has the looks of a runway model with her extremely thin body and long legs. I think she's far too thin but when I tell her that she scolds me and tells me I shouldn't comment on her size. But it's less about her appearance and more about her health. To maintain that level of thinness she barely eats, but she needs to in order to keep up with such a demanding job with long hours.

Why am I thinking about Lauren right now? And why I am comparing her to Star? Why am I even looking at Star this way? She's a girl I hit with my car. I can't be attracted to her. It's wrong. Isn't it?

There's a knock on the door and when I turn I see Lauren standing there wearing her white lab coat, her straight blond hair pulled up in a bun.

"Corbin!" she says in a hushed but demanding tone, the kind you'd use when calling a dog to come inside. She always uses that tone with me and I'm sick of it. But out of habit I respond, finding myself already out of my chair and meeting her at the door.

"What is it?"

"What the hell is going on?" she hisses.

"Not here," I say quietly as I go past her out to the hall.

Lauren pivots on her heels and strides over to me. "Are you seriously going to just sit there all day with that girl? You're missing work!"

"That's not your concern," I tell her, folding my arms over my chest. "What I do is none of your business anymore."

"It sure as hell is," she says, keeping her voice down and moving closer. "I don't know what's going on with you but you are done acting this way. You're going to go home, get showered, put on some decent clothes, and get to the clinic. And when your shift is over, I need you to pick up my things at the dry cleaners. Oh, and I need you to go down to the storage locker and get my suitcase for our trip this weekend."

"We're not going this weekend," I remind her. "And I'm not getting your dry cleaning. I'm done taking orders from you, Lauren." I notice her thin red lips pursing in anger. She's not used to me talking to her this way. "We're no longer together. You'll need to start doing your own errands."

A man comes around the corner with a yellow lab. It's one of the therapy dogs brought in to cheer up the patients.

"What's his name?" I ask the man.

"Buddy." The man smiles and stops next to Lauren. The dog goes up to her and sniffs her leg.

She shudders and moves aside. She hates dogs and refused to let me have one. I didn't fight her on it because with my residency schedule I didn't have time for a dog, but now that I have regular hours and am no longer with Lauren, I could actually get one.

"Hey, Buddy," I say, petting the dog. His nose rises, trying to lick my hand. "Going to visit some patients?"

"We're starting here today," the man says, "then we'll head over to pediatrics." He turns toward Lauren. "Would you like to pet him?"

"God no," she mutters, taking a step back as the dog looks up at her, tail wagging.

The man tugs on the dog's leash. "Let's go, Buddy."

They continue on to the nurses' station.

"Cute dog," I say.

"You know I hate dogs," Lauren snaps. "Back to what I was saying. My dry cleaning should be ready by five but if it's not, you'll need to go back later. I need my navy skirt for tomorrow."

"I'm not getting your dry cleaning."

She huffs. "I don't have time to stand here and argue about this. Just get the damn dry cleaning and we'll talk later."

"I'm not doing your errands, Lauren. And there's no need to talk later. This relationship is over. There's nothing more to say."

"This is NOT over. You're simply not thinking straight because of the damage you've caused from your careless behavior."

I know I was careless and I already feel terrible about it. I don't need to be reminded of it. My father's already given me a lecture and now Lauren's doing it. I'm starting to realize the two of them are very alike. She's condescending and controlling like my father. So why did I ever go out with her? Was I so used to being treated that way that I didn't even notice when Lauren did it? If so, it just proves how badly I needed to get out of this relationship.

"My thinking is very clear when it comes to this," I tell her. "And my decision is made. We're not getting back together."

"You've lost your damn mind," she whispers as a nurse passes behind her. She waits until the woman is gone, then says, "First you hit a girl with your car and now you're missing work, babysitting her? Corbin, you have to admit, that's not you. It's obvious you're having some kind of mental breakdown."

"It's not a breakdown. It's a break-THROUGH. I'm finally waking up and seeing how destructive this relationship was. It needed to end, and now it has. As for Star, staying with her and making sure she's okay is the right thing to do. Ignoring her and going back to work is what YOU would do, which is why you expect me to do the same. It's just another example of how you really don't know me. You never did. You didn't want to. You'd rather turn me into the man you want me to be instead of accepting who I am."

"Enough of this psychobabble," she scoffs. "I have rounds in ten minutes." She storms off, then turns back as I'm heading to Star's room. "What are you doing? You're not seriously going back in there, are you?"

"Goodbye, Lauren." I open the door and go in Star's room, my anger and frustration with Lauren immediately easing when I see Star. She's still asleep, a slight smile on her face that makes me wonder what she's dreaming about. Maybe her Hot Stuff doctor.

I laugh to myself when I think about that. She was so out of it yesterday, saying all those things about me. It was even funnier seeing her reaction when I told her what she'd said. If it'd been Lauren, she would've scolded me for telling her what she said, saying I should've spared her the embarrassment and acted as though it never happened. But Star begged me to tell her, then laughed about it.

Why do I keep comparing those two? Lauren is history and Star is a patient. Well, she's not MY patient but I should still think of her in a strictly professional manner.

My phone rings and I quickly exit the room to keep from waking up Star.

"Hello?"

"Corbin, it's your father. I'd like to meet you for lunch today. What time is your break at the clinic?"

"I can't meet for lunch. And I'm not at the clinic. I took today off."

"Why is that? Are you not feeling well?"

"I'm with Star. I want to keep an eye on her. Make sure she continues to recover."

"You're still with the girl? Corbin, stop acting like a fool and get your ass back to work."

"I'm not leaving her until I know she's okay. I hit her with my damn car. I'm not just going to leave her here alone. She has no family in town. No friends."

"That's HER problem, not yours. She has a staff of nurses to care for her. It is not your responsibility to watch over this girl. In fact, doing so could be to your detriment."

"Because I'm missing work? I've already talked to my boss at the clinic and he completely understands."

"That's not what I was referring to, although it does reflect poorly on you to miss two days of work when you're not even ill. But what I meant is more serious than that. By staying with this girl, you're admitting guilt. You're proving to the court that you're responsible for this."

"I AM responsible. I didn't look before turning. And this isn't going to court. She's not going to sue me."

"Don't be an idiot. Of course she will. She's young. Has no job. The girl needs money."

"She's not the type of person who would do that. I've gotten to know her and she's not like that."

"All it takes is one lawyer to show up and tell her just how much she could make off of this and soon she'll be

41

exaggerating her injuries in hopes of a bigger check. She probably already has lawyers calling, offering to take her case. Any lawyer in town would love to take on the Sterlings."

"Dad, relax. That's not going to happen." I knew he'd bring this up and I'm not going to get into it with him. But like Lauren, he'll keep fighting me until I do what he asks. "So about lunch. Friday might work. I'll have to check my schedule."

"Friday doesn't work. Thomas will be out of town. He can meet today at noon. He'd like to meet somewhere close to his office."

"Thomas? Your lawyer?" I blow out a breath. "I'm not meeting with your lawyer. Star is not going to sue me. This is ridiculous. You're getting way too involved in this. I'm an adult, and if I feel I need a lawyer, for this or anything else, I will find one myself."

"Don't be so goddamn stubborn. This is serious, Corbin. You could lose everything. I don't care what this girl says. She may seem all sweet and innocent now but once a lawyer's involved, she'll turn on you. I guarantee it. We have to be prepared. And you need to get out of her room. You not only admit guilt being there but might say something she could use against you later."

"I'm not talking about this. I don't need your permission to stay with her and I'm not meeting with your lawyer. Have a good day." I end the call and when he calls back, I let it go to voicemail.

"Sterling."

I look up from my phone and see Leo walking up to me. He's in the residency program with Lauren.

"How's it going, man?" He gives me his usual big, happy smile. Leo's one of those guys that doesn't let stuff get him down. He had a heart defect as a kid and spent most of his childhood in the hospital. He's fine now but the experience taught him life's too short to let things bother you. So no matter what's going on in his life he's always smiling. Because of that, Lauren can't stand him. She said all his smiling isn't professional. She thinks doctors should be serious and never show their lighter side. I totally disagree.

I point to Star's room. "You heard about the accident, right?"

"No. What happened?"

"Lauren didn't tell you?"

"She hasn't said anything about you in weeks. I was thinking maybe you two broke up."

"We did, but it happened yesterday."

"Oh. Sorry to hear that."

"Nothing to be sorry about. It needed to end. Lauren doesn't agree. She hasn't accepted the breakup yet."

"Is she moving out?"

"I told her to, but you know Lauren. It has to be on her schedule, not mine. And I can't just kick her out. She needs time to find a place."

"That'll be awkward. Broken up but still living together? Can't she go stay with her parents?"

"She could, but I doubt she will. She'll want to drag this out to get back at me for breaking up with her."

"Don't take this the wrong way but I could never figure out why you two were together."

"Really?" I ask, surprised he never told me this before. Leo's not a close friend but he's a good enough friend that we can talk openly about stuff. "Why couldn't you see us together?"

"You just seem really different. Lauren is always so serious, like she never lets herself have fun. Does she even do anything besides work?"

"She shops and goes to spin class. That's about it. But she doesn't really have time for anything else with her schedule."

"I have the same schedule and I have plenty of fun," he says with a laugh. "Em had me on one of those paddle boards last weekend. Never done it before. Water was freaking cold but we had a blast."

Emma, or Em for short, is his fiancé. She's a personal trainer and she's always getting him to try new activities. I've met her a few times and she's just like him. Full of energy, always smiling.

"So what were you saying about an accident?" he asks.

"It happened yesterday on my way to work." I explain the story up until the part where they took Star away in an ambulance.

"Shit, is she okay?" he asks, and I realize he's the only person I've told so far who's asked about Star. Lauren and my parents only asked if she was suing me. That was their main concern. They didn't care about her health.

"She's doing better," I say. "She has a concussion and some stitches but it could've been a lot worse."

"Sounds like she's lucky to be alive."

"Yeah, I know."

"How about you? You doing okay?"

He's the only person who's asked me that too. Lauren didn't even bother. When I told her what happened she scolded me for not being careful, then asked how much damage there was to my car.

"I'm feeling really guilty about what happened," I say. "Not only did she get hurt, but she lost her job because she missed work. She moved to Boston for that job and now she doesn't have it. Because of me."

"It was an accident. Feeling guilty won't make it any better. Have you been checking on her?"

"I've stayed with her since it happened. Haven't even been home since yesterday morning. My dad and Lauren are giving me shit about it but I don't care. I'm not leaving her. She doesn't have any family in town so if I wasn't here she'd be all alone. I'm not leaving her when she's hurt and scared and alone."

"This is why I never saw you with Lauren," he says with a smile. "If she was the one who'd hit the girl, she wouldn't even be checking on her. She'd probably be suing her for being in the street."

"She actually suggested I do that. She said I should blame Star for not looking before going into the street, even though she had the walk signal."

"Cool name," he says.

"Star?"

"Yeah. I never met anyone with that name. Is she as cool as her name?"

"She's awesome." I smile. "She's funny. Has a beautiful smile. Great laugh. And when she's embarrassed, her cheeks turn bright pink. It's adorable. She just has this...I don't know....gentle sweet way about her. Kind of like Emma."

"If she's like Emma I like her already." He grins. "Sounds like you do too. Is she around your age?"

"Younger. She's 23."

He shrugs. "That's not too young."

"Too young for what?"

"To date her."

"Date her? I'm not dating her. Why would you even you suggest that?"

"Because of the way you talk about her. You never talked about Lauren that way."

"I'm sure I did a long time ago."

"You couldn't have. Lauren's not anything like what you just described. You obviously like this girl. When she's better why don't you take her for lunch? Lunch isn't really a date and it'll give you a chance to see if there's anything there."

I'm not going to tell him this but there's definitely something there. There's attraction, for one, but it's more than that. There's an energy to her. An energy that makes me want to be around her. She's injured and lost her job but she's still hopeful. Still laughing. Still showing off that smile. When I'm with her I feel...present. That's a strange way to describe it but it's the most fitting. Instead of thinking of all the things I need to do or where I need to be, I'm just in the moment when I'm with her. Like my mind shuts off all distractions. That's something I've never been able to do so I'm not sure why I'm

45

able to do it when I'm with Star. Maybe because she's so different than what I'm used to. I'm captivated by her energy. Her spirit. And that bright beautiful smile.

"Hey, I gotta get going," Leo says. "Tell Star I hope she feels better."

"I will. See ya," I say as he hurries down the hall.

Does Leo really think I should ask Star out? He seemed serious when he said it. But I can't do that. It wouldn't be appropriate. But what if I hadn't hit her? If I'd just met her at a bar, would I ask her out?

I don't even want to answer that question. It'll just get my mind going places it shouldn't. She's a girl I hit with my car. That's it. She can't be anything more.

CHAPTER SIX

Star

"You can go home now," I tell Corbin.

It's five o'clock and we just finished watching a movie that I didn't really see because I kept falling asleep. They cut back on my pain meds so I'm more awake now but I still feel weak, probably because I haven't eaten much since yesterday morning. The food here is really bad and my appetite isn't back to normal yet. Even if it was, I wouldn't want to eat tonight's dinner, which consists of dry meatloaf, watery mashed potatoes, and cooked carrots that look more gray than orange.

"I'll leave after you fall asleep."

"Corbin, this is crazy. You don't even know me. Why are you staying here with me?"

"Because I want to make sure you're okay." He sets down the magazine he was reading, some kind of men's fitness magazine.

"You know I'm okay. The doctor said so."

"You're still recovering. You're not out of the woods yet. Head injuries can be very serious."

"I'm fine. Really. It's just a concussion. People get those all the time."

"You're lucky that's all it was." He looks down at the floor. "It could've been a lot worse."

He's so serious, so regretful. It's like he thought he might've killed me yesterday. I guess it *would* be pretty traumatic to hit someone with your car.

Trying to cheer him up, I say, "Maybe it was good that it happened. Maybe it was a sign telling me not to take that job."

He looks up at me. "There was nothing good about what happened. I agree that job wouldn't have been good, but as for me hitting you with my car?" He shakes his head. "I'll never forgive myself."

"Corbin, you gotta stop beating yourself up about this." I hold my arms out. "Look at me. I'm all in one piece. Sure I have a few scratches and bruises but all-in-all I'm fine."

"You're not fine. If you were fine, you wouldn't be in the hospital."

"True, but I'm considering it like a mini vacation. I get to lay in bed all day, sleep, watch TV." I point to my tray. "I even have people bringing me food."

"You're taking this really well. Most people would be yelling at me, telling me how stupid I was, how I should've been more careful."

"I think you've yelled at yourself enough. And besides, what good does it do to get mad at someone about something that can't be changed? It happened. It's over. So stop beating yourself up about it."

He looks at me, a slight smile on his face. It's good to see that smile again. I haven't seen it for hours. All afternoon he's been quiet, stuck in his own head, probably yelling at himself for what happened.

"You're amazing," he says.

I laugh. "You don't even know me."

"I know enough about you to know you're amazing."

"What exactly is it you know about me that qualifies as amazing?"

"The way you're handling this. You're hurt, sick, lost your job, and yet you're still smiling."

"What else am I going to do? Cry and complain and feel sorry for myself? I've tried that in the past and it doesn't make me feel better. When I moved here I told myself that no matter what happens I'm going to stay positive, or at least try."

"Yeah, but still. That's hard to do after everything that's happened the past few days."

He's right. How am I still smiling after all that? I'm stuck in a hospital. I lost my job. My car broke down. My resolve to be positive should've broken down by now. And given what's happened, it would've been justified.

"I think it's you," I tell him.

"What do you mean?"

"I think you're the reason I'm not a total mess right now."

He scoots his chair closer. "Why?"

I shrug. "Just having you here. It's been nice to not be all alone. You're kinda serious but when you're not being serious, you're actually kinda funny."

"Is that so?" His mouth ticks up into that smile I love.

I point to it. "And that."

"What?"

"Your smile. I like it when you smile. You have a good smile. It puts me in a good mood."

"Really?" He rubs his hand over his scruffy jaw. "I have a good smile?"

"A *great* smile. You should smile more."

"If it makes you feel better then I'll try to smile more." He smiles, which makes me do the same. "Yours is good too."

"It is?"

"It's even better than mine."

"No, it's not." I cover my mouth so he can't see it. I have a crooked smile. Always have. It doesn't bother me but I don't like people staring at it.

"Stop hiding it," he says, trying to take my hand from my face.

49

"Then stop looking at it." I push his hand away.

"You looked at mine."

"Because yours is better."

He sits back and folds his arms over his chest. "I'm not going to show it to you anymore unless you show me yours."

"That's ridiculous."

"So are you."

Watching him trying not to smile is making me laugh. He's attempting to pout his lips, which makes him start to laugh so then he tries to pout again.

"Stop it," I say, still hiding behind my hand. "Go back to being serious."

"I AM being serious. See?" He furrows his brow and frowns in an over-the-top way that's even funnier than his pout.

I burst out laughing, which causes my hand to drop.

"That's better," he says, smiling at me.

"I couldn't take it anymore. It's like I said, you can be really funny when you're not being serious."

"I'm a doctor. Being serious is part of the job. People don't want me laughing when I tell them they're having a heart attack."

"Yeah, that would be bad," I say, adjusting my pillow so I can sit up more. "So have you ever had to tell a patient really bad news?"

His smile disappears. "Just the other day, actually."

"What happened?"

"A mom came in with her daughter. The little girl had been coughing a lot. Her mom thought it was bronchitis." He stares down at the floor.

"It wasn't bronchitis, was it?" I ask cautiously.

"No. I knew as soon as she told me her symptoms. I wasn't positive it was cancer but I was pretty damn sure. I immediately called her pediatrician who scheduled tests to be run the next day."

"But you didn't know for sure, so you didn't tell the mom, right? Someone else did?"

50

"Yes, but she knew before she left my office that day. After I examined her daughter, she took me aside. She could tell something was wrong. Something bad. Apparently I wasn't able to hide it. Either that or it's just a mom's intuition."

"So what did you tell her?"

"I told her it was possible. I didn't want to say it but she kept asking, wanting answers." He shakes his head. "That's the part of the job I hate. I went into this to help people but sometimes you just can't."

"Are you saying the little girl isn't going to be okay?"

"I don't know. The test results showed the cancer had spread."

"That's so sad."

"Unfortunately, that's part of the job. And telling patients is the hardest part. You want to show compassion but at the same time, you can't get emotionally involved. If you do, you wouldn't be able to do the job."

"You're kind of breaking the rules with me then, aren't you?"

"Meaning what?"

"Staying here with me? Worrying about me? You're getting emotionally involved."

"You're not my patient. And I can't help but be emotionally involved. I'm the reason you're here. If it weren't for me, you wouldn't be in the hospital."

"Still, you don't have to stay here. You've been here long enough."

"Do you want me to go?"

"It's not that I don't want you here. It's nice having the company, but you've been here for a day and a half. You don't need to stay another night. You need to sleep."

He points to my tray. "I'll stay with you through dinner and then I'll take off. Sound good?"

"Yeah," I say, although thinking about him leaving is making me sad. Or maybe it's just the thought of being alone that's making me sad.

Picking up my fork I stare down at my tray of food, which is now cold. The mashed potatoes stick to my fork like glue and they're starting to look gray like the carrots.

"I know I said I'm trying to be positive," I say, "but this food—"

"Is really bad." He gets up and takes the tray from me. "I'll get you something else." He sets the tray down and takes out his phone. "What do you like? Name it and it's yours. I've got the number of just about every takeout place in town. I lived on takeout during my residency. You want pizza? Chinese food? Burger and fries?"

"Actually, just a sandwich sounds good. Like a good deli sandwich. With chips. And a pickle."

"A sandwich and chips? That's it?"

"And a pickle."

He smiles. "Got it. You're easy to please." He swipes through his phone, then makes a call. "Hey, Tony. It's Corbin." He laughs. "No, I'm not working today but I do need an order. Give me the number five. And add a pickle." He looks at me. "What kind of chips?"

"Barbecue, if they have those."

"Barbecue," he says to the guy on the phone. "Can you deliver or do you want me to pick it up?" He nods. "I'll meet him downstairs. Tell him to text me when he's here. Oh, and throw in one of your famous brownies. Actually, throw in two. Thanks, Tony. Tell your wife I said hi." He hangs up and turns back to me. "Should be about ten minutes."

"Is Tony a friend of yours?"

"Not really a friend. More of an acquaintance. I got to know him when I was in med school and ordering sandwiches all the time. He and his wife own a deli down the street. His son does the deliveries."

I look around the room. "Do you know what happened to my stuff? Like my keys and wallet?"

"They're at the nurses' station. Why? What do you need?"

"My wallet. I think I have a ten in there."

"You're not paying. I hit you with my car. The least I can do is buy you a sandwich." He sits down. "So while we're waiting I wanted to ask you something."

"Go ahead."

"What's going on with you and your parents?"

"Nothing. Why?"

"Why do you refuse to call them? You're in the hospital. You should at least call and let them know."

"It'd be a waste of time. And I don't want to hear them lecture me."

"About what?"

"About how I was stupid for riding my bike in the rain."

"Just explain that your car broke down."

"They'd tell me I should've taken the bus. Actually, the conversation wouldn't even make it that far. I'd call, they'd ask what I want, I'd say nothing, and then they'd hang up."

"So you don't get along with them."

"It's not that we don't get along. They're just not the type of parents that want to deal with their adult kids. They told my brother and me we're on our own when we turn 18. I didn't make enough money to be on my own so I've been living in their basement, which they were NOT happy about. They were thrilled when I finally got a decent job and moved out but I've only been here a week and already lost my job so calling them will just result in another lecture about how I'm irresponsible and can't take care of myself. Plus, my mom has a new boyfriend and I think they were going to Florida this week, and my dad is working overtime at his job so he's probably not even home."

"I still think you should tell them. At least call your mom. Moms like to know stuff like this."

"My mom doesn't want me calling and interrupting her trip to tell her something she doesn't need to be told."

"Would you just humor me and call her?" He hands me my phone.

"Fine, but I'm putting it on speaker to prove my point."

I call my mom. It rings forever before she finally picks up.

"Star, I can't talk now. Bruce took me to a dance club and it's very loud in here."

Music is blaring in the background and I hear a woman yell out a drink order, then the sound of glass breaking.

"Are you in Florida?" I ask.

"Yes, we got here last night. What do you need?"

I look at Corbin, who's motioning me to tell her. "I got in an accident."

"What'd you say? I can't hear you."

"Can you go somewhere quieter? I need to tell you something."

"Hold on. I'll go outside." The noise in the background gets even louder before quieting down. "Okay, what is it?"

"I got hit by a car yesterday. I'm in the hospital."

"Are you okay?"

"I'm fine, other than some stitches and a concussion."

"Why'd you get hit?"

I roll my eyes. "It wasn't my fault, Mom. My car didn't work so I had to bike to work and this guy just didn't see me."

"Were you wearing black? That's probably why he didn't see you. And why were you riding a bike? You should've taken the bus. You wouldn't have been hit on a bus."

"Yeah, I guess I should have. Well, I just wanted you to know."

"I gotta get back in there. Bruce will be looking for me. If you need something, call your dad."

"Yeah. Got it. Bye, Mom."

I set the phone down. "Told you. It went just like I said. She asked what I want, I told her the news, then she tells me what I did wrong. Do I know my parents or what?"

"At least she knows now. What about your dad?"

"My mom will tell him, if she remembers. They're still married by the way."

"They are? And your mom is dating?"

"My parents are separated but they don't have enough money for each of them to get their own place so they both still live at the house but stay in different rooms."

"They could still finalize the divorce."

"They could, but they never seem to get around to doing it. They've been separated for five years."

"That's odd."

"What about *your* family? Are your parents still together?"

"My mom passed a few years ago. My dad's remarried."

"Sorry about your mom."

He just nods.

"Do you like your stepmom?"

"She's okay. I was in med school when she married my dad so I haven't spent much time around her."

"Do you have brothers and sisters?"

"A sister. She lives in Denver."

"Let me guess. She's a doctor?"

"Brain surgeon."

"Like your grandpa. So you were supposed to copy your dad and be a heart surgeon."

"That was the plan until I broke my finger."

His phone rings.

"You can answer it," I say.

He sees who it is and sends the call to voicemail just as a text chimes.

"It's the food," he says. "I'll be right back."

A few minutes later he returns with a footlong sub, a bag of chips, and two giant brownies.

"Dig in," he says as he takes a brownie for himself.

"Why didn't you get yourself a sandwich?"

"I'm not that hungry."

"So you're just eating a brownie? That's not a very nutritious dinner. As a doctor, aren't you supposed to set an example for healthy eating?"

"I usually do but today I needed the brownie. It's been a bad week."

"Because of the accident?"

"Because of a lot of stuff," he mutters as he unwraps his brownie.

"What else happened?"

"Well, for one, that little girl I told you about. The one with cancer? I know it's part of the job but it still bothers me. She's so young." He shakes his head. "This is why I shouldn't get emotionally involved with patients."

"There's nothing wrong with feeling compassion for your patients. You're human. It's normal. You wouldn't be a very good doctor if you didn't care about your patients."

He points to my sandwich. "What do you think?"

"I've only had one bite but so far it's good. You want some?"

"The brownie's enough."

"No, it's not. C'mon. I can't eat this whole thing. Take the other half." I hand it to him. "If you don't eat it I'll just throw it out."

He takes it from me. "You can't throw out one of Tony's sandwiches."

"You good at word puzzles?" I ask.

"Not really. Why?"

I flip the TV to Wheel of Fortune and we try to guess the puzzles as we eat our sandwiches. He may be a smart doctor but I'm better than him at solving word puzzles. It comes from years of eating dinner in front of the TV, watching Wheel of Fortune and other game shows. My parents and brother aren't big talkers so the TV was always on during meals.

"I should get going," Corbin says, getting up from his chair. "I'll stop by in the morning to see how you're doing. I've asked them to let me know when you're being released so I can come get you and take you to your apartment. If you need anything, like groceries, we can stop at a store on the way to your place."

"You think they'll send me home tomorrow?"

"That's the plan unless something changes. Need anything else before I leave?"

"No. I'm fine. Thanks. And thanks for being here with me. It made the time go faster. And, well, it was just nice having someone here. See you tomorrow."

I don't want him to leave but I know he needs to. He hasn't been home in almost two days.

He's at the door now, looking back at me.

"Aren't you going?" I ask.

He looks down a moment, then back up. "You good at trivia?"

"Not really. Why?"

He points to the TV. Jeopardy is starting. "You kicked my ass at Wheel of Fortune. I need to earn back my dignity."

I laugh. "You can't handle a girl winning?"

"I'm all for girls winning but that doesn't mean I'm not competitive. What do you say? Rematch with Jeopardy?"

"I still might beat you. You're not going to know the popular culture categories."

"How do you know? I go to movies. Watch TV."

I shrug. "Okay. Let's do it."

I'm surprised he doesn't want to go home. Is he staying because he wants to spend more time with me? Or is he just being nice? Either way, I'm thrilled he decided to stay. I didn't want him to go.

I'm falling for this guy. I just met him and I'm already falling for him, which is really bad because after tomorrow I'll probably never see him again.

CHAPTER SEVEN

Star

"Ready to go?" Corbin walks in my room, a big smile on his face. He's all cleaned up, his dark hair neatly in place, wearing dark gray dress pants and a white button-up shirt. He looks more like a doctor than he did yesterday, or maybe it's just the lab coat he has on.

"What do you mean?" I sit up.

"Dr. Miller just told me you're cleared for release. The nurse will be in shortly to go over care instructions for when you're home."

I'm not ready to go home. I don't want to. Not yet. Going home means having to find a new job, figuring out what's wrong with my car, and enduring my very loud roommates when my head is still pounding. And at home I have to sleep on an air mattress that doesn't hold air.

Sad as it sounds, I'd rather spend another day at the hospital. At least here I get to sleep in a real bed and can put off having to find a job. And being here means being able to see Corbin. I want another day with him. He stayed here last night until I fell asleep. We watched TV and talked, and although he kept telling me to rest I couldn't do it. I knew if I fell asleep he'd leave and

I didn't want him to. I finally dozed off around ten and when I woke up in the night he was gone.

"What time is it?" I ask, searching for my phone.

"Just after nine," Corbin says. "The release paperwork should be done by ten and then we can go."

"Don't you have to work?" I ask, pointing at his lab coat.

"I told them I needed a few hours off. Leah will cover for me. She's one of the other doctors."

"You really don't need to do all this. I could just take a cab back to my apartment."

"Not an option." He goes over to the window and opens the drapes, filling the room with sunlight. "I'm the reason you're here. I'm going to make sure you get home safe and have everything you need."

My throat tickles and I cough, which triggers more coughing and I can't make it stop. Corbin comes over and hands me the cup of water that was on my bedside table.

"Try to drink." He sits down on the bed and waits for me to gulp down some water.

"Thanks." I hand him the glass, my other hand rubbing my sore ribs which took a beating from all the coughing.

"They're gonna hurt for awhile," he says, setting the cup down. "Bruised ribs take time to heal. We'll get you some medicine to help with the cough."

Thinking of my very limited cash supply, I say, "I'll be fine. It's just a cold."

He places the back of his hand on my forehead. "You still have a slight fever." He lowers his hand to my arm, gently rubbing it. "I just have to say again how sorry I am. If there's anything you need, don't hesitate to ask."

I want to ask him to keep rubbing my arm in that slow gentle way that's comforting but also slightly arousing. I know he's just doing it as part of the whole beside manner thing, trying to comfort the patient, but my attraction to him is making it more than that. I'm sure that happens a lot with his patients. He's too good looking for it not to.

He lets go of my arm as his phone dings. He checks it and stands up. "I need to go back to the clinic. It shouldn't take long."

"Corbin, if you need to—"

"I'm taking you home," he says sternly. "You're not taking a cab."

I nod.

"I'll be back soon." He walks to the door, then stops and turns back to me. "I almost forgot." He points to a blue sack sitting on the chair next to my bed. "I brought you some clothes. Yours were ruined in the accident."

"Mine were ruined?" I ask, saddened because I spent a good chunk of my savings on those clothes, wanting to impress my boss on my first day of work.

"Your pants and coat got torn on the bike when it flipped over."

"What about my blouse?" I ask, because it cost more than the pants and coat combined. I figured I'd wear it a lot so it was worth the price.

"I had to rip it open to see assess any damage to your ribs before I performed CPR."

He ripped open my blouse? So he saw me in just my bra? Or did he take that off too? I'm too embarrassed to ask.

"You did CPR on me?"

"When you passed out. Star, I have to go deal with this issue at the clinic. I'll be back shortly."

"Yeah, bye."

I watch him leave, the door slowly closing behind him.

He saw me topless. And gave me mouth-to-mouth. And it didn't even affect him. To him, I'm just a patient. Nothing more. Yet I keep imagining him as more than that. It must be that thing where patients fall for their doctor. There's a name for it. I can't remember what it is but I obviously have it because I can't stop thinking of him as more than just a doctor.

The nurse appears and does a final check of my vital signs, then gives me care instructions for my stitches and concussion.

She schedules my follow-up appointment for a week from today although I doubt I'll go. I can't afford it.

"You can go ahead and get dressed," the nurse says as she leaves.

Still feeling weak, I slowly get up and make my way to the bathroom.

"Holy crap," I say, seeing myself in the mirror. I look terrible. My hair's sticking up all different directions, there are bags under my eyes, and the only color in my face is from my nose, which is red from my cold. There's no way Corbin's attracted to me. How could he be? I'm a mess. His caring, gentle touches were simply meant to comfort me. Just something he learned in med school. Beside manner 101.

After a quick shower I return to my room and take out the clothes Corbin left me. They still have the tags on. There's a pair of black sweatpants, a white t-shirt, and a gray hoodie, all with the hospital logo. They must be from the gift shop, the only store he could get to in between seeing patients this morning.

It's nice of him to do all this for me. I know he feels guilty for the accident but he could've just left me with the number of his insurance company and never spoken to me again, like most people would do.

After getting dressed I wait in bed, my hair damp because there wasn't a blow dryer in the bathroom. It feels good to be in real clothes again instead of a skimpy, scratchy hospital gown.

Right before ten, Corbin shows up. He's not smiling this time and seems to be in a rush, walking fast as he hurries in my room.

"You okay?" I ask as he checks his pockets for something.

He looks up at me and his smile appears. "I'm fine. Ready to go?"

"Yeah." I point to myself. "Thanks for the clothes. They're a little big but way better than a hospital gown."

"I would've got you something better but I had to be at work at seven and nothing was open but the hospital gift shop."

"It's fine." I smile. "Now I'll have something to remember my visit here."

"I'm sure you'd rather forget." He searches his lab coat pocket and takes out his keys. "So that's where I put them. I'm a little out of it today. Didn't get much sleep last night."

"Why didn't you sleep?"

"I keep thinking about the accident and how I could've prevented it. If I'd just paid more attention..."

"Corbin, it's over. You can't keep reliving it. And besides, I'm fine." I shove the covers back and stand up on my good leg. A wave of dizziness hits me and my vision blurs. I wobble until I feel strong arms go around me and gently sit me back on the bed.

"You can't get up that fast," Corbin says. "Even if you're feeling okay, you need to take things slow the next week or two. Nothing strenuous. Nothing too physical. And you need to rest your brain."

"So no Jeopardy?"

"Shit." He scrubs his hand through his hair. "I wasn't even thinking of that. We shouldn't have watched that last night."

"I'm kidding. Watching Jeopardy with you didn't hurt my brain. It was fun. And better than sitting here alone all night. I'm sure you had better things to do but—"

"I didn't," he interrupts, then smiles. "Have better things to do. I liked being here."

We exchange a look. A gaze that lingers and makes me wonder if maybe he actually does feel something for me. Something more than what he'd feel if I were just a patient. But then he looks away as the door swings open.

The nurse comes in with a wheelchair. Corbin insists on helping me into it, which seems ridiculous but given my recent dizzy spill, maybe I need the help.

"What about shoes?" I ask, noticing my feet are bare.

Corbin looks at the nurse. "Did Kylie remember to bring them?"

"Yes. I'll grab them along with her phone."

The nurse takes off, then returns moments later with a pair of socks and bright pink running shoes.

"This doesn't mean you can run," Corbin jokes as he slips the socks over my feet, then works my foot into the shoe, which has scuff marks and a smudge of dried dirt along the toe.

"Whose shoes are these?" I ask.

"Kylie's. She's one of the nurses."

"And she's okay with me borrowing her shoes?"

"She said you could have them. She runs all the time and is always getting new shoes. She said she hasn't worn these in months. I'll get you new ones but for now, these will have to do."

Both shoes are on now and feel good on my feet. They fit perfectly.

"Tell her thanks," I say, checking out my new shoes.

"All set?" the nurse asks as she goes behind my wheelchair.

"Yeah. I'm ready."

The three of us go to the elevator and take it down to the first floor. Corbin races ahead to get his car while the nurse wheels me to the exit. The moment we're outside I breathe in the fresh air, happy to no longer be breathing the hospital air which is stale and filled with whatever cleaners they use.

A large black SUV pulls up beside me and parks. Corbin appears and opens the passenger door, then helps me inside. He's being so careful with me. It's sweet and caring, but again, I can't read anything into it. He's a doctor. He's trained to treat patients with care.

As he goes around to the other side I notice my crutches in the back seat. I totally forgot about them. He must've packed them before coming to my room to get me.

"New car?" I ask as he puts his seatbelt on.

"It's a lease. Short term. Just until I figure out what I want."

"Is your old car too damaged to drive?"

"Actually, there wasn't much damage at all. I just don't want to drive it anymore."

"What kind of car was it?"

63

"Audi. It was a gift from my parents when I finished my residency."

"So it's not that old. And it was a gift? You should keep it."

"Driving it would just remind me what happened. Every day I'd be reliving the accident." He shakes his head. "I never want to see that car again." He wakes up the dashboard navigation system. "I need your address."

I give it to him and he punches it in, then looks at me.

"What?" I ask, confused why he's not driving.

"Seatbelt."

"Oh." I reach back and pull it over me, then click it in place. "Better?"

He smiles, then turns his attention to the road and finally takes off.

"So Dorchester, huh?" He glances at me as we wait at a stop light.

"It wasn't my first choice but I needed a place to live and the rent was cheap."

"That street you live on," he says, driving forward as the light turns green. "Not in the best neighborhood."

"No, but I couldn't afford to be picky. It hasn't been bad so far."

"How long have you lived there?"

"A week. Not even that long if you take out the days I spent at the hospital."

"You have roommates?"

"Two. A guy and his girlfriend. The guy's in a band. I don't know if he does anything besides that. I don't think he does because he's home all day either sleeping or banging on his drums. His girlfriend comes and goes throughout the day so I'm not really sure if she has a job."

"So you basically know nothing about these people."

"I don't have to. It's not like we're going to be friends. I'm just renting out a room. Once I get a job I'll never even be there, other than to sleep."

"That guy can't be banging on his drums when you're trying to rest. Loud noises aren't good for your concussion."

"I can't ask him to stop. It's his apartment. He can do what he wants."

"Then *I'll* ask him. I'll explain that I'm your doctor and you need quiet in order to recover."

"He's not going to care. He doesn't even know me."

"If he's that loud he could be violating a noise ordinance. We'll file a complaint with the city."

"Corbin, no. I don't want him mad at me. I have to live with the guy."

"He doesn't have to know we reported him. We can do it anonymously."

"I'd rather just let it go. I'll wear earplugs or cover my head with a pillow." I sneeze, then realize I didn't cover my face when I did it. "Sorry. I just got germs on your new car."

"Don't worry about it. I'm surrounded by germs all day." He points to the glove compartment. "There's tissues in there."

I open the compartment and find a mini package of tissues. I take it out and attempt to quietly blow my nose.

"We should probably stop and get you more."

"Thanks, but I'd really just like to get home." I lean my head against the seat. "I'm more tired than I thought I was."

"How about I drop you off, then go get whatever you need? You can make a list, or I'll just figure it out."

"I don't want you doing all that. You've done enough."

"I'm not taking no for an answer. You need stuff and you don't have a car."

"But you have to get back to work."

"I took the rest of the day off."

"You did?"

"I'm really tired and I can't do my job well when I'm tired. I'm going to go home and try to sleep."

He checks the nav system, which shows we're almost there.

"It's that one," I say, pointing to the rundown building. "My apartment's on the third floor."

He slows the car and eyes the building, like he's not sure he even wants to go in it. I felt the same way when I first saw it. The inside is a little better but not much. The walls are cracked and the carpet is stained and the whole building has a weird odor I can't identify.

Corbin parks the SUV, then hops out and grabs my crutches, meeting me at the passenger door.

"You good?" he asks, as I take a few steps with the crutches.

"Yeah, I'm okay. Let's go."

Once we're inside we take the elevator to the third floor.

"Right there." I point to my door and give him my keys. "Number 320."

He goes ahead of me to the door. He puts the key in but it doesn't turn.

"Sometimes it gets stuck," I tell him. "You have to jiggle it a little."

He does but it still doesn't work.

I'm beside him now and take the key. "There's an art to opening it. Took me days to figure it out."

Sirens blare outside, which happens all the time, day and night. It bothered me at first but now I'm used to it. Corbin apparently isn't because he seems to be getting more and more anxious the louder the sirens get.

"You all right?" I ask, still struggling with the key. "They're not coming to get you, are they?" I tease.

"No, but I think they're stopping at your building."

I pause to listen and hear, "Stop! Police!"

"Yep, they're here," I say. "But outside on the street."

"Some guy's probably stealing my SUV."

"More likely a drug dealer got caught."

He holds my arm. "You've got drug dealers living here?"

"I'm not sure. I'm just guessing. Doesn't it look like a place drug dealers would live?"

"Yeah, which is why you shouldn't be living here."

"I'm safe. I rarely leave the apartment, especially at night." I take the key out. "Something's wrong. It's not working." I bang on the door. "Moon? Are you home? It's Star."

I don't hear anyone inside but they could be sleeping.

"His name's Moon?" Corbin asks.

"It's what he goes by. I don't know his real name. His girlfriend is Sun. Well, her name is Sunny but she goes by Sun."

"So you're Star, and you live with Moon and Sun?"

I laugh. "I know. I thought *I* had a crazy name but then I met those two. My name is actually why they let me live here. They needed a Star to go with the Moon and Sun."

His brows furrow. "Are you sure you want to live with these people?"

"Let's go downstairs and find the building manager. He'll be able to get the door open."

Back on the first floor, we go to Larry's door and knock several times but he doesn't answer. He's got the TV blaring so loud he'll never hear us. I get out my phone and text him that I'm outside his door.

He finally answers, wearing a dingy white t-shirt and jeans held up by red suspenders stretched over his big belly. He's holding a bag of barbecue flavored potato chips, his fingers covered in orangish-red seasoning. He's old and only has a few strands of hair left on his head but he combs them over the top as if trying to hide the fact that he's bald.

"What do you want?" he barks.

"I can't get my key to work." I hold it up.

He snatches it from me. "That's because it doesn't. And if you hadn't returned this one, you would've owed me ten bucks."

"What do you mean it doesn't work? Is the lock broken?"

"The lock is fine but it only works with the new key." He shoves my key in his pocket, then digs his hand in the chip bag and shoves some chips in his mouth.

I glance at Corbin, who looks annoyed with Larry. I'm annoyed with him too but I have to be nice so he'll let me in the apartment.

"So can I have the new key?" I ask, holding my hand out.

"Not unless you live there." He munches on his chips while wiping the chip dust off on his jeans. "I gotta get back to my program." He grabs hold of the door to close it.

"Wait! What about my key?"

"I just told ya. You don't get a key. You don't live there no more."

"What do you mean I don't live there? You know I live there. I just had you up there last week to fix the sink. My name is Star. I live in 320."

"You *used* to live there. You don't now."

"I don't get it. What do you mean?"

Corbin nudges me. "Was your name on the lease?"

"No, but I was paying rent. I paid for two months when I moved in." I look back at Larry. "Are you saying Moon gave my room to someone else?"

"Moon ain't there no more." Larry stuffs more chips in his mouth. "Said he got a gig in New York. He and the girl moved out yesterday morning."

"Wait, what? They're gone? But why didn't they tell me?"

He shrugs. "Beats me. All I know is he's gone and I've got two new people living there. I gotta go. I'm missing my show." He shuts the door.

"I don't have an apartment," I say, staring at Larry's closed door. "I'm homeless."

CHAPTER EIGHT

Corbin

"Don't worry," I say to Star. "We'll figure this out."

"How?" she asks, sounding defeated. "Do you have any idea how hard it is to find a place to live in this city?"

"There are plenty of places. We just have to look."

"Let me clarify. An *affordable* place to live. Do you know how hard it is to find an *affordable* place to live? And by affordable I mean affordable for a person with hardly any money and no job?"

Police sirens start up outside, followed by the sound of a couple screaming at each other as they come down the stairs.

I take hold of Star's arm. "Let's get out of here. We'll find you something else. Anything's gotta be better than here."

"Wait." She knocks on the landlord's door.

"What are you doing?" I ask.

"All my stuff was in the apartment. I need it back."

"Star, I—"

The landlord yanks open the door, a bottle of beer in his hand. "Now what?"

"My stuff," Star says.

"What stuff?"

"My clothes and my iPad and all my other stuff. Where is it?"

"Hell if I know. The place was empty when they moved out."

Her shoulders slump. "Empty? Are you sure? Maybe they put my stuff in a closet. Could I go check?"

"Not with new tenants living there." He takes a swig of his beer.

"I only need to be in there a minute. Or you could go in and check. I just need to know if there's anything left."

"Trust me, kid. There was nothing in there. I checked every closet, every cupboard. The place was cleaned out. "

"Star, let's go," I say.

The guy closes the door and clicks the lock shut. The volume on his TV rises, making it clear he doesn't want to be bothered again.

Star collapses back against the wall. "My stuff. It's gone. It's all gone. You know how long I saved to buy that iPad? And now it's gone, along with all my clothes and shoes and whatever else I had."

"I'm sorry this happened, Star, but you really should've gotten to know those people better before moving in with them. You should've at least been on the lease so that—"

"You're seriously lecturing me right now?" She rights herself on the crutches and hobbles as fast as she can to the door.

"Star, wait!" I catch up to her and block her path. "I'm sorry. I shouldn't have said that. I sounded like my father just now, lecturing you when I should've been trying to help." I take a deep breath and let it out. "Okay, so here's the plan. We'll go back to my place and get on the internet and find one of those apartment search places. Then we'll—"

"Hold on."

"Why? What's wrong?"

"Nothing. I'm just trying to figure out what you said."

"What did I say?"

70

"I'm not sure. You kind of mumbled it when you were taking a breath."

Damn, did I say that out loud? I didn't mean to but I must've if she heard it. Now I have to explain, which is embarrassing.

"Oh. That." I laugh it off. "Forget it. It's just something I do when there's a lot going on and I need to refocus."

"What was it? What did you say?"

"It doesn't matter. Let's get going. We have a lot to do." I walk to the door but notice she's not beside me.

"Happy little trees," she calls out.

Shit. She DID hear me.

I turn back to her. "What about 'em?"

"That's what you said, isn't it?"

"Forget it. Let's go."

"Happy little trees," she repeats. "Why does that sound familiar?"

I walk back to her. "Bob Ross. The painter. He had a show on TV. I watched reruns of it all through college and med school. Whenever I was feeling overwhelmed it calmed me down and helped me refocus."

"That was one of his phrases, right? Happy little trees?"

I smile. "It was one of my favorites. He had several good ones but I always liked the tree one the best. When I say it I imagine Bob at the canvas, talking in that calm, quiet voice, focusing on one part of the painting at a time. The mountain tops, the clouds, the shadows on the trees. It reminds me to do the same. To calm down and focus on one thing at a time."

"Hmm. Maybe I should try that."

"Go ahead." I fold my arms over my chest and wait.

"Right now?"

"Sure. Why not?"

"Okay." She takes a deep breath, and on the exhale she quietly says "happy little trees." She smiles, then laughs.

"Feel better?"

"Actually, I kinda do. I'm still feeling overwhelmed but that did help a little."

"Keep saying it, along with the deep breaths. The more you do it the better you'll feel."

Lauren hated it when I did that. She told me I sounded ridiculous so I trained myself to think the phrase and not say it out loud. But just now I let it slip. Is it because of my lack of sleep? Or because I feel comfortable around Star? Because I knew she wouldn't judge me or ridicule me for it the way Lauren would?

We leave and when we get outside I immediately check to see if my SUV is still there.

"You really thought someone stole it?" Star asks.

"In this neighborhood? I wouldn't be surprised."

Star looks up and down the street, then yells, "My car! It's gone!" She hobbles down the street, searching for it. "It was parked down the street and now it's gone!"

"Star, slow down! You're going to fall!"

Just as I say it her shoe gets stuck on a piece of broken sidewalk and she trips and falls to the ground.

"Star!" I kneel down in front of her. "Are you okay?"

"I think so."

"Let me see your knee." She puts her leg out and I carefully lift her pant leg up to expose her knee. "The stitches are still intact. It's just a little scraped up. I'll clean it when we get home. Does it hurt?"

"Yeah, but it's not bad." She reaches for her crutches. "I might need some help getting up."

I lift her to standing.

"So your car is gone," I say with a sigh.

"The way things are going I shouldn't be surprised."

"You think it was stolen?"

"I don't know why anyone would want it. It was a rusted-out piece of crap that kept breaking down. I'm guessing it got towed."

"Then we'll call all the tow lots and see if it's there. But first we need to get you back to my place so you can rest and I can clean up that knee. You okay to walk?"

"Yeah, but give me a minute."

"Why?"

She doesn't answer. Instead she closes her eyes, takes a deep breath and exhales while whispering 'happy little trees', then opens her eyes.

A smile spreads across my face. If I didn't love her before I do now. Well, not love in a romantic sense but love as in love her as a person. She's so different than what I'm used to. Maybe that's why I like spending time with her. I never know what she's going to do next. She intrigues me and makes me smile, and I'm not one who smiles a lot. I'm usually much more serious.

"Better now?" I ask.

"Better enough to keep myself from having a complete meltdown."

"I have to say, you're taking this really well."

"Only because you're here helping me. If I was trying to figure this out on my own, I'd be sitting outside my apartment crying right now. Maybe not crying. I'm not much of a crier, but I'd definitely be a mess right now."

"We're going to figure this out, Star. I'll help you get back on your feet. I promise."

We return to my SUV and I turn on the heated leather seats after noticing Star shivering. It's spring and the days alternate between warm and chilly. Today it's chilly.

On the way to my apartment I glance over at Star. She's staring straight ahead like she's deep in thought.

"What are you thinking over there?" I ask.

"I'm not really thinking anything." She lowers the visor to shield her eyes from the sun.

"Liar," I say, putting my signal on to turn.

The car gets quiet, the only sound being the ticking of the blinker. I never liked that sound. It reminds me of being a kid in the car with my dad. He wouldn't let us listen to the radio so we had to sit there and listen to the sounds the car made, like the annoying tick of the blinker.

Glancing at Star again I see her chewing her lip. She's worried. She has no job, no apartment, no car, and she's injured. And it's all caused by me. I need to help her. I need to make her feel better.

"You need the dark in order to show the light."

My words wake her from her thoughts and she looks at me. "What?"

"It's another Bob Ross quote. You need the dark in order to show the light. He was talking about painting but it applies to life too."

She pauses a moment. "You really think that's true?"

"Definitely. If everything was great all the time you'd never know it was great. Great would become the norm. Or if you were never sad, would you really know what it felt like to be happy?"

"I guess not."

"So in a way, you're in a good spot right now."

"Meaning what?"

"You're in the dark, which means there's light ahead."

"Or more darkness," she mutters.

"Maybe, but realistically, what else could happen? You got hit by a car, lost your job, lost your apartment, your car, all your possessions. There's not much more that could happen."

"You'd think that, but the way things are going I wouldn't be too sure."

"Trust me. Things will get better. They already are. You met me, right?"

"Only because you hit me with your car."

"True," I say with a sigh. "Bad example."

"I wasn't trying to make you feel bad. I just meant that if it weren't for the accident, we never would've met. But I'm glad we met."

"You are?" I ask, glancing at her.

74

"I wish we'd met under different circumstances but it is what it is. And if anyone was going to hit me with a car I'm glad it was you."

I chuckle. "I'm not sure that's a compliment but I'll take it."

"I'm serious. Other people would've just had their insurance deal with me. They wouldn't have even checked if I was okay. But you stayed by my side the whole time. And you're still here, helping me when you really don't have to."

"I'm not going to just leave you with no place to live. I caused all this and now I need to fix it."

I stop at the light and notice Star looking around.

"You live in Cambridge?" she asks.

"Yeah. A few blocks from here."

"In an apartment?"

"I guess you'd call it that. My grandfather owns the building. I live in the top floor and he rents out the rest. There's a coffee shop on the street level."

"Does he make you pay rent?"

"No. He doesn't need the money. He made a fortune investing in real estate. Made way more than he ever made being a surgeon."

"Does he live here?"

"He has a home here but spends most of his time traveling with my grandmother. They're currently in Dubai."

"How long have you lived there?"

"In the building?"

"Yeah."

"Since college. Well, med school."

"Let me guess." She smiles. "Harvard?"

I nod. "My father went there too. And my grandfather."

"What about undergrad?"

"Columbia."

"So you're really smart."

"In some things, yes. In other things, not so much."

"Like what?"

"You're really going to make me admit my weaknesses?" I shoot her a smile as we wait for the light to turn green.

"Just one or two. I'd like to know what doctors aren't good at."

"Okay, well, for one, painting."

"Like Bob Ross painting?"

"Any kind of painting. I tried painting my bedroom and had to get it fixed by a professional. The guy said it was the worst paint job he'd ever seen."

"That wasn't very nice."

"He wasn't trying to mean. He was just being honest. I did a horrible job. And don't even get me started on my attempt at painting landscapes. No amount of Bob Ross instruction could make my trees look happy. They turned out looking like sad sticks that'd been burned in a forest fire."

She laughs. "So you'll never be a painter. At least you have the doctor thing to fall back on. What else aren't you good at?"

"I don't like this game. Can we quit now?"

"C'mon. Just one more thing."

I take a moment to think. "Pasta."

"Pasta?"

"I either overcook it or undercook it. I set a timer and it still doesn't come out right."

"I can help you with that. Pasta's cheap so I eat it all the time. I've become an expert at making it."

We approach the gate of my parking garage and I swipe my key card to open it. The building I live in is old but kept up. It has great architecture and beautiful stonework, which is what drew my grandfather to buy it. That and the fact he knew it'd increase in value given the location.

"Maybe we'll make some tonight," I say as I park in my reserved spot.

"Make what?"

"Pasta."

I give her a smile, trying to put her at ease. She's still stressed out from everything that happened today. But we'll figure it out.

She can stay with me tonight, or all week if that's what it takes for her to find a new place.

We go in the elevator and I punch in my code. The elevator doors open to a small foyer with slate tile floors and a dark wood bench with a tall back that has hooks on it. Next to that is a small table with a lamp and the black bowl where I drop my keys.

"Come on in," I say to Star, leading her to the living room which is open to the kitchen and dining area.

"I like your place," she says, looking around.

"I didn't decorate it. Decorating is another thing I'm not good at."

"It's very manly," she says, her eyes going to the dark leather sofa and thick wood tables.

I chuckle. "It's not everyone's taste but I like it."

Lauren didn't. She kept threatening to hire a decorator but I wouldn't let her. That should've been a clue I didn't see a future with her. If I had, I would've been open to her making this place ours and not just mine.

"I meant manly in a good way," Star says. "It's woodsy, like a cabin. We had a cabin growing up and I always liked going there."

"You don't have it anymore?"

"My dad had to sell it. He went through a gambling phase and needed the money to pay off his losses."

"That's too bad. Is he still gambling?"

"I don't know. I don't ask." She walks over to the large window opposite the couch and looks out at the garden below. It's too early in the year for the flowers to be up but when they are, it's really beautiful.

"Nice view," Star says.

"It's better when everything's in bloom. I'm gonna go change. Feel free to make yourself at home."

I go down to my room and change into jeans and a t-shirt, then wash my hands and grab my first aid kit. When I get back

77

to the living room Star is sitting on the couch, checking her phone.

"You need anything?" I ask, setting the first aid kit on the coffee table.

I feel her watching me, and when I look up at her, I swear she's checking me out. Or maybe I'm imagining it.

"Star?" I say, getting her attention.

Her eyes dart to the coffee table and she grabs the remote. "The TV. I found the remote but where's the TV?"

I take the remote from her and press a button. The TV slowly rises from the top of the media cabinet that's across from the couch.

"That explains why I couldn't find it," she says. "That's really cool."

"It's hidden so it doesn't obstruct the view of the gardens. I don't watch a lot of TV so I usually leave it in the cabinet."

"Why don't you watch TV? You just don't like it or what?"

"I don't have time. I'm either at work or the gym or just out doing stuff." I sit beside her. "Let me see your knee."

She yanks up her sweat pants, exposing her knee. I carefully lift up her leg and rest it on mine.

"Does it hurt?" I ask, running my finger around the cut, gently pressing the skin in certain spots.

Her body stiffens and she pulls back. "It's just a scrape." She tries to put her leg down but I keep hold of it.

"Keep it extended," I say, reaching forward to open the first aid kit. I take out a cotton ball and soak it in the antiseptic. "This may sting a little." I push her sweats up higher on her leg, exposing part of her thigh. She sucks in a breath and I glance up at her? "You okay?"

"Yeah." She forces out a smile. "Go ahead."

Looking back down at her leg, my eyes catch on her exposed thigh and I feel a twitch below the belt. Shit. That's not supposed to happen. I can't be thinking of her that way.

Redirecting my attention back to her knee, I dab the cotton ball over the cut.

My hand stalls as my eyes wander up to her thigh again, noticing the shape, the gentle curve, her smooth skin. I feel another twitch of my cock and force my eyes back to her knee.

"Still okay?" I ask, reaching for the bandage.

"Yeah." She sounds breathless and when I lift my eyes to hers, we pause a moment, gazing at each other, and I'm suddenly very aware that it's not just me having these feelings. Star feels it too.

What am I doing? I just broke up with Lauren. I can't be interested in another woman, especially not the woman I hit with my car.

I blink away from her and clear my throat as I secure the bandage in place.

"All done," I say with a smile, pulling her pant leg down.

My phone rings and I see Lauren's name on the screen. She texted me earlier to talk about our living arrangements going forward. I don't want to talk to her but we need to get this settled.

"I need to get this," I say to Star.

"Go ahead." She smiles. "I'll watch TV."

I go down to my room and shut the door. "Hello, Lauren."

"Why didn't you return my texts?"

"I've been busy."

"Busy doing what? Your nurse said you took the afternoon off."

"There were some issues with Star. It ended up taking longer than I thought."

"Star? The girl you hit with your car? Why were you with HER?"

"It doesn't matter. Just tell me why you called."

"I've decided to acknowledge your need for some time apart," she says in a business-like tone. "I think it'd do us both some good to have a little space. Time to think about our future and where we want to take it. I think it might even strengthen our relationship."

I sigh. "Lauren, this isn't a temporary break. It's over. We're not together anymore."

"Whatever you need to tell yourself," she says, dismissing me as usual. "We'll discuss it later. For now, I'll be taking some of my things and staying with a friend."

It's a start. I want her to take everything, but at this point, I'm not going to push her to do more.

"When will you be over?"

"I don't know. Why do you ask?"

"I'm just wondering. I don't want you just dropping by without telling me."

"Why? Are you planning on having someone over?" she asks, a hint of jealousy in her voice.

"What I do or who I see is none of your business. We're not in a relationship anymore."

"So you DO have someone," she huffs. "I knew you were cheating on me!"

"I was not cheating on you. And if I decide to date again, it will not be cheating because our relationship is over."

"It's not over. We're simply taking a break."

"Lauren, I don't have time for this. I have to go."

"This isn't the end, Corbin," she snaps, then hangs up.

I take a calming breath, then return to the living room. Star is still on the couch but the TV isn't on.

"I thought you were watching TV," I say.

"There was nothing on," she says, tossing the remote aside.

Sitting beside her, still angry from Lauren, I force out a smile. "You ready to search for apartments?"

"Um, sure," she says, staring at me like she wants to ask me something.

I wait but she doesn't say whatever she's thinking so I get up. "I'll grab my laptop."

"Corbin?"

"Yeah?"

"Is everything okay?"

"It's fine. Why?"

"You seem kinda angry."

"I'm not angry. Why do you think I'm angry?"

"You just seem different."

My brows lift. "Different how?"

"You were all happy trees and then you took that phone call and now you're kinda crooked angry trees."

I wonder if she heard me talking to Lauren. I did raise my voice toward the end of the call.

"Sorry. No more angry trees." I smile. "Back to happy."

"Is there a problem at work?" she asks, seeing through my fake smile. How is she able to read me so well? We just met. "Do you need to go back to the clinic? If so, I can go somewhere else, like a coffee shop or the library."

"It wasn't work." I rub my hand over my jawline, which is scruffy because I didn't shave this morning.

Star's waiting for me to say more. Should I tell her what's going on?

My phone rings. I get it out and see it's Lauren calling again. I send it to voicemail, then text her, *Can't talk now. Text me before you come over.*

"Is it her again?" Star asks.

Her? So she DID hear me talking on the phone. And she knows I was talking to a woman.

I put my phone away. "It was Lauren."

"And she's your..."

"Girlfriend," I say without even thinking.

Disappointment falls over Star's face and I suddenly feel the same way. Not because I have a girlfriend. Because I *don't* have a girlfriend. Not anymore. My disappointment is because I'm single now but can't act on my feelings for Star. It wouldn't be right. Not right after a break-up. Not after hitting her with my car. And now I'm letting her stay with me. I'm more involved with her than I should be and yet I want more. I just can't let myself have it.

CHAPTER NINE

Star

He has a girlfriend. Of course he does. He's gorgeous, smart, rich, successful. I assumed there was a woman in his life but part of me held out hope that he was single.

"Lauren's your girlfriend?" I ask casually, trying to hide my disappointment.

"EX-girlfriend. We broke up the morning of the accident. It was another reason I wasn't paying attention that day."

They broke up? Then why was she calling? Maybe the breakup is more of a break. Some time off, and then they'll get back together. What girl would ever give up a guy like Corbin?

"Did you guys have a fight?" I ask.

"Yes, but that's not why we broke up. It's a long story. Things haven't been good for a long time. So long I don't even remember them being good."

"How long have you two dated?"

"Years. We started dating in med school."

"She's a doctor too?"

"She's finishing up her residency. She'll be done in a few months. You might've seen her at the hospital. She stopped by your room but I think you were asleep."

"So why the other day? Why'd you pick then to break up with her? Or should I not be asking?"

"You can ask. As for the answer, I'm not entirely sure. I spent that whole night before thinking about it, wondering if there was anything I could do to save the relationship. I realized there wasn't, because my feelings for her were gone. They'd been gone a long time but I tried to deny it. I woke up the other day and realized how unhappy I was. I couldn't take another day of it so I ended things with her."

"But didn't she just call you?"

"She's not accepting the breakup, which doesn't make sense because I know she was just as unhappy as I was in the relationship, but for some reason she's not willing to let it go. I think it'll just take time."

So they broke up but she's not letting him go. I wouldn't want to either. I've only known him a few days and already miss him when he's not around. I shouldn't be getting this attached to him but I am. Maybe because he stayed with me in the hospital, and because he's the only person I know in Boston.

"Want something to drink?" he asks, walking to the kitchen.

"No, thanks."

I watch as he takes a glass from the cupboard and fills it at the water cooler that's next to the stove. He's wearing faded jeans and a white t-shirt and damn, he looks good. He looked good in his doctor clothes but I like this casual look even more. I can get a better look at his body. Maybe I shouldn't be focusing on that but he's got a great body so it'd be a shame not to look. He obviously works out a lot so I'm simply admiring his hard work.

When he touched me earlier to bandage my knee I almost passed out. It could have been due to my concussion but I think it was more about how I felt when he touched me. I wasn't expecting my body to react that way. Breathless. Heat flooding my core. When he pushed my sweat pants slowly up my leg, his warm hands sliding up my thigh, I was so aroused I had to pull back before I kissed him. He noticed and looked up, our eyes meeting, and for a moment I felt like he was just as aroused as me. I was convinced of it. But then he went into doctor mode and my fantasy ended, reminding me he's not interested. It's just my imagination telling me so because I want it to be true.

He just broke up with a girl he dated for years. He'll need time before he's ready to date again.

"I'll be right back." Corbin goes down the hall and returns with his laptop. He brings it over and sets it on the coffee table in front of me. "I have two so we can each search. It'll go faster with us both looking."

He seems to be in a hurry to find me an apartment. He wasn't before, but then his girlfriend, or EX-girlfriend, called and now he wants me out of here as fast as possible. Maybe she said something to him. Maybe she told him it's not right to help a patient this way. Maybe it's against some doctor code of ethics. But he's not my doctor. He's just helping me out.

I wake up the computer. "I need a password."

Looking behind me I see Corbin sitting at the breakfast bar in the kitchen, his laptop open. Why is he sitting way over there? There's plenty of room on the couch.

"Hold on." He comes up behind me and reaches over to put the password in, then quickly returns to his spot at the breakfast bar.

"I'm not sure where to start," I tell him. "Any suggestions?"

"Search apartment rental agents. We'll have better luck going through an agent than using one of those apartment search sites."

"I can't just look for apartments. I need to look for a roommate. I can't afford to live by myself."

"If you do that you risk getting another roommate who'll take off with your stuff."

"I don't have a choice. I can't afford to live on my own. I need to find a college student. If they're here for college, they're not going to take off mid-semester."

"Those people already have roommates. You're not going to find someone looking for a roommate this time of year."

"You could be a little more positive."

"I'm just saying, it's not likely. And if you have to find a place with a roommate, we're not going to get this done today. It's going to take time."

"Then I don't know what to do. I don't have money for a hotel. And I can't go home. My parents would kill me if I showed up there again. I already stayed five years past their 18-and-you're-out rule. Even if I *could* live at home I don't have a car to get there." I sigh. "I'm so screwed. I have no money. No place to sleep. No car."

"Hey." Corbin appears beside me. He takes the laptop and sets it on the table. "I told you I'd help you and I will."

"I know but there's only so much you can do. Like you said, it'll take time to find a roommate. And I don't just need a roommate. I need a job. Fast. Except nobody's going to hire a girl with a concussion who has to use crutches to walk. And I have nothing to wear to an interview except these sweats, which I really appreciate by the way. I'd pay you back if I had the money. Actually...." I reach in my pocket and dig out the money I stuffed in there from my wallet. "Here's ten." I shove the wadded up bill into his hand. "It's not much but it's something. Anyway, to find a job I'm gonna need—"

"Okay, stop." He takes my hand and gives it a gentle squeeze. "Take a deep breath."

I do as he says, watching as he does it with me. On the exhale we both whisper 'happy little trees' which makes me laugh.

"Feel any better?" he asks.

"A little, but I still don't know what to do. I don't even have a place to sleep tonight."

"You'll sleep here," he says.

"Here? I can't do that."

"Why not?"

"Well, for one, I don't think your girlfriend would like it."

"She's not my girlfriend. She's my ex. And it's not her decision. This is my place and I can have whoever I want stay here."

"But it might be a few days before I find a place. I can't inconvenience you like that."

"You're seriously worried about being an inconvenience?" He lets out a laugh. "Are you kidding? I've completely turned your life upside down. Because of me, you lost your job and everything else. If anyone's been inconvenienced, it's you. I owe you a lot more than a room in my apartment." He stands up. "You feeling okay or do you need to rest?"

"I'm okay. Why?"

"We're going out." He holds his hand out. "C'mon."

I take his hand and stand up. "Where are we going?"

"Shopping. You need clothes."

"I don't have money."

He smiles. "Luckily, I do. Lots of it. So buy whatever you want. And feel free to toss out the hospital sweats. Those were just meant to get you home. I didn't expect you to ever wear them again."

"I'm not throwing them out. I only wore them one time."

"Which is plenty. You really want to walk around covered in the hospital logo? Those clothes don't even fit you. They're way too big and the fabric is scratchy."

"It IS kind of scratchy."

"Hold on." He races to his room and returns holding a gray hoodie. "Try this."

I take off the hospital hoodie, leaving the t-shirt on, and put on Corbin's hoodie, which is softer than any sweatshirt I've ever owned.

"It's too big on you," he says, "but it's gotta feel better, right?"

"It feels great. It's really soft."

"Sorry I don't have pants that'll fit you but we'll remedy that. Ready to shop?"

"Okay, but let's just go somewhere cheap. I don't want to spend a lot."

"I'm the one paying and I don't care what it costs. You seem to be forgetting I hit you with my car."

"I think you've already made up for that."

"Not even close. You need to use the restroom before we leave?"

"Actually, yeah."

"Down the hall on your right."

His bathroom is immaculate. The sink and fixtures are clean and shiny and there's nothing on the counter except for a soap dispenser. I know I shouldn't but I sneak a peek in the cabinet drawers. There's nothing in there. I thought maybe his girlfriend would have left some stuff here but I guess not.

When I return from the bathroom Corbin is in the kitchen, going through his mail.

"You have a really clean bathroom."

He chuckles. "I can't take credit for that. The cleaning lady was here yesterday. And that's not the bathroom I use. It's the guest bathroom. The one in my room isn't that clean."

That must be where his girlfriend keeps her stuff. I'm guessing she used to stay here. I wonder if her stuff is still here. If they just broke up, she probably hasn't had time to come get her things. What if she shows up while I'm here? That would be awkward.

"Let's head out," Corbin says, pushing the elevator button. "We'll get you what you need and grab some lunch, then get you home so you can sleep."

Corbin starts driving to the mall but I insist we go to a discount store where I can get more for the money. After just a few minutes of being there I can tell Corbin doesn't like shopping. He keeps looking at his watch to check the time, but he doesn't rush me at all. Still, I try to hurry, finding some jeans, t-shirts, and a couple sweatshirts. For now, I just need the basics, including underwear and some bras, which I snuck in the cart when Corbin took off to make a phone call.

"I think I have everything," I say.

"You sure?" Corbin looks at the cart. "What about girl stuff?"

I laugh. "Girl stuff? What girl stuff? It's not that time of the month."

"I meant other girl stuff, like shampoo, conditioner, shower gel, makeup. You need all that stuff, right?"

"Um, I guess, but I don't have to get it right now."

"We're here. You need it. You might as well get it. Or if you want to go to a better store for that stuff we can."

"I can get what I need here."

As he's pushing the cart to the shampoo aisle, he says, "Lauren would never buy shampoo here. Or makeup. She wouldn't even buy her shower gel here."

"Where does she go for that stuff?"

"She has different stores for all of them. She special orders her shampoo off the internet. And she has some special store for her makeup where they blend it just for her."

"That's a thing? I've never heard of that."

"It's a thing but it costs a lot."

"Good thing she has a good job. Does she have a job for after her residency?"

"Not yet. She's been talking about looking for jobs in New York." He stops the cart in front of the shampoo. "Want to pick one out?"

After we finish shopping and ring everything up at the checkout, I go in the bathroom and put on my new jeans, a t-shirt that actually fits, and a hoodie so I can give Corbin's back to him. I'd love to keep wearing it but that seems like something a girlfriend would do, which I am not.

For lunch we go to a deli next to his apartment building. It's busy and loud but the lunch crowd is starting to leave, quieting the place down. I've had a headache all morning but I didn't want to tell Corbin because I knew he'd make us go home and I really needed some different clothes. I feel a lot better knowing I have stuff now. After losing everything, I'll never again take for granted things like clean underwear and warm socks. And jeans. The sweatpants were huge on me. It feels good to be in jeans again.

As we're finishing lunch one of the deli workers walks up to our table. He's around my age with shaggy blond hair, an eyebrow ring, and black and brown leather bracelets lining his wrists. "Sterling, what's up? Haven't seen you for a while."

"I've been working a lot." He motions to me. "Lars, this is Star."

He gives me a nod. "Hey." Turning back to Corbin, Lars folds his arms over his chest. "So I heard you hit some girl with your car."

"Where'd you hear that?"

"Lauren and I had spin class this morning. She said the chick was on a bike and ended up in the hospital." He smacks Corbin's shoulder. "Better lawyer up, man. That girl finds out you have money she'll be all over that, suing your ass for as much as she can get."

Corbin clears his throat. "Star is the girl I hit."

"Oh, shit!" Lars takes a step back, briefly glancing at me before looking back to Corbin. "Sorry, man, I had no idea."

"Don't worry about it."

Lars looks at me. "You okay? I mean you look good to me but what do I know?" He laughs.

"I'm fine. Just a few scrapes and bruises." I glance at Corbin. "And don't worry. I don't plan to sue anyone. Corbin's more than made up for what happened."

"He has, has he?" Lars looks back at Corbin and I realize he took what I said a different way.

"I'm helping her find an apartment," Corbin explains. "When she got out of the hospital, she found out her roommates took off with all her stuff and rented the place out to someone else."

"That sucks," Lars mutters.

"And because of me, she lost her job so I'm trying to help her get back on her feet."

"You're a good man, Sterling." Lars pats him on the shoulder. "I gotta get back to work."

"Hey, before you go," Corbin says, "What else did Lauren say this morning?"

He shrugs. "Not much. She just told me about the accident. She seemed pissed you were missing work."

"Yeah, well, that's not something she should be worrying about. She told you we broke up, right?"

"You guys broke up?" he asks, sounding surprised.

"A few days ago. Lauren hasn't quite accepted it yet."

"That's why she was in a bad mood. I thought she was just tired from her double shift. The girl works constantly. I don't know how she does it."

"It's just until her residency is over. After that she'll have more regular hours. Lauren's tough. She can handle it."

"Yeah. Hey, sorry about the breakup."

"It was time. We both need to move on with our lives." Corbin gets up from the table. "We should get going. Star needs to rest."

"So where are you staying?" Lars asks me.

"With me," Corbin answers. "Just until we find her a place."

He nods, then looks at me. "Hope you feel better."

"Thanks."

Lars walks back to the kitchen.

"How long have you known Lars?" I ask Corbin as we're leaving.

"About a year. We're not really friends. I just see him at the deli. I eat there a lot since it's so close to my apartment. Lauren knows him better than I do."

"Because of spin class?"

"That, and they do other stuff sometimes. When she has a night off Lauren likes to go to clubs. I'm kinda done with clubs so if I don't feel like going she goes with a group of friends. Sometimes Lars tags along."

"He's kinda cute."

90

"Cute?" Corbin wrinkles his nose in disgust. "You think he's cute?"

"Cute in a grungy, laid-back kind of way."

"I'm laid-back," he insists.

"Yeah? So?"

"You don't think I'm cute?"

"Um, no, not really."

It's true. Cute is not how I'd describe him. Hot. Smoldering. Burning with masculinity. Those are words I'd use to describe him. Cute doesn't cut it.

He huffs. "I have a history that says otherwise."

"Meaning what? You've slept with a lot of women?" I don't know where that came from. It just shot out of my mouth. I blame the concussion.

"Meaning I've been told I'm cute many times."

"What's cute to one person isn't cute to another."

"True." He glances at me with a smile. "I'm still disappointed you don't think I'm cute."

"Why do you care?"

"Because it means I'm getting old. Losing my looks."

I laugh. "You're a guy. You're not supposed to care how you look."

"Of course I care. All guys do."

"Not my brother. He'll go out with his hair a mess, wearing clothes that are ripped or stained or both. It doesn't bother him at all."

"Does he get girls looking like that?"

"He already has one. Don't ask me how he got her. It's a mystery. I'm thinking he must've brainwashed her somehow."

Corbin laughs. "Well, girlfriend or not, I still want to look good. It's how I was raised. We couldn't leave the house unless we were what my mother considered to be presentable. She would've rolled over in her grave if she saw me in your hospital room the other day, wearing those wrinkled clothes."

We're in the elevator now, going up to his apartment.

91

"What happened to your mom? Or do you not want to talk about it?"

"I can talk about it. My mom had a stroke and never recovered." The elevator doors open and we go into his apartment. "My dad's new wife was one of my mom's friends."

"That's kind of weird, isn't it? Your dad marrying your mom's friend?"

"Not really. I don't think they married for love. It was more for companionship. They both go to a lot of parties and fundraisers and like to travel. They didn't want to do those things alone." He drops his keys in the bowl by the door, then walks over to me. "Time to rest. Doctor's orders."

"You're not my doctor."

"But I'm *a* doctor and I know you need rest. It's been a busy morning."

"I really should try to find an apartment."

"I'll search while you sleep. Follow me."

He walks down the hall to the room at the very end. It has a queen-sized bed, nightstand, and TV on the wall.

"Will this work?"

"It's perfect. Way better than an air mattress."

"You slept on an air mattress?"

"I moved here with just my car and whatever I could fit in it."

"When we find you an apartment I'll get you a bed. You need to sleep on a real mattress."

"I'll get one after I find a job."

"It can't wait. Sleep is important for health. This is another doctor's orders thing. Now stop arguing with me and get some rest."

He gives me a smile, then leaves, shutting the door behind him.

Out of all the people who could've hit me with their car I really lucked out having it be Corbin. He's done so much for me and keeps offering to do more. I just don't know how long it'll last. I can't expect him to keep helping me. I need to find my own way out of this mess. But for now I need to sleep.

CHAPTER TEN

Corbin

While Star is asleep I do a quick search for apartments. Finding one that's affordable is going to be difficult. The Boston housing market is one of the most expensive in the country.

My quick search brings up websites for luxury apartments downtown. They don't even bother to list the rent, meaning if you have to ask, you can't afford it. The next few listings are also for luxury rentals. Clicking to the next page of search results I see a place that looks old and rundown but it's in a safe area and close to the subway, a plus since Star doesn't have a car. Scrolling down to the rent I see the cheapest apartment is $1600 a month. That's nothing for me but way too much for her. She'd need a roommate, but how do I find her a roommate she can trust? I know a lot of people in town but none who need roommates.

Shutting down my laptop I grab my keys and take the elevator to the first floor. Not having slept the past few nights, I'm exhausted and need some caffeine to keep me awake. There's a coffee shop on the street level of my building. I go there every morning and love the place but it's going to be awkward going there now that I broke up with Lauren. Her best friend, Alexis, is the manager.

I see her as soon as I walk in. She's behind the counter, refilling the coffee machines.

"Alexis," I say, getting her attention.

"Corbin." She sounds surprised, but I'm sure Lauren told her I wasn't at work. Lauren tells her everything.

"I'll take a double espresso." I get out my wallet.

She stands there, not getting my coffee. "I heard about you and Lauren."

I nod. "I assumed you did."

She cocks her head. "Why the break? You need time to think, or what?"

I sigh, not wanting to discuss this with her. "Lauren and I broke up. It's not temporary."

"She said you just needed some time alone."

"That wasn't the reason. Now could I get my coffee please?"

She remains in front of me, her hand on her hip. "I don't get it. You two have been together forever. Why end it now?" She narrows her eyes at me. "You're cheating."

"I'm not cheating. Now could I please have my coffee?"

"Why would you break up with her? Why now? Right before your engagement?"

"We weren't getting engaged. Just because her mother was planning an engagement party doesn't mean I had plans to propose. Her mother never should've done that."

"It wasn't just her mother. Everyone thought you two were headed to the altar. Lauren and I were already looking at dresses. We even went to bridal shops and she tried some on. But don't tell her I told you that. She wouldn't want you to know."

That doesn't surprise me. I always felt like Lauren was hiding stuff from me.

"What else wouldn't she want me to know?"

"What's that supposed to mean?"

I shrug. "I just wondered if there were other things Lauren didn't tell me. You would know. You're her best friend. She tells you everything."

"Lauren doesn't have secrets," she says, walking over to the espresso machine.

"If she did, you wouldn't tell me," I say, keeping my tone light so she doesn't think I'm accusing her of anything. Because I'm not. I'm just curious if Lauren told her things she didn't tell me.

"What could she possibly be hiding?" Alexis asks, her back to me as she waits for the machine to finish.

"I don't know. Maybe *she* was the one cheating."

"Lauren cheat?" She laughs. "When would she have time? She works like a hundred hours a week." Alexis returns with my espresso. "You look like shit today."

I hand her the money. "Keep the change."

As I'm leaving I hear her talking. "Heard you almost killed someone."

Lauren always makes things sound worse than they are so I'm not surprised Alexis said that.

I turn back around. "She's fine. Just a little banged up."

"Have you talked to your lawyer yet? Because my father has a friend who specializes in these types of cases. I could give you his number."

Why do people keep assuming Star's going to sue me? Not everyone is out to get money. Star didn't even want me buying her a sandwich.

"I won't be needing it," I say to Alexis as I walk to the door. She says something else but I pretend I didn't hear and continue out the door.

Alexis is from a wealthy family of lawyers. She was headed into a law career herself but then changed her mind and got a degree in women's studies. After college she moved back in with her parents and spent her days shopping. A year later her father told her he'd cut off her allowance if she didn't get a job, which is why she's managing the coffee shop. She's 28 and still gets an allowance to pay for her designer clothes and more shoes than she could ever wear.

Back at my apartment I go check on Star. She's sound asleep. I close the door and return to the living room.

Sipping my coffee, I get out my phone and check for messages. There's nothing from work. I didn't think there would be. Working in urgent care you see people once and that's it. It's not like having your own practice where patients are contacting you day and night with questions. My father was always on call. He could never relax. Now my sister's that way. I don't want that to be my life but it's exactly what Lauren wants. She's all about her career and has no problem working around the clock. It's another reason we weren't a good fit.

My phone rings and I see Lauren's name on the screen. I'd rather not answer but I pick up because she might be calling to tell me when she'll be by to get her things.

"Hello, Lauren."

"She's LIVING with you?" she yells.

"Lauren, if you're going to scream like that I'm hanging up."

I hear her blow out a breath, then calmly say, "I heard the girl you hit is now living with you. Is that true?"

"Where'd you hear *that*?" I ask, because I haven't told anyone. Did she bug my apartment? It wouldn't surprise me if she did.

"Lars told me. He called to tell me Kari from spin class broke her ankle and wouldn't be teaching tomorrow. Then he mentioned seeing you at lunch and said you had that girl with you."

"It's just temporary. Until she finds a place of her own."

"She's homeless? You're living with a homeless girl?"

"She wasn't homeless until this morning. She had an apartment but her roommates took off when she was in the hospital. She doesn't have anywhere to go so unless you know of somewhere she could stay, rent-free, she'll be staying here. Is that the only reason you called? To ask about Star?"

"Star," she mutters. "What a stupid name."

"Lauren, why did you call?"

"You better not be sleeping with her. We're on a break. That doesn't mean you can date other women."

"For the last time, this is more than a break. We are no longer in a relationship. It's over. I'm sorry you're having a hard time with this but this isn't the first time we've talked about it, Lauren. Just last year you talked about us not having a future."

"That was during a fight. I was angry. It doesn't count."

"The topic came up more than once, and every time it did you told me I needed to change. Our entire relationship you kept trying to make me be someone else. I'm tired of it, Lauren. I can't make you happy and I accept that. We're just not right for each other."

She sniffles, a sign she's about to fake cry. When she doesn't get her way in an argument, the fake crying begins and doesn't end until I give in. But I'm not giving in. Not this time.

The fake crying gets louder, her breath hiccuping, followed by sniffling. Even though I know it's fake, I still feel bad hearing her cry. That's why she does it. She knows I don't like hurting her.

"Lauren, I'm sorry. I really am. It just wasn't meant to be."

"But I love you," she says, sniffling.

If she loved me she wouldn't have treated me the way she did all the years we were together. She would've supported me the way I've supported her. She would've listened to me and let me be who I am instead of trying to change me into someone else.

Lauren doesn't love me. She loves what she imagines me to be, which is not who I am.

"Lauren, why don't you take some time off? Go home and get some rest. You'll feel better tomorrow."

She sniffles, then gets quiet.

"Lauren?"

Checking my phone, I see she hung up. I don't know what that means. Is she telling me she's angry at me? If so, I already know that. I'm angry at her too for making me feel like this is all my fault when really it's nobody's fault. The relationship just wasn't working. All we did was fight. There was no love left between us. It got to the point we didn't even like spending time together. We're both better off with someone else.

In the short time I've spent with Star I already feel more like myself again. The real me, not the one Lauren kept trying to create. I've smiled and laughed more the past few days than I have in months. Everything was so serious with Lauren. We couldn't just relax and have fun.

Lauren's call has me feeling stressed and when I'm stressed, I like to work out. I go in my room and change into my gym clothes, then check on Star in the guest room. She's still asleep so I leave her a note telling her where I am in case she wakes up.

The gym is on the second floor. My grandfather added it a few years ago as a birthday gift to me but it ended up benefitting him as well. It made the apartment building more attractive to renters so he was able to raise the rent. It's not a large gym but it has all the basic cardio equipment and enough weight machines for a good workout.

"Sterling." Kent smiles when he sees me walking in. "What are you doing here?"

Kent's a grad student, working on his PhD. He comes here during the day between classes. Last year he worked out in the mornings, same time as me, which is how we got to know each other.

"Taking the day off," I tell him.

"Oh, yeah?" He picks up a towel, a grin on his face. "Lauren let you?"

I laugh, but it's not funny. It's true. Lauren tried to control my schedule and everything else in my life.

"Lauren and I aren't dating anymore," I say, going to the treadmill to warm up.

"Seriously?" he asks, sounding surprised. "When did that happen?"

"A few days ago. She hasn't moved out yet but she's staying with a friend until she finds something."

"Are you seeing someone else?"

"No." I laugh. "It's only been a couple days since I ended things with Lauren. I'm not quite ready to date again."

"Then who was the girl?"

"What girl?"

"I saw you with a girl earlier. She was going up to your apartment."

"She's just someone I'm helping out. I don't like telling this story but you might as well know. I hit her with my car."

"The girl I saw?"

"Yeah. She was on a bike when I hit her."

"Is she okay?"

"She has some cuts and bruises and a mild concussion but it could've been a lot worse."

"Shit, that would mess me up if I hit someone like that."

"Believe me, I'm still feeling sick about it. Haven't slept since it happened. And then she lost her job and her apartment. I'm trying to help her get back on her feet."

"Is there anything I can do to help?"

"Know anyone who needs a roommate?"

"Actually I do but the rent's $2800. She'd have to pay half. Is that too much?"

"Yeah. She can't afford that. But if you hear of anyone else, let me know."

"I will. Hey, now that you're single again, any interest in going out with someone?" He grins.

"I think it's too soon, but who are we talking about?"

"Brynn. My cousin. You met her at that party I had last summer."

He had a party in the garden out back and invited a ton of people. I'm sure he introduced me to her but I don't remember her.

"Blond hair," he says. "Tall. Thin. She kind of looks like Lauren."

"Yeah, now I remember. She DID look like Lauren."

"Is that a bad thing? Because personality-wise, she's nothing like Lauren. I think you'd really like her. And she already likes you. She's still talking about you."

"She is?"

"Yeah. She's always asking me about you. What do you think? Want to meet her for coffee sometime?"

"Sorry, but I have to say no. I'd rather not date a Lauren lookalike."

"No problem. I totally get it." He wipes down the weight machine he was using. "I'm going to head out."

"See you later." I up the treadmill speed.

He walks over to me. "So the girl who's staying with you. Is she seeing someone?"

I want to smack him for even asking, but why? Why would I be angry about that? Star could date him. He's closer to her age than I am. And he's a nice guy. Smart. Getting his PhD. He's in good shape. But I still don't want him dating her.

"She's never mentioned a boyfriend," I tell him, "but that doesn't mean she doesn't have one."

"I'd be surprised if she didn't. She's gorgeous." He smiles. "Guess you're more into blondes but I prefer brunettes, myself."

I've only dated blondes but that doesn't mean I prefer them. I'm more attracted to Star than I ever was to Lauren, but maybe that's because she's different than what I'm used to. I don't know what's causing this attraction I have to Star but I need to get it under control. I can't be getting aroused every time I'm around her.

"Maybe when she's feeling better, you could introduce us," Kent says.

"Yeah, sure," I say, but I have no intention of doing so.

"Okay, well, have a good workout."

He leaves and I bump up the treadmill speed until I'm running at an all-out sprint.

Kent wants to go out with Star. Of course he does. She's gorgeous. Her face. Her body. That smile. Any guy would want to date her. Including me.

CHAPTER ELEVEN

Star

I wake up and notice it's dark outside. Checking my phone I see it's after five. I slept the entire afternoon and it was the best sleep I've had in years. The mattress is just the right level of firmness, the sheets are buttery soft, and the pillows are perfect. If I could, I'd buy this bed from Corbin and take it with me when I leave.

My phone buzzes. I find it on the nightstand and see it's Haley calling. I sent her a text before I fell asleep telling her I was staying with Corbin.

"Hi, Haley."

"Hey, I just got home from work. What the hell's going on there? You're seriously hanging out with the guy who put you in the hospital?"

"Yeah, but it's not as bad as it sounds. He's a doctor and he works at the same hospital they took me to after the accident. He felt horrible about what happened. He stayed by my side the whole time, then took me back to my apartment this morning and that's when I found out my roommates had moved out and taken all my stuff."

"I told you not to trust people named Moon and Sun."

"You could say the same thing about people named Star. You can't judge people by their name."

"You said you got a bad vibe from them when you met them."

"Yeah, well I didn't have a lot of options and the rent was cheap."

"So they took *everything*? What about your car?"

"I think it was towed. I don't have the money to get it out of the impound lot so I'm just going to leave it. I can't afford to fix everything that's wrong with it so they might as well take it."

"So you have no place to live, no car, and none of your stuff?"

"I still have my phone and my wallet. And Corbin took me shopping this morning and got me clothes and shampoo and other stuff I needed."

"He took you shopping? Doesn't he have to work?"

"Yeah, but he took today off to help me."

"And you're staying at his place?"

"Just for tonight. Or until I find an apartment."

"Star, this isn't right. Something's going on with this guy."

"What do you mean? He's just being nice."

"No guy is that nice. He has a motive. He wants something."

I roll my eyes. "And what could he possibly want? I don't have anything."

"Uh, let's see...you're young, hot, vulnerable."

"You think he's doing all this for sex?"

"Seems pretty obvious to me."

"If he wanted sex he could go to a bar and get any girl there. He's really hot. Tall. Muscular. Gorgeous face. Rich. He doesn't need me for sex. He has plenty of options."

"He's rich? Like how rich?"

"I don't know. He just made it sound like his family has a lot of money."

"So some rich doctor hit you with his car and put you in the hospital."

"I'm not going to sue him if that's what you're thinking."

"But maybe he *thinks* you're going to, so to protect himself and his rich family he's playing the Nice Guy role so you won't go after his money."

"He's not being nice to save himself from a lawsuit. He's just a nice person."

"I swear, Star, sometimes you're so naive."

"I'm not being naive. You don't know him like I do. He feels really bad about what happened and wants to make things right. He's out in the living room right now trying to find me an apartment."

"Yeah, let's see how hard he tries," she mutters.

"He can't have me staying here more than a few days. His ex-girlfriend wouldn't allow it."

"If she's his ex, why would she care?"

"She hasn't accepted the breakup. And I don't think she wants me here. I overheard them fighting."

"This is way too much drama. The last thing you need right now is his psycho ex-girlfriend coming after you. You need to get out of there as soon as possible."

"I have nowhere to go and I don't have money for a hotel."

"Maybe you could stay with Roy."

Roy is a friend of hers from college. He parties all the time and sleeps with as many women as possible.

"Are you kidding? Roy's a total pervert. He'd be trying to crawl into bed with me every night."

"He's changed. He's more laid back now. Doesn't drink as much. And he has a girlfriend. If I asked, I'm sure he'd let you crash on his couch for a few nights."

"Forget it. The few times I've met him he couldn't keep his hands off me. Remember when he put his hand up my skirt at your birthday party?"

"And I totally yelled at him for that. I even yelled at him again the next day when he was sober."

"I'm not living with Roy. I'll find someone else. How about that girl you roomed with junior year?"

"Kristy? She got married and moved to Virginia."

"What about your other roommate? From sophomore year?"

"Got a job in Texas. She's been there over a year."

"You don't know anyone else in town I could stay with?"

"Sorry, but no. Everyone took off after graduation."

"How am I going to find someone who needs a roommate?"

"You could forget finding a place and just go home."

"You know my parents' rule. I already broke the rule once. They're not going to let me do it again."

"But this is a special situation. You lost everything. You have no place to live."

"Which I don't want them knowing. If they found out, they'd give me yet another lecture on how I'm irresponsible and immature and need to get my life together."

"Parents always say shit like that. Just ignore it and hide in your room until you figure out what to do."

"No way. I'm not going back there. That house is completely dysfunctional. Did I tell you my mom has her boyfriend sleeping over now? With my dad, her husband, just down the hall?"

"That's messed up. They need to get divorced or at least stop living together."

"I keep telling them that. Hey, I should go. I've been sleeping all afternoon. I need to look for apartments."

"Call me if there's anything I can do to help."

"I will. Thanks."

"And be careful. This doctor guy could be psycho. Lock your door when you go to sleep."

"You watch too many of those murder shows."

"If it happened to those people it can happen to you."

"Great. Now I'll have nightmares."

"Bye! Get better soon!"

As I set my phone down I hear a knock on the door. "Star? Are you awake?"

"Yeah, come in."

Corbin opens the door. He has on the hoodie I was wearing earlier. It looks better on him. Then again, he looks good in anything.

"I assumed you were awake," he says. "It sounded like you were talking but I wasn't sure."

"My friend, Haley, called to check in. I was asking her if she knew anyone who might need a roommate. She went to college here so she knows a lot of people. Well, she used to. She said everyone she knew doesn't live in Boston anymore, except for Roy."

"Who's Roy?"

"This guy she met at college. He's fun to party with but he tries to sleep with every woman he meets."

"And she thinks you should live with him?"

"Just until I find a place. I told her I wouldn't do it. But if you need me out of here by tomorrow I guess I could consider it. She said he's changed but I have a hard time believing that."

"You can stay here as long as you want. There's no hurry to leave."

"How'd the apartment search go? Any luck?"

"Not yet. All the ones I found online were too expensive. I called one of my contacts at Harvard to see if he knew anyone but he said all the students he knows already have roommates. He suggested I search through some roommate wanted forums, which I did, but everyone on there sounded even crazier than your last roommates."

"There's gotta be someone normal out there."

"I'm sure there is. I just didn't have time to go through all the listings."

"I'll search after dinner tonight."

"Speaking of dinner, I was thinking of ordering something in."

"I thought I was teaching you how to make pasta."

He smiles. "You don't have to do that. And you shouldn't be cooking after just getting out of the hospital. How are you feeling?"

"Better after the nap, although my ribs are really sore."

He comes over to the bed and sits down. "Show me where it hurts."

I move the covers back and point to the right side of my ribcage. "Right here, but like the doctor said, I can't do anything about it. I just have to let it heal."

"You landed on your left side. The right shouldn't hurt. Can I see?" He goes to lift up my shirt.

"Um, yeah, okay."

When I came in here to sleep I ditched my jeans and sweatshirt along with my bra so I'm only wearing a t-shirt and panties.

Corbin raises my shirt to just under my breast and lightly presses his hand along my ribcage.

"Tell me when it hurts."

My heart is racing at the feel of his hands on my skin. I look up at the ceiling, trying to focus on the light fixture but all I can think about is where his hands will go next. They continue down my ribcage, his fingers pressing just below it.

"Ow!" I cringe. "Right there."

He presses lower. "How about there?"

"That doesn't hurt."

He moves the sheet down farther and presses along my hip area, and then lower. Heat floods my core, moving between my legs where I'm feeling sensations I shouldn't be feeling. He's just examining me. It's not sexual, but my body doesn't seem to get that.

His fingers press down near the center of my pelvis and I twitch.

His brows furrow. "That hurts?"

"No. Just tickles a little."

"How about here?" His fingers press on the other side of my pelvis and I stiffen up.

"It hurts but it's not bad."

"Huh. It could just be bruising from the accident but you should keep an eye on it." He lifts the sheet back over me, leaving me yearning to feel his hands on me again. "If it doesn't feel better in a few weeks, go see your doctor. When's the last time you saw your gyno?"

"My what?"

"Gynecologist," he says casually, as if it's not at all a personal question. He's in doctor mode, which means all that touching was nothing more than a doctor checking a patient. "When was your last appointment?"

"I don't know. Probably three or four years ago."

"You haven't been to the doctor in three or four years?"

"I couldn't afford to. I don't have insurance."

"You should see a gyno. That pain could be from a cyst or something more serious. I could refer you to one of the women's clinics in town that charge based on what you can afford. It may even be free."

"Great, now can we stop talking about cysts and gynos?"

He smiles and sits back. "Sorry. Sometimes I go into doctor mode before I can stop myself. But I would keep an eye on that spot that hurts. And the area below your rib. I'm guessing they're both just bruised, but if the pain doesn't go away you'll need to get it checked out."

"Yes, Dr. Sterling." I crack a smile.

He shakes his head. "You're a terrible patient, aren't you? Never listens to your doctor?"

"I listen. I just don't want to talk about my lady parts anymore."

"Lady parts?" He chuckles.

"I'm not good with medical terms so lady parts it is. Now can we talk about something else? What are you thinking for dinner?"

"I was going to ask you. After being forced to eat hospital food because of me, I think you should be the one who gets to pick what we have for dinner."

"Then I pick pizza. Really cheesy pizza with lots of red sauce."

"That's my favorite kind too but I never have it."

"Why not?"

"In the rare times Lauren and I ordered pizza she'd only get the kind with a gluten free crust and olive oil, no sauce."

"What about toppings?"

"Usually broccoli and red peppers with goat cheese."

"Ugh, that sounds disgusting."

"It's not bad but I do miss having just a basic pepperoni with red sauce."

"Then let's get that. With extra cheese."

"Sounds great." He shoots me a smile as he stands up. "I'll call the order in. You get dressed and meet me out in the living room."

Get dressed. He said it because he knew I was only wearing panties. His hand almost touched them when he was pressing on my pelvis. If he'd gone a few inches lower he would've been to third base!

I'm still breathless from him touching me. And wet. God, he turns me on. Everything about him is sexy. His body. His smile. The way he carries himself. And his touch. The feel of his hands on my skin, pressing, probing, going lower and lower. I'm getting aroused just thinking about it. And yet he didn't seem affected at all. He just sees me as a patient. Nothing more.

"Fifteen minutes," I hear Corbin yell from the living room.

"Okay!" I yell back.

Damn. Even his voice is sexy.

When I get to the kitchen, I see him looking in the fridge. "What do you want to drink?"

"Got a beer?"

He turns to me and smiles. "No alcohol when you're on those pain meds."

"How about a soda?"

"How about sparkling water?" He holds up the bottle.

"Let me guess. Soda has too much sugar?"

"Sugar. Fake colors. Fake flavors." He grabs a glass from the cabinet. "I'm a health nut about some things but not everything."

"Like pizza?"

"And beer. But I won't have one tonight since you're not able to."

"You can have one. I don't mind."

"You sure?"

"Go ahead."

He takes a bottle of beer from the fridge. "I really needed this tonight."

"Why? Did something happen? Besides getting stuck having to help out the girl who got kicked out of her apartment?"

"It's not that. It's other stuff."

"You want to talk about it?"

"Not really. Actually no, I'd rather not."

His phone rings and he checks it. "It's Lauren again. I'm not answering." He sends it to voicemail.

"Is she coming over to get her stuff?"

"Probably not tonight." He pours sparkling water in a glass and hands it to me. "She has to work another double shift. She'll get almost no sleep before having to be back there tomorrow but she'll still insist on going to spin class at seven."

"I wouldn't want a doctor working on me after only having a couple hours of sleep."

"I kept telling her to get more sleep but she wouldn't listen. It's not like she's flipping burgers. She's being trusted with peoples' lives. She needs to be awake and alert."

"Has she ever made a mistake from being tired?"

"If she has she wouldn't tell me. Lauren's a perfectionist. She doesn't want anyone seeing her flaws."

"Even you?"

"Especially me. She's very competitive. She was always trying to beat me. She wanted to work at a more prestigious hospital than me. Make more money than me. I kept telling her none of that stuff mattered to me but it matters to her so nothing I said would change her mind."

"Did you like that she was competitive like that?"

"I did when we first started dating. I thought it was sexy. A strong, beautiful woman determined to do better than anyone else? But then it got old. I couldn't imagine the rest of my life like that, constantly feeling like I was competing with her."

The pizza arrives and the smell of it has my stomach growling. I'm getting my appetite back and the pizza looks so good I could eat the whole thing.

Corbin grabs some plates from the cupboard.

"We can just use paper," I say.

"Paper what?"

"Plates. That way we don't dirty any dishes."

"I don't have paper plates." He hands me a plate and I help myself to the pizza.

"Can I take this to the couch?" I ask.

"Um, I guess. Why do you want eat over there?"

"So we can watch TV. If you don't want to, we can eat at the table."

"The couch is fine. It's just not something I normally do."

"Really? Growing up, we always ate in front of the TV. My parents would be on the couch and my brother and I would sit on the floor. We only ate at the table for holidays."

"My parents wouldn't allow us to eat anywhere but the dining room table. It's what I'm used to, so even though I can sit wherever I want now, I always sit at the table. But what the hell? Let's sit on the couch."

We take our plates to the couch and watch the end of a movie. Actually, we spend more time talking than watching the movie. Corbin tells me about his sister and I tell him stories about my brother, Seth. For whatever reason Seth always has crazy stuff happen to him. Not bad crazy, but good, like meeting his girlfriend when he went to get his oil changed. They've dated for years and will probably get married. Or there's the time he went into a rest stop on the way to Pennsylvania and found a hundred dollar bill on the floor. Nobody was around so he kept it.

Good stuff like that happens to him all the time. Me? I get hit by a car and lose my job all in one day. Then I lose my apartment and all my possessions. The family luck definitely went to Seth and not me.

Except for Corbin. He's the first good luck I've had in a while. I just hope the good luck keeps coming my way.

CHAPTER TWELVE

Star

"Hey." I feel Corbin nudge my arm. "Why don't you go to bed?"

I rub my eyes. "Was I sleeping?"

"For the last half hour." He grabs our plates from the coffee table. "I'll clean up dinner. You go ahead and get to bed."

"I can't. I need to look for apartments. Besides it's too early to go to bed."

"You need your rest. It'll help you heal faster." He stands up, the plates in his hands, and nods toward the hall. "Go. Get to sleep. Doctor's orders."

"You keep forgetting you're not my doctor," I say, getting up.

"Well, while you're here under my care, I am. So go get some rest."

He takes the plates to the kitchen and rinses them in the sink.

"Corbin?"

"Yeah?" He looks back at me as he sets the plates in the dishwasher.

"I just want to thank you again for helping me out like this. I don't know where I'd be tonight if you hadn't let me stay."

"You're welcome here for as long as you need." He closes the dishwasher and wipes his hand on a dishcloth.

"Thanks, but I really am going to try to find a place as soon as possible. I didn't do much today on my search but I promise I'll put my full effort into it tomorrow."

He leans back against the counter. "Star, I don't want you taking the first place you find just to get out of here."

"I know, but I told you I'd only be here a night so—"

"I'm not counting how many nights you're here. If you need a week, or even two, it's fine. I'm not keeping track. Now would you please go get some rest?"

He sounds so exasperated with me it makes me smile.

"Goodnight, Dr. Sterling."

He smiles back. "Goodnight, Ms. Jenkins."

I feel him watching me as I go down the hall. When I'm in my room I shut the door and crawl into the big, comfortable bed.

I fall asleep and wake up to light peeking through the shades. I sit up, which causes a coughing fit, followed by sneezing. It's just a mild cold but really annoying and the last thing I need right now.

Turning on the light by the bed I see a small tray on the nightstand that wasn't there last night. On it is a glass of water, cough drops, cold medicine, and a note. I pick up the note. It's from Corbin.

Hope you got some rest. Take the cold meds and drink plenty of water today. There's food in the fridge. Help yourself. I'll stop by at lunch to check on you. - Corbin

It's after nine. When did he leave all this? Last night? This morning? I didn't even hear him come in my room.

After a quick shower I put on my new clothes and head to the kitchen. His fridge is stocked with healthy food, except for the leftover pizza from last night. I grab a slice and sit down at the breakfast bar.

"Making yourself comfortable, I see," a voice says.

Looking up, I see a woman walking toward me. She's tall and beautiful, her shiny blond hair pulled back into a long sleek ponytail. Her makeup is flawless, like it was professionally done, and she's wearing black yoga pants and a hot pink zip-up jacket that fits tight to her lean frame. A giant black purse is slung over her shoulder and she's holding a silver water bottle.

Where'd she come from? I didn't even hear the elevator door open.

"Hi." I jump off the barstool and quickly wipe my hands on my jeans. "I'm Star." I go to shake her hand but she pretends not to notice.

"I'm Lauren," she says as she sets her purse on the table. "I assume Corbin told you about me?"

"Yes. Hi." I fake a smile, suddenly feeling nervous and like I shouldn't be here. "He didn't mention you'd be stopping by."

"I didn't tell him. I just finished my spin class and need to shower." She goes to the fridge and grabs a bottle of organic juice from the shelf. "It's too far of a drive to go all the way back to my friend's place."

I wish she'd told Corbin. I don't think he wants her just stopping by like this but if I told her to go I doubt she'd listen to me.

"So Corbin said you stayed here last night." She shakes the juice then twists open the cap.

"I didn't plan to but I didn't have anywhere else to go."

She raises her perfectly trimmed brows. "No friends? No family?"

"Not in Boston. I just moved here from Worcester. I came for a job but missed the first day because of the accident so they gave the job to someone else."

"Yes, Corbin mentioned that." She takes a sip of her drink. "So any leads on apartments?"

"Honestly, I haven't had much time to look. But I will today. In fact, I should probably start looking right now." I pick up the laptop Corbin left, hoping to escape to my room before Lauren asks me more questions.

116

"If you'd like I'd be happy to help." She unzips her pink jacket revealing a white tank covering her flat chest. She's very thin.

"Um, thanks but I think I can manage. Besides, Corbin said you work a lot. I don't want to take up your time."

"I can ask around. See if anyone I know needs a roommate. It wouldn't take any time."

"Oh, then sure, that'd be great. But the place has to be cheap."

"What's your budget?"

I tell her and she almost laughs, but then stops herself and says, "You do know the average rent in Boston is around $2500 a month."

Actually I didn't know that but pretend that I do. "That's why I need a roommate, or maybe two."

She comes out of the kitchen to where I'm standing. "I'll ask around but really, why are you staying?" She tilts her head to the side, her eyes doing a quick scan of my clothes before returning to my face.

"I'm not sure what you mean."

"Why are you staying in Boston if you have no friends or family here and no job?"

"I've always wanted to live here," I tell her, although it's not really true. I just wanted to get out of my hometown. I didn't really care where I ended up. "I like the city."

She shrugs. "It's okay. I, myself, find it a little stodgy. Everyone's so academic here, which was fine when I was a student but now that I'm older and beginning my career I want a city that's more alive. More vibrant."

"Like New York?" I ask, remembering what Corbin said about her wanting to live there.

"Exactly. New York has an energy to it that no other place seems to have. I'm still trying to convince Corbin of that. Once he's living there, he'll see how great it is and eventually come around."

"Corbin's moving?"

"Not yet, but once I get a job there he'll have to."

"Um, I guess I'm confused. I thought you two weren't dating anymore."

"It's only temporary. Corbin and I have a tumultuous relationship. We're just taking some time apart."

I don't think Corbin would agree with that. He made the breakup sound permanent.

"You really think he'd move to New York?"

She eyes me suspiciously. "You're awfully concerned about Corbin and his future plans."

I shake my head. "I didn't mean anything by it. I was just thinking that his family lives here and he's from here so maybe he'd want to stay."

"Men don't know what they want. It's up to us to tell them. Corbin may think he wants to remain here but he'll change his mind when we get to New York."

She's really in denial. Corbin said she wasn't accepting the breakup but I thought that meant she was just sad about it, not that she was thinking they were still together.

"So any ideas about what you'll do for a job?" she asks.

She won't stop asking me questions. I really just want to go down to my room and get away from her. She's making me nervous.

"I haven't given it much thought," I say. "So much has happened the past few days I haven't had time."

"Do you have time now?"

"Um, yeah, I guess. What are you thinking?"

"Come with me." She starts walking to the elevator.

"Wait. Where are we going?"

"Downstairs. C'mon." She holds the elevator door open for me.

Downstairs? What's downstairs?

We take the elevator to the first floor and I follow her to the coffee shop that's on the street level of the building. It's bustling with men in suits talking on their phones.

The squeal of the espresso machine greets us as we walk in. That sound always hurts my ears, which is why I tend to stay out of coffee shops. That and the fact I don't have money for coffee.

"Alexis!" Lauren yells over the machines, waving her hand at a girl who could be her twin. They both have the same long blond hair and matching makeup, like they use the same brand and colors. Alexis is shorter than Lauren but just as thin.

Alexis turns and spots Lauren. "Sister!" she squeals, coming around the counter to give her a hug.

"You two are sisters?" I ask.

"No." Lauren laughs. "But we act like it so we've declared ourselves sisters. "Alexis, I want you to meet Star. She's the one I told you about that's looking for a job."

That's why Lauren took me here? For a job interview? I'm not dressed for an interview and I didn't really want to work at a coffee shop. It doesn't pay enough and the squeal of that machine all day would drive me crazy.

"Oh, um, I wasn't—"

Alexis interrupts. "Nice to meet you." She shakes my hand. "So I was thinking we could start you in the back. The kitchen could really use some help in the mornings. And then as you learn more, maybe we'll put you out front."

"Wait—you're giving me the job? You just met me."

Alexis and Lauren laugh. I'm not sure what they're laughing about.

"If I recommend someone, you're basically hired," Lauren says. "You seem hardworking and responsible, which is better than half the people who apply here. Right, Alexis?"

"Totally." She rolls her eyes. "You should hear the stories of the college kids I've hired. They think they're too good to have to lift a finger at work. Seriously, this one guy just sat in the corner and read a book all day and then wondered why I fired him."

"He thought reading a book was considered working?" I ask.

"He said he was working by giving the place character. Drawing in customers with his presence. So anyway, when can you start?"

Alexis and Lauren both look at me, wide-eyed and smiling with their matching pink lipstick.

"Um, well, I just got out of the hospital." I sniffle. "And I'm fighting a cold so—"

"She could start Monday," Lauren says, then turns to me. "Trust me. I'm a doctor. You'll be fine by then."

"Great!" Alexis says. "Then I'll see you at seven."

"Hold on," I say, stopping her before she goes behind the counter. "I'm not sure this will work out. I mean, I'm hoping to find an apartment soon and I doubt it'll be anywhere near here. I don't have a car, and subway fare will eat up all my money. Plus I was really hoping to find something that—"

Lauren and Alexis are laughing again so I stop to see what's so funny.

"It's only temporary," Alexis says. "Lauren said you needed cash fast so she thought this would be a good solution. And as long as you're living upstairs it'll work out perfectly. But if you really don't want the job, then—"

"No. I do! I just didn't understand. Temp work is great. And yes, I do need cash fast, so thank you. And if I'm able to come in before Monday I'll let you know."

Alexis hands me her business card which lists her as the manager. "I need to get back to work. See you Monday!"

"Isn't she the greatest?" Lauren asks as we ride the elevator back up to Corbin's apartment.

"Yeah. She's really nice. Did you two meet in college?"

"Yes, at Columbia. We roomed together for a year and then she moved in with her boyfriend. They're no longer together."

"She went to Columbia but works at a coffee shop?"

"She's only working there until she finds a husband. Her family is loaded. She doesn't need the money."

"I can't believe she just gave me a job. Thanks for the recommendation."

We step off the elevator into the apartment.

"Whatever I can do," she says as she checks her phone. "I'm going to go shower."

She goes into Corbin's bedroom, leaving me alone in the living room. Why would she get me that job? She doesn't even know me. Maybe she wants me to work so I can get money and move out faster. I can tell she doesn't like me living here.

Sitting on the couch I start up Corbin's laptop then realize I don't have the password. Corbin forgot to leave it so I search on my phone instead, starting with the roommate site I used before. Given my previous luck I probably shouldn't use that site again but I'm desperate.

Nearly an hour later Lauren appears again, ready for work in black pants and a light blue dress shirt. Her hair is pulled back and she's lightened her makeup. Why was she wearing so much makeup to spin class?

"How's the search going?" she asks, her heels clicking on the wood floor.

"I might have found one in Jamaica Plain. But I'd have two guys as roommates."

"Is that a problem? Do you only want girls?"

"I can't be picky so I'm fine living with guys, as long as they aren't perverts."

"Aren't all men?" She laughs. "Good luck with the search," she says as she walks to the elevator.

When the elevator door closes I realize I forgot to ask her for the laptop password. I'm sure Corbin gave it to her.

My phone rings, the call coming from a number I don't recognize.

"Hello?" I answer.

A deep voice replies, "Star, how's it going?"

"Who's this?"

He laughs a little. "Corbin. Who'd you think it was?"

"I wasn't sure. We've never talked on the phone."

"I just wanted to check in and see how you're doing."

121

"I'm doing okay. The swelling in my leg is going down and my cold seems to be getting better."

"Good. Keep resting and drinking fluids and be sure to eat something."

"I will. Hey, Lauren was just here."

"Lauren was there?" he asks, sounding angry. "What the hell was she doing there?"

"She came by to shower after spin class. She said it was too far to go back to her friend's place."

"She could've showered at the hospital. Damn, that pisses me off. She can't just be stopping by like that. She doesn't live there anymore."

"Sorry, I should've called you. I didn't know what to do."

"Don't be sorry. It's not your fault. She knows she's not supposed to be there without telling me. I'll have a talk with her. If she shows up again, text me and I'll call her. Did she give you any trouble while she was there?"

"No, she was fine. But you were right about her not accepting the breakup. She told me it's only temporary and that you'd be moving to New York with her when she gets a job there."

"Yeah, well, that's not happening. She just needs more time to accept it."

"Speaking of jobs, she got me one."

"What are you talking about?"

"Lauren took me downstairs to that coffee shop her friend works at and her friend gave me a job."

"Huh." He pauses. "Why would she do that?" He asks it like he's talking more to himself than to me.

"I don't know but I could use the money so I told her I'd do it. I start Monday, or sooner if I'm able to."

"Don't rush it. You need to get better. Are you sure you want to do this?"

"Well, yeah. I don't have any other options and it's right downstairs. It's just short term until I find something else."

"Any luck on the apartment search?"

"Not yet. Oh, could you give me the password for the laptop?"

"Sure, it's shandy14. No caps."

"Great, thanks! I'll talk to you later."

He hangs up and I try the password. It works and I'm greeted by a screensaver that's a picture of Corbin and Lauren on a sailboat. They look like the perfect couple. Beautiful, tan, wearing big sunglasses, Lauren's hair blowing in the breeze. She's wearing a white bikini on her perfect body and Corbin has on navy swim trunks. I'm trying not to stare at his chest and chiseled abs but my eyes won't let me. Damn, he's hot. And kind, generous, funny.

My attraction to him is making it hard to live here. And I feel like I'm in the way as he tries to settle things with his ex.

I shouldn't be staying here. I pick up the laptop and begin my search again, determined to find a place.

CHAPTER THIRTEEN

Corbin

"Hey, Star," I say as I walk in the apartment. She's sitting on the couch with my laptop.

"Hi!" she says, greeting me with a smile.

It's nice coming home to someone who isn't yelling at me the minute I walk in the door. Lauren always skipped any kind of greeting and went straight to giving me orders, which I didn't take, so then we'd fight.

"Any luck?" I ask as I set the takeout sacks on the kitchen counter. I'm exhausted from work and didn't want to cook so I picked up dinner on the way home.

"A little," she says as I walk over to her. "I called two people looking for roommates and they said I could come see the apartments this Saturday."

"That should work. In the morning?"

"Oh, you don't have to come with me. I'll just take the bus."

"I'll drive you. I don't trust your judgment in apartments."

"Hey!"

I laugh. "What? Like you really think you made a good decision last time?"

"Okay, maybe it wasn't the best, but how was I supposed to know they were going to take off like that?"

"So what are the options?" I ask, sitting beside her.

"Some girls in Brookline and a couple guys in Jamaica Plain."

"Guys? You want to live with two guys?"

I shrug. "I can't be picky. As long as they're halfway normal I'd consider it an option."

"You shouldn't live with guys you don't know. It could be dangerous." I get up and walk back to the kitchen. "You hungry?"

"Yeah. I was just about to make a sandwich."

"I brought home Italian. Enough for two."

"You didn't have to do that." Star meets me at the table where I'm dishing out the pasta.

"Have a seat." I set a plate down in front of her, along with a fork and napkin. "Try it. Let me know what you think."

She takes a bite. "It's *really* good. I love Italian food."

"Me too but Lauren never wanted it," I say, joining Star at the table. "She said it had too many calories."

"She could use some calories. She's really thin."

"That's right. I forgot you met her today. Sorry about that. I texted her and told her to stop coming over."

"Did she text back?"

"No, but I'll call her later and tell her again. It'll take several tries to get her to listen."

I rip open the bag of garlic bread and set it between us. "Help yourself."

She takes a piece. "Can I ask you something?"

"Go ahead."

"If Lauren and you were still together and she got a job in New York, would you move with her?"

"Probably not."

"You'd be okay dating long-distance?"

"If she moved, we would've broken up. The breakup was inevitable. My feelings for her just weren't there anymore. They haven't been for a long time but sometimes you get so used to the relationship and the routine of it that you don't even realize

125

you no longer love the person. When Lauren started all this talk about moving to New York I was forced to really look at our relationship and what it'd become. That's when I realized there was nothing left."

She nods and looks down at her plate, twirling her fork in the pasta. "You think you'll start dating again soon?"

"I didn't think I would but now I'm more open to the idea."

I shouldn't have said that. When she asked, I was thinking about *her* and how meeting her has made me want to start dating again. But not just anyone. I want to date someone like Star. Someone who lets me be myself and doesn't judge everything I do. Someone who laughs and smiles and doesn't take everything so seriously. Someone who stays hopeful even when things aren't going her way.

"What changed your mind?" she asks.

"I just don't want to wait. That car accident really shook me up, then *woke* me up as I realized how short life can be. I'm tired of doing what's expected of me, and right now, everyone expects me to wait before dating someone new after being with Lauren for so long. But why wait? Why wait to be happy?"

"I agree," she says.

The table gets quiet, neither one of us knowing what to say next. We both know there's something going on between us, something more than just attraction, but neither one of us wants to admit it or act on it. Maybe because we don't know what this is or if it's real. Are we only feeling this way as a side effect of the accident? She's drawn to me because I'm helping her and I'm drawn to her because of my guilt? Or would we have felt this way if we'd just met on the street? I really don't know and I don't think she does either so we keep those feelings hidden and continue on as friends. But that's getting harder to do when she's living here. The more I'm around her, the more I want to take this beyond a friendship.

"So about my job," she says, breaking the awkward silence. "I was thinking I could start Friday, maybe just for an hour or two. See how it goes."

"It's too soon. You need to rest."

"The job won't be anything strenuous. She's having me work in the back. I won't be straining my brain trying to make coffee drinks or run the register."

"Let me talk to Alexis before you start."

"So I could maybe start Friday?"

"Maybe, but that's only a day away. We'll see."

We finish dinner and I get up and take our dishes to the sink. I rinse off the plates and wipe down the counters, occasionally glancing over at Star. I keep catching her watching me. I do the same to her when she's not looking. Not being able to act on our attraction to each other is only making it stronger. And touching her makes it almost unbearable. When I tried to examine her the other day I was aroused to the point I had to get up and leave.

Shaking that memory from my mind I go over to Star. "I've got a surprise for you."

"A surprise?" Her face lights up. "What is it?"

"Follow me."

We go to the elevator.

"Wait." She stops. "Do I need a coat?"

"No, we're staying in the building but grab your crutches if you need them."

"I don't. I haven't used them all day."

We take the elevator to the basement storage area. I lead her to my storage room and unlock the door.

I point to the bike. "What do you think? It's yours if you want it."

"The bike?"

"I ruined yours so I owe you a new one. This one technically isn't new. It was my sister's but she only used it a couple times so it's like new. But if you want a new one I'll get you one. It's the least I can do. Or if you decide to take this one I'll have it fitted for you. There's a bike shop just down the street."

She walks over to the bike and lifts up the handlebars. "It's really lightweight."

"Let's see if it fits." I take the bike out to the hallway. "Go ahead. Try it out."

I hold the bike steady while she swings her leg over the bar and sits on the seat.

"It's perfect," she says, smiling. "Like it was made for me."

"I thought it might work. My sister's about the same height as you. But like I said, I'm happy to get you a new one if you don't like this one."

"Are you kidding? This is great. Way better than my old one. This is like a thousand dollar bike."

I chuckle. "More like three so make sure to lock it up when you leave it somewhere."

"A three thousand dollar bike? Corbin, I can't take this. It's more than my crappy car cost."

"Don't worry what it cost. If you want it, it's yours. But I don't want you riding it until you get your stitches out and your leg is fully heeled. Hopefully it'll get you around until you get a car. Just beware of idiots who don't check before turning."

"Corbin." She puts her hand on my arm. "It was an accident. You don't have to keep feeling bad about it."

"I'll always feel bad. I turned your life upside down because of one stupid mistake."

"But it's getting better. I already have a job, and a new bike. And hopefully after this weekend I'll have a new apartment."

"We should look for some other options just in case the ones you found don't work out."

"We can, but I already spent all day looking and couldn't find anything else in my price range."

I put the bike away and we go back up to the apartment. I show her where I keep the extra key for the storage locker so she can get to the bike when she needs it. I also gave her a key to the apartment so she can come and go when I'm gone during the day. My father would tell me I'm making a huge mistake, trusting a girl I just met, especially one in desperate need of money. But oddly enough, I trust Star more than I trusted Lauren. I never felt like she was being honest with me.

"So who's Shandy?" Star asks as we're sitting on the couch later.

My brows rise. "Shandy?"

"The laptop password. I assume shandy has some kind of meaning behind it."

I smile. "Shandy was my dog growing up. She was a mutt. A German Shepherd mixed with something else. My sister found her during a storm, hiding by our house, trying to stay dry. We took her inside and tried to hide her from my parents but of course they found out and demanded we take the dog to the shelter."

"But they obviously didn't."

"They did. My parents didn't like dogs, mainly because of the mess they make."

"So you only had Shandy a day?"

"Twelve years, actually. When my parents took the dog away my sister cried for days. They couldn't take it anymore so they went back to the shelter and got the dog. My father built a dog wing onto the house. Shandy wasn't allowed anywhere else but there."

"A dog wing?" Star laughs. "What's a dog wing?"

"An addition onto the garage. It was heated. Had water. It was actually really nice. Way nicer than your typical dog house."

"So if you wanted to see her you had to go to the dog wing?"

"Yes, which my sister turned into a playhouse. She'd have her friends over and they'd all hang out there. My mother hated it. She'd spent all this money making a playroom in the regular house that looked like a princess castle and all my sister wanted to do is hang out in the dog's house."

"That's funny. So why the name Shandy?"

"It's a combination of Shannon and Mandy. My sister couldn't decide which to name her so she combined the names." He smiles. "Shandy was a great dog. I really miss her. I miss having a dog."

"Why don't you have one?"

"Lauren wouldn't let me. She hates dogs. She said they're too loud and she doesn't like all the shedding."

"But you're not dating her anymore. If you want a dog, go get one."

"I've thought about it but I'm away from home so much it wouldn't be fair to the dog."

"Put him in doggy day care. They have them all over the city. And if you get one now I'll watch him for you until I move out. I love dogs. We had a black lab growing up. He died when I was twelve and my parents wouldn't let us get another."

"Huh. Maybe I should consider it. I really do want one." I smile at her, my excitement building. "You want to go to the shelter with me this weekend? Just see what they have?"

"I'd love to! But you know it'll be nearly impossible to go home without one. You may end up leaving with a dog."

A buzzer rings and I get up from the couch.

"What's that?" Star asks.

"Someone's downstairs." I walk over to the speaker on the wall and push the talk button. "Yeah, who is it?"

"It's your father. I know it's late but I was in the area. Do you mind if I drop in?"

I glance at Star. He doesn't know she's staying here. This is going to turn into a fight but I can't avoid it so I say, "Yeah, come on up."

"I'll go in my room," Star says, hurrying to leave. "Goodnight."

"Star, wait. I want you to meet him."

"Oh, um, could we do it later?"

The elevator door opens and my father appears, wearing gray dress pants and a black overcoat.

"Hello, Father," I say, going to take his coat.

"Corbin." He nods his hello, his eyes going to Star. "You didn't say you had a visitor."

"This is Star." I motion her to stand beside me. "She's staying with me for a few days until she finds an apartment."

"Is that so?" He looks her up and down. "A friend of Lauren's?"

"No," Star answers. "I, um—" She looks at me to answer.

"She's the girl from the accident," I say. "When she was released from the hospital she found out her roommates had taken off and left her without an apartment. She didn't have anywhere to go so she's staying here for now."

My father narrows his eyes at Star. "How fortunate of you to have someone like Corbin take you in. Almost like winning the lottery."

"What?" she asks, seeming confused.

"Dad," I say under my breath, begging him to be nice.

"Could you excuse us, please?" he says to Star.

"Sure. I'll be in my room." She races down the hall.

As soon as we hear her door shut, my father starts in. "What the hell are you thinking?"

"Dad, keep your voice down."

"I will NOT keep my voice down. Why the hell should I? She knows what she's doing. Why let her think we don't know? Better to be on the offensive. Let her know we're on to her."

"Dad, it's not like that."

"How stupid are you, son? Do you even know how the world works? People like her live for moments like this. For all we know, she threw herself in the street, hoping someone with money would hit her."

"That's completely ridiculous and not at all what happened. She crossed the street when the light told her to go. I was the one in the wrong."

"And have you told her that?" He huffs. "I'm sure you have. You have no sense when it comes to these things. What have I always told you? Play innocent. Never admit guilt. And yet here you are housing the girl in your apartment! What the hell is wrong with you? Have you not listened to a word I've said all these years?"

"Of course I have but this is different. She's not trying to get our money. She didn't even want to stay here. I had to convince her to. She's been looking for apartments and as soon as she finds one she'll be out."

"And that's when we'll get the letter from her ambulance chaser lawyer demanding everything we have. And in their quest to get our money, they'll destroy you! They'll destroy your character. Your career. Everything you've worked for!"

I walk to the living room, putting my back to him. "We're not talking about this. I'm an adult and I can handle this myself."

"You're handling it like a child. And this doesn't just involve you. It involves the entire family. You're not the one with money. I am! So if she comes after you, she's coming after me!"

I turn to face him. "You need to stay out of this. I told you, I'm handling it."

"Like you handled Lauren?"

"What's that supposed to mean? I told her it wasn't working anymore. It's not my fault she refuses to accept it."

"You were supposed to get married! And then you just end things with her?"

"Lauren and I never talked about marriage. She just assumed that's where we were headed."

"The girl is completely distraught over what you did to her. So is her mother, and your stepmother. Do you really think I trust you to handle this after the disastrous way you handled the situation with Lauren?"

"Lauren's creating drama so you'll feel sorry for her. It's what she always does and we both know it. Stop giving her attention and she'll eventually accept the breakup and move on. As for Star, you need to stay out of it."

He points his finger at me. "Get rid of her! Or I will!

He goes to the elevator and I storm off the other direction, too angry to say another word to him. When he's gone I take a few deep breaths, then go down to Star's room and knock on the door.

"Come in," she says.

I walk in her room and see her sitting on the bed.

"Sorry about all the yelling. For the most part, my dad and I get along, except for when he doesn't agree with my choices. I don't know how much you heard but—"

"Don't worry about it. I didn't really hear that much and it sounds like something that should stay between you and your dad."

"He doesn't understand. He always thinks people are out to get him. He had a patient sue him once and ever since then he's been overly cautious. Anyway, I just wanted to make sure you're okay, given what you heard."

"I'm fine." She gets up. "I know it's only nine but I think I'll go to bed."

"Me too. It's been a long day." I walk to the door, then stop. "I didn't ask. How are you feeling today?"

"Better. I really do want to start that job soon so I can get some money. Do you think maybe I could go down there tomorrow? Just see if she has anything easy I could do?"

"I'll talk to Alexis on my way to work. Let her know what you can and can't be doing. But I don't want you working more than an hour or two. You need to rest."

"And look for apartments." She smiles. "Thanks for all your help, Corbin. And for the bike."

"You're welcome. Goodnight."

I close her door and go to my room, still angry at my dad but feeling better after seeing Star. I hope she didn't overhear too much of what my dad said. If she did, I hope she doesn't think I agree with him. I'm not worried about her suing me or stealing from me. She's not that kind of person. Since I've met her she's never asked for anything, and she keeps thanking me for helping her even though she only needs the help because of me.

If only my father could see her the way I do, but he never will.

I don't care what he thinks. I'm doing what makes me happy, and that's helping Star.

CHAPTER FOURTEEN

Star

"So all you have to do is portion whatever coffee bean they ordered into the bag, seal it shut, then label it with the customer's name," Alexis says as she hands me the stack of order sheets. "Any questions?"

"No, I think I got it."

She takes off, leaving me alone in the back room.

It's Friday, my first day on the job. I got here at ten. I asked Alexis if she had anything she'd like me to do for an hour or two and she said I could fill coffee bean orders. It's easy and I'm able to sit while I do it so I'm thinking I could work longer than I'd originally planned. The job pays fifteen dollars an hour which is way more than I expected. Knowing that, I might keep working here even after I move.

After an hour of packing coffee, Alexis comes back to check on me.

"How's it going?"

"Good. Hey, I was thinking I could stay for the afternoon if you need the help."

"I'd have no problem with it but Corbin would. He came down here this morning and gave me strict orders not to let you work too much. He said two hours max."

"He's just being overprotective. Between my cold and my injuries he thinks I need to rest but I'm feeling much better today. My cold is almost gone and as for my injuries, I have meds to help with the pain."

She rests her hip against the counter and folds her arms over her chest. "So tell me, Star, what's your story?"

"What do you mean?" I set the bag I was holding down on the table. I don't like the way she asked the question, as if I'm hiding something.

"I mean, you just show up in town with basically nothing and no reason for being here other than some job you claim to have had, and now you don't even have the job and you still want to stay here? With no friends or family in town? It doesn't seem to add up."

"What are you implying?"

"Nothing," she says with a shrug. "I'm just curious. That's all. Why stay here when you could go back home? Wouldn't you be more comfortable recovering at home with your family than with some stranger?"

"My family isn't around. My brother lives with his girlfriend, my mom's in Florida with her boyfriend, and my dad works all the time. Plus, I'm not allowed to live at home. My parents have this rule about no adult children living at home."

"Still, an apartment *there* would be cheaper than here." She tilts her head. "It's really odd the way your roommates just took off like that. And the timing...right after your accident?"

What is she accusing me of? Does she think I arranged all this so I could somehow get closer to Corbin? To get to his money? I can't believe she would think that! She doesn't even know me. Did Lauren tell her to do this? Lauren seemed suspicious of me when we met. She put on a phony smile but I know she didn't like me.

I walk over to Alexis. "Listen, I don't know what you think is going on but whatever you're thinking, it isn't true."

"And what am I thinking?"

135

"That I somehow arranged for all this to happen." I throw my hands up. "Why would I do that? Why would I purposely put myself in this situation?"

"Hey, calm down." She puts her hand on my shoulder. "That's not what I meant. I wasn't trying to accuse you of anything. Let's just forget I said anything, okay?"

I can't tell if she's being sincere or not. She's one of those people who seems like a good liar. I'll keep working for her but I need to keep an eye on her. Or maybe she's keeping an eye on *me*. Maybe that's why she hired me. I should just quit right now but I can't pass up fifteen bucks an hour.

"I need to get back to work," I tell her.

"Feel free to take a break if you need to." She clicks away on her heels back to the front of the coffee shop.

That was really strange. I didn't expect her to attack me that way. I'm just going to keep quiet and do my job and make as much money as I can until I can find something else.

I work until three, then race upstairs to call Haley, hoping she'll take my call even though she's at work.

"Haley," I say when she answers. "Can you talk?"

"Yeah. What's up? How are you feeling?"

"Better. Hey, remember how I told you I got that job at a coffee shop?"

"Yeah. Did you start yet?"

"Today. Just for a few hours. I'm working for Lauren's friend, Alexis. I swear she only hired me so she could spy on me."

"Spy on you? For what?"

"To see if I'm trying to scam Corbin to get his money."

"What are you talking about?"

"The other night Corbin's dad came over and they had this big fight. His dad basically said I was going to sue the family and that by having me stay here, Corbin was making things worse. Like he was exposing me to all this stuff I could use against him later. Then today Alexis starts asking me what my story is, implying that I set up the whole roommates taking off thing so I'd end up homeless and need a place to live."

"Are you kidding me? She actually said that?"

"Well, no, but she implied it. The way she was asking the questions, it was like I was on trial."

"You need to get out of that place, and fast. Even if you end up living with some old lady with ten cats it'd be better than living there. Those people sound creepy."

"They're not creepy. They're just suspicious of people who don't have money."

"That's ridiculous. You've done nothing to even hint that you'd try to take their money. If you were going to sue them, you would've done it by now. And you definitely wouldn't have agreed to live in the guy's apartment with him. That doesn't even make sense. Does Corbin think this about you too?"

"No, not at all. That's why he was fighting with his dad. He was trying to tell him it wasn't true but his dad didn't believe him. He wants me to move out."

"Well, I agree with his dad on that. You need to move. Have you found any apartments that might work?"

"Not yet. Corbin and I are going to look at some places this weekend."

"Why don't you just go alone? Take the bus. The faster you get this guy and his family out of your life the better."

"Corbin's not the problem. He's a nice guy who genuinely wants to help me and I could really use his help. And after we look at apartments we're going to the shelter to look for dogs. He's really excited about it. I don't want to cancel on him."

"You're helping him pick out a dog? Isn't that something a girlfriend should do?"

"Or a friend."

"Sounds like you two are more than friends."

"Nothing's happened between us. I swear."

"Do you want it to?"

I hesitate, not answering her.

"Star, is that what you want?"

"Maybe, but it's not going to happen. Corbin's not interested in me that way."

"You sure about that?"

"Yeah. Why?"

"He keeps having dinner with you. Finding ways to spend time with you."

"He's just being nice."

"So he hasn't shown any interest in you? None at all?"

"Not that I can tell. And even if he did have feelings for me, he wouldn't act on them. He can't. He's my doctor. I'm sure dating your patient is against some doctor code of ethics."

"But he's not your doctor."

"That's true. I keep forgetting that."

"So if he wants to start something with you, he can."

"If he wanted to, he would've by now."

"Or he might be waiting until you're better."

"I don't think so."

"Just be careful, okay? I don't want him charming you into doing something you shouldn't. Or worse, just using you for sex."

"Haley, I should let you go. I don't want you getting in trouble at work."

"Call me this weekend. Let me know if you get an apartment."

"I will. Bye."

Does she really think Corbin would use me that way? He's not that type of guy. I know I've only known him a short time, but in that time he's been kind, considerate, caring, and concerned only about my health, not what I can offer him. He hasn't even made a pass at me.

Corbin gets home at six, looking tired but still really hot in his work clothes, a five o'clock shadow covering his face.

"Feeling up for a movie?" he asks, tossing his keys in the bowl. He looks down at the mail in his hand as he walks to the kitchen.

"A movie? Tonight?"

He shuffles through the mail, then drops it on the counter. "If you're not feeling up to it I can go by myself."

I can hear Haley telling me not to go. To keep my distance from this guy. But she doesn't know Corbin like I do.

"I could go. What are we seeing?"

"Maybe that new spy one? Unless you're not into those."

"I like spy movies."

"Then we'll go to that one. I need to take a quick shower and change. We'll stop somewhere and eat on the way." He takes off for his room.

We're going to dinner and a movie? Sounds like a date. I know it's not, but still, I'm not going to tell Haley about this. She'll definitely think it's a date.

I change into a different shirt and meet Corbin in the living room.

"You sure you're okay to go?" he asks. "I don't want to push you to do too much, especially after you worked today."

"All I did was sit in the back and fill coffee bags. It was easy." I stuff my phone in my pocket. "I'm ready to go if you are."

"Sit down a minute." He pulls out a chair at the dining room table.

I take a seat. "What are we doing?"

"I just want to check this." He kneels down and pulls up my pant leg, exposing my knee. He lifts my leg and rests it on his, then gently presses around my stitches with his fingers.

I know he's just doing the whole doctor thing but his touch always gets me aroused. And he's not even touching me in a sexual way.

"Any pain?" he asks.

"Not really. Just some soreness."

"The swelling's really come down." His fingers move over my skin, causing my heart to speed up and a warmth to spread through me. I love the feel of his hands on me. Even just having him touch my leg makes me want him to do so much more. I wish I didn't think that way about him but I can't help it. I have a huge crush on him. I know I can't act on it but that hasn't stopped me from fantasizing about it.

"We should go," I say, pulling my leg back and lowering my jeans back to my ankle.

As he stands up, his eyes go to mine and for a moment I think he can tell he turned me on just now. I haven't been able to figure out if he knows I like him that way. I'm trying to hide it but sometimes I fear my expression gives me away. Or my fast breathing. Or the flush of my cheeks. If he notices, he doesn't say anything.

We go to dinner at a trendy sushi place. We're surrounded by couples, all on dates, and I feel like I'm on one too. Obviously I'm not but if I were, this would be a good one. Corbin is so easy to talk to. There aren't any awkward pauses. We always find things to talk about and he's always making me laugh.

"So how'd you meet Lauren?" I ask on our way to the movie theater.

"You really want to talk about Lauren?" he asks.

"Sorry, I shouldn't have brought her up. There were just all those couples on dates at the restaurant and it made me wonder how you two met."

"Our parents are friends. I've known Lauren since we were kids."

"Let me guess, her family's rich like yours?"

"Yes, but that's not why I dated her." He glances at me. "I'm surprised you said that."

"What?"

"The money thing. It's the first time you've mentioned the fact I have money." His tone is almost accusatory, like I'm interested in his money. Maybe what his dad said to him is starting to sink in. Maybe he believes him.

"I only said it because people from rich families tend to marry people from other rich families. Or maybe that's not true. It always seems to happen in the movies." I nervously laugh, wishing I hadn't said anything.

"You can't trust what you see in movies. Like tonight, when you see the spy kick a guy in the head ten times and the guy's still standing? It'd never happen. After the first kick, the guy would likely have a concussion, or at the very least head trauma that would confuse and disorient him to the point he'd fall down. He might get back up but the second kick would definitely knock him down."

I smile. "Do you always analyze movies like that? From a doctor's point of view?"

"Not usually, but sometimes if I'm watching with med school friends we do. It used to be a game we'd use to help us study. We'd watch an action film for the fights and list off all the possible injuries the guy could have. It turned out to be a good way to study. Now it's just something we do for fun."

"Do you have a lot of friends here?"

"I do, but I never see them. When I was dating Lauren she'd insist we hang out with her friends, not mine. Or she'd make us hang out with her parents."

"Did her parents like you?"

"They did until I broke up with her. They wanted us to get married."

"How about your parents?"

"Same thing. They've always thought Lauren and I are a perfect match. We're both goal-oriented, high achievers."

"Did having that stuff in common help your relationship?"

"Not really. In some ways I think it harmed our relationship because we both put too much emphasis on our careers. It would've been better if one of us was more laid-back and could help the other person be more that way. I used to think it was good to be with someone who's just like you but now I'm thinking it'd be better to be with someone who's different. When you're too similar you butt heads."

We arrive at the theater, and just like the restaurant, the place is full of couples, kissing and holding hands in the lobby as they wait to be let in. Corbin and I keep our distance but when I'm sitting next to him in the theater, in the dark, I have this urge to reach over and hold his hand. I wouldn't actually do it but my stupid body has a mind of its own, so just to be safe I keep my hands folded safely in my lap for the entire movie.

"What'd you think?" Corbin asks as we get back to his apartment.

"It was good. I haven't been to the movies forever. Thanks for taking me."

"Thanks for being my date." He realizes what he said and laughs. "Not my actual date. You know what I meant."

"Yeah. It was fun." I go in the kitchen, and as I reach up to get a glass a sharp pain shoots through my rib.

"Ow!" I say, bending over, holding my ribcage.

Corbin races over. "What happened?"

"It's my rib. I shouldn't have reached so far." I slowly straighten up. "I'm fine now."

"Let me see." He goes to lift my shirt.

"No, really, I'm fine."

"You wouldn't have reacted that way unless it really hurt."

"You told me how much my ribs would hurt. You said they'd take a while to heal."

"Just show me where you felt the pain." Before I can protest, he lifts me up on the counter.

I raise my shirt and point to the spot. "Right there."

He does that thing with his fingers where he gently presses them along my skin. It gets me all hot and bothered, which I wish I could control but I just can't seem to do.

"It doesn't seem to be anything serious. I think you just aggravated the bruising when you reached up to get the glass."

I lower my shirt. "It's nice to have a doctor around every time something hurts."

He smiles. "I'm happy to make house calls once you move out. Feel free to call or text me if you need me to check anything, at least until you find a job that has insurance." He pauses, his eyes on mine. "Or if you just want me to stop by. Say hello. Go to lunch."

"Are you saying we'll be friends?" I ask in a tone that sounds flirty even though I didn't mean for it to.

"Given the past few days I think we could definitely be friends. I think we already are. We may not have a lot in common but I like spending time with you."

"I like spending time with you too."

Our eyes lock and I feel myself moving toward him. Toward his face. His lips. Before I can stop myself, I kiss him. It's a hesitant kiss, my lips barely touching his, afraid he might reject me. But he doesn't. So I kiss him again, for real this time, and feel his hand on the back of my head, tangling through my hair. I'm still on the counter and feel his other hand nudge my legs apart so he can get closer. The kiss becomes hotter, deeper. I move to the edge of the counter so I'm right up against him. He runs his hand up my leg, his fingers wrapping around my thigh, gently squeezing, as his thumb reaches over and presses the sensitive spot between my legs.

My desire for him explodes, my body craving him, wanting him. I feel like I'm losing control but it feels so good I don't care. I knew we had a spark but this is more like a burning flame. He's got me hotter than I've ever felt, wanting him so bad I can't stand it. There's no going back. We have to do this.

"Corbin?" I hear Lauren's voice behind me.

Corbin quickly steps back. "Lauren, what are you doing here?"

"I came to get my things." She glares at me as she drops her purse on the bench across from the elevator.

Corbin walks over to her. "Why didn't you call first?"

"I did, but you didn't answer."

He checks his phone. "I turned it off at the movie."

"You two went to a movie?" she asks. "Was this a date?"

"No," I say with a nervous laugh as I get down off the counter. "Corbin was just getting me out of the apartment."

"How long will this take?" Corbin asks Lauren.

She shrugs and walks past him. "If I do it all tonight it could take hours." She turns back to him, glancing at me. "Or if you two would like some time alone, I could get what I need and come back later."

"Just get what you need and go," he says. "And next time you need to check with me before you come over."

She walks off.

"Oh, and I need your access card for the building," he says but she's already in his room and probably didn't hear him.

"I'm going to bed," I say to Corbin.

"Star." He walks up to me and lowers his voice. "About what happened."

"Forget it." I laugh. "It was all that romance in the movie. Guess it just got to me." I go around him. "Goodnight." I hurry to my room and shut the door, still out of breath from what happened before Lauren walked in.

Holy shit, that was intense. That kiss. The way he touched me. The way my body reacted. It only made me want him more.

I can't live here. It's too tempting. I'm too attracted to him and falling for him way too hard. And now his ex knows. She looked like she was going to kill me.

Haley was right. I've got enough going on. I don't need all this drama. I need to move out.

CHAPTER FIFTEEN

Corbin

It's Saturday morning and I'm taking Star to look at apartments. This is the first time I've seen her since last night. We usually have breakfast together but today she stayed in her room. I think she was avoiding me because of that kiss. Because she's not sure what to do now or where we stand. I'm not sure either. I didn't expect her to kiss me last night but after she did, I couldn't stop thinking about it. And now, being around her, all I can think about is how much I want to do it again.

That kiss. Damn. It sparked a fire that's been burning ever since. I've never felt that much passion. That much desire. I tried to control myself, limiting it to just a kiss, but my hands just had to touch her. I've felt her body many times while assessing her injuries but this was different. This time I let myself feel my attraction to her. I let my hands go places I've only allowed them to go in my dreams.

Neither one of us wanted it to end. Our desire for each other was finally being quenched and there was no way we could stop it. But then Lauren walked in, and just like that, it was over.

Now it's like we're pretending it didn't happen. I want to talk about it but I don't think Star does, so for now I'm going to leave it alone and see what happens.

"How was that event the other night?" she asks as we drive through the narrow streets trying to find the building for the apartment she's considering.

"It was fine," I say.

Thursday night I had to attend a charity function for the hospital. It was so boring I'd already forgotten about it.

"Did you have fun?"

"I don't know if I'd call it fun. It was the typical charity event. You go there to meet people and make connections, not to enjoy yourself. I really don't have a need to go out there and sell myself anymore. I'm done with med school. I have a job. There's no reason for me to spend my night networking so I hung out by the bar and talked to the bartender." I chuckle. "He had a lot of good stories."

"Was Lauren there?"

"No, she had to work. But a lot of her friends were there. They didn't speak to me, which I knew they wouldn't. There was a ceremony after the dinner so I had to sit through that."

"Sounds really boring."

"It was. Thank God for the bartender. He was the only entertaining person there."

"Did your parents go?"

"Yes. I avoided them. They're not too pleased with me right now."

"Because of me?"

I glance at her. "Why would you think that? They don't even know you."

"Your dad met me and I could tell he didn't like me."

"That has nothing to do with you. It's more about his need to control me. He wanted me to be with Lauren, even if I wasn't happy with her."

146

Star's quiet, then says, "I heard him that night he came over. I tried not to listen in but he was yelling and, well, I heard what he said."

I sigh. "I'm sorry. I really am. He shouldn't have said what he did but if you knew him, you'd understand. It's just the way he is. He always assumes the worst."

"You know I'd never do that, right? Go after your money?"

"I know you wouldn't." I smile at her but she's looking down, her face full of worry. I reach over and put my hand around hers. "Star, relax. I don't think that about you. I know you're not trying to go after my family's money. You get mad when I try to buy you dinner."

She cracks a smile. "I don't get mad. I just feel bad making you pay."

"Don't. I'm happy to take you to dinner. Or to a movie. I like doing things with you. I'm going to miss you when you move out."

She nods, seeming uncomfortable. I wish she'd just tell me how she feels. If she thinks our kiss last night was a mistake I want her to tell me. I don't think it was a mistake at all. She doesn't fit the mold of someone I'd normally date but I don't care about that anymore. I'm doing what I want now, not what everyone else expects me to do.

"I think that's the one." She points to a brown brick building. "I'll text her and let her know we're here."

We go inside the building and I'm immediately hit with the smell of mold. I look up and notice water spots on the ceiling. Star notices them too.

"Maybe it's just on this floor," she says.

"Doesn't matter. You'd still have to walk through here everyday to get to your place. Do you know how bad mold is for your health?"

"To you, everything is a health hazard," she says in a kidding tone, but it's not a joke. Mold really is a health hazard.

There's no elevator so we take the stairs to the third floor. Star knocks on the door and an old lady answers. She's very large and wearing a pink robe and slippers.

"You must be Star," she says, holding her hand out.

"Um, yeah. Is Judy here?"

"I'm Judy. We spoke on the phone."

That's Judy? Star made it sound like the person we were meeting was much younger, like in her twenties. This lady has got to be at least sixty.

"Come on in." She steps back, pushing something aside with her foot so she can open the door.

That's when I notice the floor is covered, completely covered, in stacks of newspapers, craft supplies, stuffed animals, dishes, and just about anything else you could imagine. Whatever furniture is in there is covered up with piles of clothes, old books, magazines, shopping sacks, and plastic bins overflowing with more stuff. The place is straight out of one of those hoarder shows you see on TV. And the smell...it's a mix of rotting food and a sweaty locker room.

"Are you the boyfriend?" Judy asks me.

"No," I say as I continue to scan the room. I've never seen anything like this. And someone else lives here too?

"Linda will be out shortly," Judy says to Star. "She's in the bathroom. Would you like to see your room? Or we could go see the kitchen."

Star looks just as horrified as I am. "Actually, now that I think about it, I think this place is too far from my job, but thanks for showing us. Sorry to take up your time."

"Oh, it's no trouble at all. If you change your mind, just let us know."

"I will. Bye!"

We hurry out of there, racing down the stairs. When we're out of the building I reach in my pocket and take out my hand sanitizer.

"Hands." I hold the sanitizer out and when Star places her palms out I cover them in sanitizer.

148

"I don't need that much," she says, trying to rub it in.

"Did you see that place? We need the whole bottle. I feel like I need a shower now."

"It *was* pretty bad. I don't know how she lives like that. There wasn't even anywhere to sit. And what was that smell?"

"I don't know. I was trying not to breathe. Let's check out the next place. It's gotta be better than the last one."

The next apartment is in a building that looks fairly new but it's in a bad neighborhood.

"You really want to live here?" I ask as we watch a cop arrest a guy across the street.

"You don't know what he's being arrested for. Maybe he just shoplifted."

"Or murdered someone."

She shoves me. "What the hell? Why are you trying to scare me?"

"Because you shouldn't be living here. It's not safe."

"The safe neighborhoods cost too much. I'll buy some pepper spray and learn self defense."

I just shake my head. I know this is her decision but I don't want her living here. If she does, I'll be worrying about her constantly, which just shows how much I've fallen for her. I didn't try to. I wasn't even aware it was happening. But it has, and now I care about her way too much to let her live in a dangerous neighborhood.

We go in the building. It's nothing great but at least it's clean and has an elevator. We take it to the fourth floor and Star finds the apartment and knocks on the door.

"Come in," a guy says.

She opens the door to a mostly empty apartment, the complete opposite of the last place. There's almost nothing there—just a couch and a TV. A shirtless guy around my age is sprawled out on the couch smoking a joint.

I grab hold of Star's arm. "Let's go."

She turns to me and whispers, "Maybe he has a health condition. Maybe it's medicinal." Turning back to the guy, she says, "Are you Ty?"

"Yeah." He sighs and pushes himself up to standing. "This is the living room. Kitchen's over there." He motions to it. "Bedroom's down the hall. You can go take a look."

"I don't think we need to," I say.

Star looks at me, annoyed. "I'm going to at least check it out."

Ty collapses back on the couch while Star and I go down the hall. The first bedroom has the door open and we see a guy passed out on his bed. That must be the other roommate. He's only wearing boxers. Nothing else.

There's no way she's living here.

"The place reeks of pot," I say quietly to Star. "I'm getting high just being in here."

She opens the door of the last bedroom. It's empty except for a dingy stained mattress on the floor.

"It has two windows," she says in a cheery tone.

"Which you'll need to use to escape when the cops come raid the place."

"Pot's legal here. They're not getting arrested."

"You really think pot's the only thing they do?"

She glances around the room. "It's not bad. If I get a new mattress and maybe a lamp, it could be okay."

She's trying to be positive, a trait I admire about her, but there's nothing positive about this place. She needs to see it for what it is; a hangout for drug addicts and their drugged-out friends.

"This place is a shithole and I don't trust either one of those guys. You could wake up one night and find them on top of you."

"You're being very negative," she says, her hands on her hips. "It's almost like you don't want me to find a place."

"I do, but I want you to find a decent place in a decent neighborhood."

"Decent places in decent neighborhoods cost way more than I can afford, even with roommates."

"We've only looked at two apartments. Let's do more searching tonight and maybe tomorrow we can check out some more places."

"What do you think?" Ty asks as we're leaving.

"It's not really what I'm looking for," Star says, "but thanks for showing us."

Ty yawns and curls into a ball on the sofa, his eyes closed.

We let ourselves out and return to my SUV.

"Now what?" Star asks.

I smile. "Want to look at dogs?"

"Yes! I forgot we were doing that. Actually, I didn't think you were serious. Do you really want to get a dog?"

"I've wanted to for years. I just couldn't because I was never home and Lauren forbid it."

"What if you guys get back together?"

"Not going to happen. The idea hasn't even crossed my mind. I've moved on. Lauren is history. We're never getting back together."

"Never say never."

Is that why Star won't tell me how she feels about me? Is that why she made light of our kiss? Because she thinks I'll get back with Lauren?

I wait until we're at the animal shelter, then shut off the car and turn to her.

"Star, I just need to say this."

"What?"

"It's over with Lauren and me. The accident changed me. I almost killed you because I was driving without even thinking. Without looking where I was going. It made me think of my life and how I was just going through the motions. Letting Lauren and my parents take the lead and not really caring where I ended up. I don't know how I got to that point but I finally woke up when I was with you in the hospital."

151

She takes her seatbelt off and turns to face me. "What do you mean?"

"When Lauren found out I was staying with you at the hospital, waiting for you to wake up, she was furious. She said I shouldn't be there. That I was getting too involved. And in the past, when we were dating, I would've agreed with her just to avoid arguing with her. But that's not me. That's not who I am. I'm the guy who stays. The guy who does the right thing. I had to take responsibility for what I'd done and part of doing that was staying with you. You were all alone and I knew you'd be scared and confused when you woke up so there was no way I was just going to leave you."

"Did you and Lauren fight about it?"

He huffs. "Big time. I'd broken up with her that morning but she was still trying to tell me what to do. She even called my father and tried to get him to convince me to leave your room and go back to work. But I wouldn't do it."

"So you fought with your dad too?"

"Yes, which when you think about it makes no sense."

"In what way?"

"In the sense that we're all doctors. My father, Lauren, me. We all swore to take the best possible care of our patients. We work to help people. And here I am trying to help a woman who I, myself, injured, and my father and Lauren are yelling at me for being by your side."

"They don't want me staying with you, do they?"

"It doesn't matter. I don't care what they think. I'm done doing what everyone tells me to."

"I didn't realize I was causing so many problems. If I'd known I would've—"

"It's not you. You didn't do anything wrong. It's the other people in my life. The people who don't accept my choices. But that needs to end. I'm done letting other people control my life, especially Lauren."

"Does a part of you still love her?" Star looks down. "Sorry, that's too personal. I shouldn't have asked."

"I don't love her. Not even a little. And when I did love her, it was more because of our history. All the time we spent together. The memories we share. But it wasn't the kind of love I'd need to feel in order to marry her. I know that now more than ever. When you finally meet someone you—" I stop before I say too much. It was Star that made me realize my love for Lauren wasn't the right kind of love. But I can't tell her that. I'm still trying to figure out my feelings for Star and understand why I feel more for her after just a short time than I felt for Lauren after years of being together.

"That you what?" Star asks.

"That you click with. That you feel something for. That you..." I stop and clear my throat. "What I'm trying to say is that sometimes you don't realize what you're missing until you finally experience it. And then it's like a light goes off and you no longer want to continue on the path you were on. When you know there's something better, you want to go out and get it."

There. I said it. But I kept it general. I didn't say I was talking about her.

"Anyway," I say, wanting to get off this topic. "Ready to go check out the dogs?"

We go in the animal shelter and a girl leads us back to the kennels where the dogs are kept.

"Corbin, look at the puppy!" Star squeals, running up to one of the kennels. The dog is full of energy, jumping around his crate.

"Yellow lab?" I ask the girl.

"Yeah. Came in the other day. This is the first day he's up for adoption. He's a cutie. He'll go fast."

"Can we see him?" Star asks.

The girl goes to get him.

"I don't think I can handle a puppy," I say to Star. "I was thinking of getting an older dog."

"We can at least look at him."

The girl hands him to Star and he licks her face.

I smile at her. "He likes you."

"He's so cute. I want him. I wish I could get a dog."

"His *is* pretty cute." I take him from her. He licks my face, his tail wagging. "What's his name?" I ask the girl.

"Lucky."

"Then he'd be perfect for me," Star says to the girl. "I have bad luck. Like the worst ever. I could use a dog named Lucky."

"Maybe you should take him home."

"I would but I don't *have* a home. That's part of my bad luck."

I look at Star. "Maybe it's time for your luck to change. I say we get him."

The 'we' came out before I could catch myself. I guess that's how I think of us. As a couple, even though we're not.

"But you said you didn't want a puppy," she says.

"No, but if I remember right, you agreed to dog sit while I was at work. You can teach him all he needs to know."

"Except I won't be living there much longer."

"Then I'll hire you to come over and dog sit. You need money and I need a dog sitter. Works out great."

"You sure about this?"

Lucky licks my face again, his tail wagging even more, like he already knows he has a home.

"Lucky's the one. I can feel it. He speaks to me."

As if on cue, Lucky barks.

Star laughs. "I guess he does."

"Can you put him on hold for me?" I ask the girl.

"I can't, but we're open until six if you want to come back later." She hands me a sheet of paper. "This is our tip sheet for new dog owners. Tells you what you'll need if you decide to adopt him. Or do you already have a dog?"

"No. I haven't since I was a kid so this would be a big change."

"Then I'd say to give it some thought and maybe come back later today or tomorrow. You don't want to rush into something like this. It's a big commitment."

"But what if someone else takes him?" Star asks.

"If Lucky's the dog for you he'll still be here." She puts him back in his crate.

I give Lucky one last look before we go. He watches as we leave, looking confused like he's wondering why we didn't take him with us.

"He's a really sweet dog," Star says as we're driving back. "Do you think you'll get him?"

"I want to, but that girl is right. It's a big commitment. I can't make a decision like that without giving it some thought." I check my phone for the time. "It's time for lunch. You want to stop and get something?"

"We could, but don't you have other things to do? I feel like I'm taking up all your time."

"I'm the one who invited you so unless *you* have other things to do, I say we have lunch."

We go to a restaurant in Cambridge. As we're waiting for our food I look across the table at Star. "What do you think I should do?"

"About what?"

"The dog."

"It's up to you. You need to decide if you're ready for that kind of commitment."

"I've wanted a dog for years but couldn't with my residency hours. Now that I have more regular hours I think I could make it work, especially if you'd agree to dog sit."

She smiles. "How much does it pay?"

"Is ten an hour enough?"

"I get fifteen at the coffee shop."

"Then fifteen. Whatever it takes to hire you."

"You don't even know if I'm good with dogs."

"You did well with Lucky today. That's all that matters." I sigh as I think of all the work it takes to have a dog. "Maybe I'm not ready. I feel like I'm rushing into this."

"Then don't do it. You have enough to deal with right now between work and all the drama with Lauren and your dad, and the girl who's living rent-free at your apartment."

155

"Hey." I reach over and hold her hand. "Don't feel guilty about that. Letting you stay with me is the least I can do given what happened."

"Corbin?"

I look to my right and see Lauren walking toward us. Her eyes go to my hand, which is still holding Star's.

CHAPTER SIXTEEN

Star

"What are you two doing here?" Lauren asks with a fake smile, pretending not to notice Corbin holding my hand. He takes his time letting it go as he slowly sits back.

"We were out looking for apartments and decided to stop for lunch," he says. "How about you? Don't you have to work today?"

"I did, but I left because I thought I was coming down with something."

"You're sick?"

"I'm probably just tired. I'm here to pick up some soup, then I'm going home to rest."

"Well, I hope you feel better."

Lauren turns to me. "Alexis said you were scheduled this afternoon."

"I am?" I quickly get out my phone and check the online schedule. "I don't see my name on the schedule."

"She said she told you yesterday," Lauren says as she types something into her phone.

I call Alexis. "Hey, was I supposed to work today?"

"You were supposed to be here ten minutes ago."

"Shit, I'm so sorry. I don't remember you telling me I had to work."

"Where are you?"

"Having lunch, but I can skip it. I'll leave right now." I end the call and get up from the table. "Sorry, I can't stay. I'm late for work."

Corbin gets up. "I'll give you a ride."

"I don't need a ride," I tell him. "It's only a couple blocks."

"But with your leg—"

"She'll be fine," Lauren says. "The exercise will be good for her."

"Star, wait!" He follows me to the door. "Just let me give you a ride."

"It's not that far. It'll be faster to walk. I'll see you later."

"You're not walking. You could make your injuries worse."

As we leave I look back and see Lauren watching us. I wish I knew what she was thinking. She hasn't been bothering Corbin as much but she still seems possessive of him.

At the coffee shop Alexis is waiting for me and takes me to the back. "I need you to wash cups. The dishwasher broke."

"I'm not supposed to do anything strenuous. I don't have the doctor's okay yet."

"What's strenuous about washing dishes?" She brings me a stool. "Here. You can sit while you wash."

"Then I can't reach the sink."

She sighs. "Then rest on the stool when you need it. I have to go deal with a customer."

When she's gone I go over and check the schedule by the time clock. I'm not listed as working today. I wonder if Alexis called me in last minute and pretended I'd been scheduled. Maybe Lauren put her up to it so I wouldn't be spending time with Corbin.

After an hour of washing cups I'm not feeling very good, my head pounding and my stomach queasy from not eating. I find Alexis out front behind the counter.

"Do you mind if I leave?" I ask.

"It's one-thirty. You've only been here an hour."

"I know but I finished all the cups and I really need to rest. My head is killing me. And I need to eat. I missed lunch."

"Have a muffin." She points to the tray. "I'm tossing them soon anyway."

I take one because I'm starving. "I still can't stay. I'm supposed to rest when my head hurts and it really hurts right now."

She stares at me, annoyed. "Fine. But I need you here tomorrow. Can you be here at six?"

"On a Sunday? I thought we didn't open until eight."

"I need help getting a catering order ready." She straightens the row of coffee cups behind the counter. "Are you really turning down work? I thought you needed money."

"I do. Okay, yeah, I'll be there." I take off before she asks me to do something else.

Back at the apartment I find a note from Corbin saying he's at the gym. Noticing I stink like coffee I decide to take a quick shower before I rest. When I get out I hear the other shower running. Corbin must be back.

I go in my room and lay down in the bed but now I'm not tired. And my head feels better. The shower really helped.

There's a knock on the door. "Star? Are you up?"

"Yeah, come in."

Corbin opens the door, wearing track pants and a t-shirt, his hair wet from the shower. "How are you feeling?"

"Okay. I left work because my head was hurting but I took a long shower and it's better now."

"How's that area by your rib? Still sore?"

"I don't know. I'm trying to avoid touching it."

He smiles. "You have to touch it to know if it's getting better." He comes over to the bed and pulls the sheet back. I'm wearing a t-shirt and panties like I was before when he did this, except now he's not in doctor mode. I can tell by the way he's looking at me. The desire in his eyes as they move slowly up my legs.

"It's up here," I say, pointing just below my ribcage.

"Right," he says, his eyes darting back to mine. "Tell me if it hurts."

He sits next to me and slides my shirt up to just below my breasts. I close my eyes as I feel his fingers gently press down on my skin. "That okay?"

"Yeah," I say, biting my lip. I'm already aroused and he's barely touched me.

He moves his hand down, his fingers making small indents along my abdomen, getting lower each time. "Any pain?"

"No." I can barely breathe I'm so turned on.

My eyes remain closed as his hand slides down to the hem of my panties, still gently pressing down.

"How about now?"

I shake my head, lifting my hips just slightly, enough to let him know I want him to keep going.

When his fingers slip under my panties I suck in a breath.

"Still okay?" he asks in a deep sexy tone that tells me this is no longer an exam.

"Uh huh," I pant, my eyes still shut.

His fingers slide over the slickness between my legs, stroking me, and I shiver from how good it feels.

I feel his breath by my ear. "You sure about this?"

I swallow and nod, unable to form words. I feel his lips over mine as two fingers dip inside me, his thumb rubbing over that perfect spot and sending me soaring. My hips buck and I feel his palm pressing me down as he continues to work me.

"Oh, God," I say, trying to catch my breath between kisses. I'm breathless, ready to burst. Corbin knows exactly what to do, where to touch. I break from his lips, grabbing the sheet and holding on as pleasure rockets through me.

He waits a moment, then his hand moves to my lower abs, gently massaging, pressing into the area that's still warm and tingling, almost too sensitive to touch. He keeps it going, those soft presses, like we're back in exam mode, except this time, there's nothing medical about it. His touch is meant to tease, torture, make me want him even more.

That hot tingly feeling remains and intensifies as he continues that gentle massage over my pelvis. My eyes pop open as I feel my panties start to lower.

He smiles at me. "I'm going to need to remove these."

I just nod, mesmerized by his deep brown eyes, that chiseled face, and that sexy smile. I lift up as he tugs my panties down and slides them off.

His hands go to the hem of my shirt. "This will have to go too."

I smile. "This is a very thorough exam."

"It is." He smiles back. "And it's barely started. Lift up for me."

I do, and he pulls my t-shirt up and over my head, tossing it aside.

"Now lie down," he says, playing doctor again. I follow his orders, then watch as he yanks off his shirt, revealing his broad shoulders and defined abs.

Leaving his pants on, he sits beside me again, his hand splayed over my hip, his thumb extending down close to the area that's still warm and sensitive. My eyes fall shut as he leans down to kiss me. He deepens the kiss, his tongue moving slowly and sensually in my mouth as his hand moves up to my breast, gently squeezing.

I break from the kiss, gasping for breath.

"Still okay?" he says over my mouth.

My lips curve into a lazy smile. "More than okay."

His body lowers and I feel his mouth at my breast as his hand massages the other one, his thumb and finger tugging and teasing my nipple. I feel like I'm going to come again. I didn't think that was possible but I can feel it building. But I don't want it yet. I want to wait until he's inside me.

"Corbin." I breathe out his name, my hips rising off the bed, trying to get closer to the part of him I so desperately want.

He kisses his way up my chest, my neck, back to my mouth. "You are so beautiful."

"I want you," I say between kisses.

He stops and smiles at me. "That's not an appropriate request for your doctor."

"It is." I smile back. "It's part of the internal exam."

He gets up and quickly drops his pants and holy hell, he's huge. My eyes can't look away, remaining on him as he grabs a condom from the nightstand. He rolls it on, smiling when he sees me staring.

"It might sting a little at first," he kids.

Hell, yeah, it might. I've never been with someone that size.

"But I guarantee it'll feel better once it's in." He lies beside me and kisses me as his hand runs down my center to between my legs. I'm wet, soaked, more than ready for him. He moves over me, his body covering mine and I feel the tip of him nudge my entrance. He pushes in just a little. It doesn't sting but I definitely feel stretched.

He thrusts all the way in and I gasp.

"You okay?" he whispers.

I nod, then pull his mouth to mine and kiss him.

He kisses me back as he slowly pulls out. When he fills me again, I suck in a breath, then smile.

"You like that?" he asks in a deep, sexy voice.

I'm lost in bliss, unable to answer. Being with him is even better than I imagined.

His soft lips brush against my neck, sending a tingle down my spine. My whole body is drenched in feelings of pleasure like I've never felt before.

I lift up, meeting his thrusts, our bodies rocking together in a fluid motion. The sensations build. I feel it coming. I grab Corbin just as it hits, holding onto him as the spasms rocket through me even stronger than before.

I collapse back on the sheets, soaked in sweat. Corbin pauses to lean down and kiss me, then starts up again, his hips bucking fast and hard.

He groans as his body stiffens, then shudders as he comes. He pauses a moment to give me a kiss, then rolls off me onto his back.

I turn and lay my head and arm over his chest. "I've never had an exam like *that* before."

"I've never given one like that." He kisses the top of my head, like it's natural, like something we always do. And oddly enough, that's how it feels. Like we're a couple and we've done this before. It doesn't feel awkward. We're not hurrying to get up or trying to explain why we did it. We're just lying here, calm and relaxed, his arm around me, my body warm and sleepy against his.

"I should probably get up," I hear him say.

I lift my head, feeling drool at the side of my lip. "Did I fall asleep?"

"Yeah." He chuckles. "You were snoring."

"I was?" I sit up. "That's embarrassing."

"Hey." He pulls me back down to him and kisses me. "Don't be embarrassed. I didn't mind. I thought it was cute. And I like that you're comfortable enough with me to fall asleep on me."

"I am." I smile and lay back on his chest. "And I was really tired after what you did to me. Twice."

"It was once but I'm happy to do it again."

"I meant two orgasms. That's never happened before."

"Then you're in for a treat. Two is nothing."

"Really?" I ask, raising my head to look and see if he's kidding.

"I'm an expert in the human body. I know the right spots."

"You definitely do." I smile as I fall back on the pillow. "I've never felt anything like that before. It's never been that intense."

He turns on his side, facing me. "I didn't hurt you at all, did I?"

"No, but I had to adjust to it. It's larger than I'm used to."

He smiles. "I wasn't talking about my penis. I meant your ribs. Your bruises. I didn't hurt you, right?"

"Not at all."

"Good." He drops a kiss on my lips. "I'm going to go clean up."

He gets up and leaves my room to go down to his own. I need a shower but I remain in bed, taking a moment to enjoy how happy I feel right now. It's not just from the sex, although that's part of it, but it's also Corbin. He makes me feel happy. Safe. Cared for.

I don't know if what we just did changes anything between us but I want it to. He's become more than just some guy who helped me after the accident. He's become someone I trust, care about, and don't want to say goodbye to. I want more time with him. I want to keep getting to know him and maybe see where this could go.

Hearing the shower turn on I decide to do the same. As I'm walking to the hall bathroom I stop and go in Corbin's room. His bathroom door is open and I peek my head in.

"Do you have any extra towels?" I ask.

He shoves the shower curtain open, wiping his eyes. "There's a whole stack of them in the—" He stops, smiling when he realizes I'm not here for towels. He holds his hand out to me. "Come here."

"I don't know," I say, playing shy. "Is it really appropriate to shower with your doctor?"

"It's completely appropriate," he says as I join him, the warm steam surrounding us. "I have to check and make sure you're okay after all that physical activity."

His warm wet hands slide over my body as he kisses me.

"How's this feel?" he asks, cupping my ass and pulling me against him.

"Mmm," I hum, wrapping my arms around him. "Perfect."

He leans down and kisses my head and I close my eyes, feeling happier than I remember feeling in a really long time.

The shower leads to sex, then we end up in his bed and fall asleep.

"Star, are you up?" I hear Corbin say in a soft voice as he moves strands of my hair off my face.

I'm lying on my side, facing him. "Kind of. What time is it?"

"Six. I'm starving. How about you?"

"I'd say I worked up an appetite."

He chuckles and pulls me into his chest for a hug. "I had a great time today."

"Me too."

"Not just the sex, but just being with you. Lying here. Spending the day together. I liked it."

I look up at him. "I did too."

He runs his hand over my hair. "I don't want you to go."

"Then I'll stay, but I don't think our stomachs will be too happy."

"I wasn't talking about leaving the bed. I meant I don't want you to move out. I want you to stay."

"Corbin, we've talked about this. I need to get my own place. I need to give you your life back."

"You already have. Since meeting you I feel like my life is my own now. I'm finally taking control and making my own decisions. Do you know how freeing that is? How much happier I am now that I'm not living my life for other people?"

"But that started before you met me. It started when you broke up with Lauren."

"If I hadn't met you there's a chance I would've gone back to her. It was the accident that changed me. And meeting you. I realized life is too damn short to be unhappy. To keep wasting time trying to make something work that never would."

"So hitting me with your car was a good thing," I kid.

He pulls me closer. "Not at all. And I'll always regret that I hurt you. But something good did come from it. Actually two things. One is the realization that I needed to get my life back. And two is meeting this girl I can't seem to get enough of. A girl I think about constantly and want to fall asleep in my arms, after a thorough medical exam, of course."

I smile, my heart swelling with joy. "What are you saying?"

"I'm saying I don't want you to leave. I want you to stay with me, and not because you're injured or jobless or need a place to

165

stay, but because I want you here. Because I'd miss you too much if you left. I know we haven't known each other long but I feel like we have. I feel like I've known you so much longer than it's actually been. If you want to move out I'll understand but I still want to see you. I want to take you out." He takes my hand and looks in my eyes. "Will you go out with me?"

I laugh. "You're asking me on a date? After we've already had sex?"

"I know it's not the conventional way to start a relationship but we didn't meet in a conventional way, so thinking of it that way it's really not that strange. What do you say?"

I smile. "Yes. I'll go out with you.'"

"What about my other question?"

"What?"

"Will you stay here? Live with me?"

"Hmm." I chew on my lip. "Can I have your bedroom?"

"Only if I get to stay here too."

"Deal."

He kisses me and my stomach growls.

"Sorry." I look down at my stomach. "Way to ruin the mood."

He laughs. "Let's go get some dinner."

Later that night, as I'm lying in bed with Corbin sleeping soundly at my side, I think this can't possibly be real. Nothing good ever happens to me and now I'm dating a doctor and living in this luxurious apartment. And I'm happy. Really happy.

Maybe my luck is finally changing for the better.

CHAPTER SEVENTEEN

Two Months Later

Corbin

"I'll take that one," I tell the guy at the flower stand just down from my building. I buy Star flowers at least once a week. I mix up what kind I get. Today it's a seasonal mix of spring flowers in pinks and purples.

Star and I have been together for two months now and every day we fall more in love. I told her I love her soon after we slept together for the first time. That day will always be one of my favorite days of all time. When I held her in my arms and we drifted off to sleep to the sound of the gentle rain falling against the window, I felt a peace like I'd never felt before. Like I was finally where I was meant to be. Holding this beautiful girl who I'd grown to love for her cheerful spirit, caring heart, and relentless optimism.

Most people would say it was too soon to fall in love. I would've agreed with them before meeting Star. It took months of being with Lauren before I felt like I loved her, and even then, I questioned it, not sure it was really love. With Star, I knew. There was no question about it. And yes, it was fast.

Faster than I thought was possible. But when I met her my heart fell for her before I even knew it was happening.

When I realized what I was feeling I wanted to tell her right away but thought I should wait. But then one night while we were making dinner, those three little words slipped past my lips before I could stop myself. Her eyes widened and she jumped in my arms and said it back. It was another moment I'll always remember and one that still brings a smile to my face.

Star's unlike anyone I've ever met and if I hadn't hit her with my car that day I never would've known what I missing. I wouldn't have known that such a perfect match for me existed. Someone who, to the outside world, doesn't seem like a match for me at all.

My parents think I've lost my mind. My father isn't even speaking to me. He won't return my phone calls. He doesn't answer the door when I go to his house. I want a relationship with him again but it won't happen if he refuses to accept Star.

As for Star's parents, they couldn't be happier we're together. We went to visit them last weekend. Star didn't want to go but I insisted on meeting her parents. She's embarrassed by them because they're still married and living together while dating other people. But they told Star they'd soon be filing the paperwork for their divorce, which she was relieved to hear. And *they* were relieved to know she has a steady job and won't be moving back in their house. Star still works at the coffee shop and also dog walks for people in the building.

"Sterling," someone calls out from behind me.

I turn around and see Kent's smiling face. "Hey, man. Where you been? Haven't seen you around."

He nods. "Been traveling. Had to speak at some conferences. I'm finally home for the week."

He follows beside me as I continue down the street, heading back to the apartment.

"Flowers, huh?" He smiles. "You and Lauren back together?"

I look at him. "Has it been that long since I've talked to you?"

"What do you mean?"

"I've been dating Star for two months."

"The girl you hit with your car?"

"Yeah. She's fully recovered now. We're living together."

"No shit?" His eyes widen. "That was fast."

"When it's right you just know."

"So what happened to Lauren? I'm sure she's not happy you found someone else. Has she been giving you a hard time?"

"She was, but I think she's finally giving up. She moved the rest of her stuff out a couple weeks ago. I haven't heard from her since."

"You sure that's a good sign?" he asks with a grin. "Not hearing from her? Maybe she's planning something."

"Like what? She knows it's over between us. Her residency ends soon and then she'll be moving. She's hoping to get a job in New York. Once she's gone, I doubt I'll hear from her again."

"So you and Star? It's going well?"

"Better than I ever could've imagined. I've never felt like this before. I never thought a relationship could be this good. Every day I can't wait to get home to her."

"That's great. I'm happy for you."

We stop at the door to our building and go inside.

"I'm going to stop and check the mail," he says. "Have a good night."

"You too." I get on the elevator and when it opens to my apartment, I'm greeted by the aroma of garlic and tomato sauce. Another great thing about Star? She loves to cook. She didn't when I met her but then she tried some recipes and now she's hooked.

"Corbin, is that you?" I hear her say.

"No, it's the guy you've been seeing from the first floor," I kid.

I hear her laughing. "Hold on. I have sauce on my hands."

169

Dropping my keys in the bowl I look up and see Lucky racing toward me at full speed, tongue out, tail wagging.

"Hey, boy." I reach down and rub his head. He jumps around like he hasn't seen me in weeks and lets out a bark. "Go get your ball."

He turns and runs off to get it. I laugh and continue to the kitchen.

I love having a dog. We got Lucky a few days after we saw him at the shelter. We went back to see him and couldn't leave without taking him home. He's been a handful, like all puppies are, but Star's been taking him to dog obedience classes and even taught him a few tricks.

"Hey, gorgeous," I say, coming up behind Star at the sink.

She flips to face me, greeting me with a huge smile and a kiss.

"For you." I hand her the flowers.

Her face brightens, her eyes wide. "Corbin, they're beautiful." She hugs me. "I love you."

"I love you too."

She lets me go. "How was your day?"

"Good. No big emergencies. I had a teenage girl who broke her nose and was crying because she said her boyfriend would break up with her with a crooked nose."

"Did you tell her she's better off without him?" Star asks as she puts the flowers in a vase.

"I did, but it didn't seem to help."

Star turns back to me, her arms around my waist. "Would you break up with me if I broke my nose?"

"Never. You were covered in bruises when I met you and I still thought you were the most beautiful girl ever."

"I looked horrible after the accident. How could you possibly think I looked good?"

Lucky comes racing up to us, barking.

Star leans down to him. "What's wrong?"

I pet his head. "Where's your ball?"

170

Lucky hears me say 'ball' and barks again, nudging me with his nose.

"What's he doing?" I ask.

"His ball probably got stuck behind something. He'll keep barking until you find it."

"Let's go find your ball," I say to Lucky. He gets excited and starts jumping around.

"Dinner's almost done," Star says.

"Okay, I'll go change."

Walking past the couch I see Lucky's ball wedged under it. I pull it out and toss it to Lucky. He grabs it and follows me to the bedroom, sitting down on the floor and chewing on it.

He makes me laugh. He's been a good addition to the family. He brings so much life and energy to the place. I used to dread coming home. It was either too quiet and lonely, or if Lauren was here, I felt tense, prepared for an argument to erupt. Now I come home and I'm greeted by Star's loving arms and Lucky's overexcited dog kisses and tail wagging the minute I walk in the door.

Things couldn't get much better than this.

My phone rings as I'm changing into a t-shirt. I pick it up and see it's my dad. He hasn't called me since I told him about Star and me. The call ended with him yelling at me to come to my senses and go back to Lauren. I'm sure his feelings haven't changed so I set the phone down, deciding not to answer.

"Who was that?" Star appears, pointing to my phone.

"My dad." I toss my work clothes in the hamper.

"You're not going to talk to him?"

"No." I meet her at the door. "Is dinner ready?"

"A few more minutes. Corbin, you should talk to your dad."

"Why? He's just going to yell at me for being with you. I'm not going to listen to it. I no longer need him to validate my decisions."

She places her hands on my chest and looks up at me. "Would you please just talk to him? Maybe he's changed his mind about us."

"He hasn't. I guarantee it." I try to go around her, but she holds onto my shirt, keeping me there.

"Please. Just see what he wants. What if it's something important?"

"Like what?"

"I don't know." She takes my phone from my pocket and hands it to me. "Call him. And then we'll have dinner." She walks out. "Come on, Lucky."

He jumps up, the ball in his mouth, and follows her down the hall.

Sighing, I look at my phone. I don't want to call him but I do because Star asked me to. It shows how much I love her. I'd do anything for her.

"Hey, Dad," I say when he answers. "I see that you called."

"Yes." He clears his throat. "I just wanted to let you know I'll be having a procedure done tomorrow. I'll be staying overnight at the hospital."

"Procedure? What procedure?"

My father's in excellent health so I'm surprised he's having something done. And now I'm worried because he wouldn't be telling me this unless it were serious.

"They found a partial blockage in an artery," he says. "They'll be putting a stent in and they want to run some tests while I'm there."

"Tests on your heart?"

"Yes. I'm sure everything will turn out to be fine but I just wanted you to know."

"Yeah, I'm glad you did. What hospital? Mine?"

"Yes. I'll arrive at the cardiac unit at seven tomorrow morning. Anyway, I just wanted you to know. Enjoy the rest of your evening."

"Dad, wait."

"What is it?"

"I want to be there. I'll be there when you arrive and stay as long as you need me."

"Corbin, that's not necessary. Helen will be there, and as you know, it's not a risky procedure."

"And as we *both* know, there's risk to any and all procedures. I'll be there."

"Very well. Then I'll see you tomorrow." He ends the call.

I go back to the kitchen where Star is stirring the sauce on the stove.

"Did you talk to him?" she asks.

"Yeah." I go up to her and hug her, squeezing her tight. "Thank you."

"For what?"

"Making me call him."

"Why? What happened?"

"He's having a heart procedure done tomorrow. I never would've known if I hadn't called him back."

She pulls away. "A heart procedure? That sounds serious."

"He's having a stent put in. It's fairly routine but it sounds like he may have some other heart issues. They're keeping him in the hospital to run some tests."

"You're going, right?"

"Yeah, I'll get there early and I might stay there after work to be with him, if that's okay."

"Of course it is. Stay as long as you need."

"I'd invite you to come with but it might be—"

"Corbin, don't worry about it. I don't need to go. I understand."

I hug her again. "God, I love you."

"I love you too."

We have dinner and watch TV but I can't stop thinking about my dad. He sounded worried, and he never sounds worried, which means he's afraid they're going to find more problems with his heart. Just the fact that he called me tells me he's really concerned.

The next morning, I arrive in his room and find Helen, my stepmom, there but not my dad.

"Helen." I give her a quick hug. We're not close but we get along okay.

"Hello, Corbin." She gives me a worried smile. "They took your father away to run some tests on him before the procedure."

"When did he find out about this?"

"A couple weeks ago."

"I wish he'd told me."

"He wanted to, but you know your father. He's very stubborn."

"He's still upset about Lauren," I say.

"We're both upset about that. We understand you two had issues but your father and I think those issues could be worked out if you put some effort toward them. Perhaps saw a couple's counselor."

I shake my head. "That wouldn't have helped. Lauren and I had more than a few issues. We didn't share the same values. We didn't want the same things. All we did was fight. I'm much happier now that we're no longer together and I'm sure Lauren is too."

Helen sits on the chair by the bed, setting her purse in her lap. "You two were going to get married. I don't understand how things changed so quickly."

"We weren't getting married. We'd never even talked about it. Helen, I know you and Dad want me to be with Lauren but it's just not going to happen. It's over."

Helen looks behind me, smiling. "Lauren, dear, come in."

I grit my teeth. I should've known they'd tell her about this. They still consider her part of the family.

"Hello, Lauren," I say, turning to her.

"Corbin." She smiles and walks up to me, giving me a brief hug. "I'm sorry to hear about your father."

"I'm sure he'll be fine. It's a routine procedure. You don't need to stay."

"Corbin, she wants to be here," Helen says, giving Lauren a hug. "It's good seeing you again, dear."

"You too, Mrs. Sterling."

She smiles. "Lauren, you know you can call me Helen. We're like family."

I fight the urge to roll my eyes.

"How is your mother?" Helen asks Lauren.

"She's doing well. Still working on getting back the deposit for the party."

"Such a shame," Helen says, glancing at me. "Tell her we'll be happy to contribute to any cancellation fees."

"I will. Thank you." Lauren turns to me. "So Corbin, how have you been?"

"Good. And you?"

"Busy as always. I've applied for several positions in New York and should hear back this week regarding interviews. Actually, I wanted to talk to you about that." She looks at Helen. "Would you give us a minute?"

"Of course." She grabs her purse from the chair and walks out of the room.

"What is it?" I ask Lauren, already feeling on edge just being around her. I never noticed how anxious she makes me until I met Star and realized that anxious feeling wasn't normal. With Star I feel calm and relaxed.

"One of the hospitals I applied at requires I submit a peer recommendation. I would like you to write it."

"Lauren, I don't think that's appropriate. Ask someone else. There are plenty of people who could write it for you."

"They don't know me like you do. They wouldn't know what to write. You've known me since we were children. Certainly you could come up with something to say."

"I really think you should find someone else. Someone you didn't used to date. Someone you know professionally."

"Corbin, don't be ridiculous. Our relationship has nothing to do with this. I'm asking you to write it because you'll do a far better job than anyone else I know."

That's one of the few compliments she's ever given me but she's only saying it to get what she wants.

"And doing this for me," she continues, "could get me the job. I'm sure that would please you." She smiles. "To get rid of me?"

"Lauren, don't start. We're not going to argue in my father's hospital room. He'll be back here any minute."

"I'm not arguing with you. I'm simply asking for a favor. Do this one thing for me and I'll never ask again."

I sigh. "Fine. Send me the details and I'll get it done."

"Thank you." She hugs me but I don't hug her back, my arms stiff at my sides.

"Corbin," my father says as they wheel him in. "Glad you could make it."

Lauren pulls away from me but stands right beside me, as if we're still a couple.

"Hello, Dr. Sterling." She smiles at him. "How are you feeling?"

"Fine, thank you." He glances at me, then back at Lauren. "Nice to see you two together again."

Lauren smiles even wider.

I step away from her. "Lauren was just leaving." I give her a look to go. "She's late for rounds."

"I can spare a few minutes," she says, ignoring my request.

Helen walks in. "The nurse said it could be another hour."

"Then why the hell am I here so early?" my father scoffs.

"Dad, just relax," I tell him. "You know they're not always on time. You want me to get you a paper?"

My father begins every day by reading the newspaper. First the local paper, then *The Wall Street Journal*.

"I've already read them," he says. "Couldn't sleep. I was up all night."

"How about some TV?" I pick up the remote. "The financial news?"

"No. I want quiet." He's cranky, which is how he gets when he's worried.

"Perhaps we should sit down," Lauren says, and when I look at her, I see she's swaying a little and her eyelids are flickering.

"Lauren?"

She sways some more, then her knees buckle. I race up and catch her before she collapses.

"Lauren!" Helen hurries over to her.

"I'm fine," she says, blinking several times and taking deep breaths as she tries to stand up. I'm still holding onto her and she grips my arm as she steadies herself.

"What happened?" I ask her.

"It's probably low blood sugar. I didn't eat this morning after spin class."

"Dear, you need to eat," Helen says, rubbing her arm. "Can I get you something?"

"Thanks, but I'll be fine."

I let go of her and stand back, watching to make sure she doesn't start swaying again.

"When's the last time you ate?" I ask her.

"Last night, probably around five."

"You haven't eaten since last night? It's no wonder you almost fainted. Why didn't you eat?"

"I've gained a few pounds," she says, looking down at herself. "I was trying to get them off."

"Lauren, don't be ridiculous," Helen scolds. "You're skin and bones. You could use a few extra pounds."

"Why don't you go get something to eat?" I take her arm and walk her to the door.

She leaves and I go out in the hall and watch as she walks to the elevator. She stops a moment like she's about to pass out, then takes a breath and continues walking. That's just like Lauren to skip eating to lose weight even though she's already stick thin. As a doctor she knows better but she always puts her appearance before her health.

Back in my dad's room I sit on the chair next to the window. Helen is sitting by the bed, searching through her purse.

My dad looks over at me. "She's not doing well without you."

I sigh. "She's fine. She just hasn't eaten."

"She's not eating because she's upset. Because she misses you."

"Dad, I don't want to get into this. Lauren and I aren't getting back together."

He stares straight ahead, his mouth tight like he's trying to hold himself back from yelling at me for breaking up with Lauren. It's completely unlike him. He never holds back from criticizing my decisions. Maybe this health scare is changing him, making him want a relationship with me again despite not liking my choices.

"So you and Star," he says, his jaw tightening as he says her name. It's the first time he's used her name. He usually calls her 'that girl you hit with your car'. "You're still together, I assume?"

"Yes, and we're very happy. I know you don't think we're a good match but we get along great. She's actually perfect for me."

"I can't imagine you two could have much in common. She didn't attend college, did she?"

"She went for a year then left because she wasn't sure what she wanted to do."

"Does she plan to go back?"

"I don't know but it doesn't matter. College isn't for everyone, and it doesn't guarantee a high paying job. Look at Alexis. She has a degree from Columbia and manages a coffee shop."

Helen looks up from her purse and turns to me. "Her father isn't doing well. Did she tell you?"

"No. What's wrong with her father?"

"His blood pressure is dangerously high. The doctors say he could have a stroke at any time."

"He needs to get some weight off," my father says. "He's gained a significant amount since retiring. Have you seen him lately?"

"No," I say. "It's been over a year."

"I'm surprised Alexis didn't mention it," Helen says. "Or Lauren. She, of course, knew, given they're such close friends."

178

"I don't talk to Lauren much anymore. But I see Alexis every day when I get coffee. And Star works for her."

"She has a job?" my father asks. "She's not just living off your income?"

"Dad, for the last time, Star isn't with me for my money. She's very independent and works hard to make her own money. She's walking dogs now too and actually makes a lot doing it."

"She could still file a lawsuit," my father says. "Do you know if she's spoken with an attorney?"

"Dad, seriously, you need to stop this. Star is not going to sue me. We're in a relationship. We live together."

"Let's change the topic, shall we?" Helen says, getting up and going to the window. "Look at the beautiful day we're having. They say it may reach 75. Wouldn't that be lovely?"

My father and I don't answer, and we remain quiet until the nurse comes and takes him away. The procedure goes smoothly and I talk to my father briefly when it's done, then head to my job at the clinic.

Star calls just as I'm getting there. I've been texting her all morning with updates.

"Hey, I'm just getting to work," I tell her.

"I'll let you go. I just wanted to see how he was doing."

"He's doing fine. I'll call and check on him later."

"Are you going back there tonight? After work?"

"Probably, so go ahead and have dinner without me."

"Okay. I'll see you later tonight. Love you!"

"Love you too. Bye."

I didn't tell Star about Lauren showing up today or that I'd be writing her a letter of recommendation. I never keep secrets from Star so I feel like I should've told her but I didn't want to upset her or make her think there's a chance I'd get back with Lauren.

Lauren is my past. Star is my future.

CHAPTER EIGHTEEN

Star

"It's just you and me tonight, Lucky," I tell him as we get home from our walk. I let him off the leash and he runs to his water bowl for a drink. "Are you hungry, Lucky?"

I know he can't understand me but I talk to him like he can. He's such a sweet dog. He reminds me of the lab I had as a kid.

"There you go," I say, stepping back to let him eat the food I just poured in his bowl. I laugh as his tail hits me in his race to get to his food.

"Now I have to figure out what *I'm* going to eat." I open the fridge. "Maybe I'll just get a sandwich."

Corbin called an hour ago and said he was going to eat dinner with his stepmom at the hospital then hang out with his dad until visitor hours are over. I wish I could be there with him but I understand why I can't. He needs to fix his relationship with his dad, and since I'm part of the reason they haven't been talking I need to stay away until things are better between them. I think his dad will accept me eventually but it'll take some time.

"I'll be back soon," I tell Lucky, putting him in his kennel. With his tummy full, he'll take a nap in there until I get back.

I go down the street to the deli Corbin took me to when we first met. I go there all the time. It's close, not too expensive, and the food is good.

Lars is working behind the counter and spots me as I walk in.

"Grilled ham and cheese," he says, trying to guess my order.

"Okay," I say, walking up to the counter.

He laughs. "I was joking. What can I get you?"

"The ham and cheese. It sounds good. And don't forget the pickle."

"Is this for here?"

"No, I'll take it to go. I have a puppy who gets mad if he's alone for too long."

Lars puts his gloves on and gets to work making my sandwich. His shaggy blond hair is pulled back in a man bun and his skin has a darker tan than when I saw him last. He's always out in the sun, biking or hiking or playing volleyball with his friends. He's in really good shape from all his activities. I saw him biking without a shirt one day and he had abs as good as Corbin's, although Corbin is still hotter. He's taller and more muscular. He's so hot. I can't believe he's mine.

"Where's your man tonight?" Lars asks as he wraps up my sandwich.

"At the hospital. His dad's there having some tests run."

"Is he going to be okay?"

"I don't know. We're waiting to find out."

He hands me my sandwich and rings me up.

"Star," I hear someone say.

I look over and see Lauren walking toward me. Has she been here the whole time? I didn't see her when I came in.

"Hi," I say, grabbing my change from Lars. I shove it in my pocket and turn to leave.

"Star, wait." Lauren catches up to me before I reach the door. "Have you heard anything about Corbin's father?"

"You know about that?"

She lets out a laugh. "Well, obviously. I was there this morning during his procedure."

"You were?" I ask, but I shouldn't have sounded so surprised. Now Lauren will know Corbin didn't tell me she was there. Why didn't he tell me? Did he think I'd be jealous? If so, he's wrong. I'm not jealous of Lauren and I don't consider her a threat. Corbin loves me and I love him. Our relationship couldn't be better. So why didn't he tell me about Lauren?

"I've known the Sterling family for years," she says. "It's not surprising they'd ask me to be there during this difficult time. I'm practically part of the family."

I ignore her attempt to make me feel bad for not being included. We both know why she was allowed to be there and I wasn't, but it doesn't change my relationship with Corbin so I really don't care.

"I need to go," I say. "I don't like leaving the dog for too long."

"You have a dog?"

"Corbin didn't tell you?" I ask, knowing he didn't. Now it's her turn to feel excluded.

"It makes sense. He's wanted a dog for years. I can't stand dogs. All that barking and shedding."

"Corbin loves having a dog. We both do. Anyway, I really should get going."

"When you see Corbin later, remind him about the letter."

"What letter?"

Damn, I did it again. I let her know Corbin didn't tell me. Now she'll think he keeps secrets from me. I didn't think he did, but now I'm questioning that.

"He's writing me a letter of recommendation for a job I applied for in New York."

"You're moving to New York?" I ask, secretly happy about it. She'll finally be out of our lives.

"That's the plan, but first I need to get a job. Tell him I need it by Thursday."

"I will." I open the door to leave, then turn back. "By the way, what are you doing here? Shouldn't you be at work?"

"I wasn't feeling well earlier so I took the night off. I nearly passed out this morning but luckily Corbin caught me before I hit the floor. Anyway, I love the soup here and thought it'd make me feel better."

"Oh, okay, well, goodbye." I walk quickly back to the apartment, simmering with anger that Corbin didn't tell me about Lauren. He caught her? In his arms? What the hell? And why was she fainting? Did she fake it so Corbin would catch her? And why didn't he tell me about this letter he's writing for her?

I talked to him several times today and he never mentioned anything about Lauren. Why didn't he say something?

He gets home at ten and takes a quick shower before joining me in bed.

"I just checked my phone," he says. "Results won't be in until tomorrow or the next day."

"But your dad's feeling okay?"

"He feels great. He wants to go home but they want him to stay overnight."

"I'm glad he's feeling better."

Corbin turns toward me, his arm going around my waist. "Goodnight." He gives me a kiss.

"Hey, um, did anything else happen today?"

"What do you mean?"

"With your dad this morning. You didn't say much about it."

"There wasn't much to say. Helen and I waited with him in his room, they took him for the procedure, and then we waited while he recovered. Then I went to work." He yawns. "Can we talk tomorrow? I'm really tired. I need to sleep."

"Yeah, okay. Goodnight."

He still didn't tell me. Why didn't he tell me? I could've asked but now I'm curious if he'll ever tell me or if he'll keep it a secret. I don't like secrets in a relationship, especially when

183

they're secrets about an ex. An ex I don't trust who I know wants him back.

The next day at the coffee shop I'm wiping down the counter when a man in a suit comes up to me.

"What can I start for you?" I ask.

I've been working behind the counter for weeks now and I'm getting really good at it. I can whip up drinks faster than anyone here.

"I'll just have a plain coffee," he says. "Dark roast."

"Room for cream?"

"No."

I get his coffee and as I'm ringing him up, he says, "I heard about the accident."

"What accident?" I ask.

"You were hit while riding your bike. Isn't that right?"

"Um, yeah, but that was a long time ago."

"I believe it was around two months ago, or is my timing wrong?"

I stare at him, wondering who he is and what he wants. "What's this about?"

"I'd like to talk to you about our services." He hands me a business card. It's for a law firm specializing in personal injury cases.

"I'm not interested," I say, shoving the card in my pocket as I turn to grab a rag to wipe the counter.

"We'd just like to meet with you. You could decide not to work with us but it would be wise for you to at least know your options. Our work is free of charge unless you receive compensation, in which case we would take a small percentage to cover our expenses."

"I told you, I'm not interested." I go around the counter to wipe down a table that has coffee spilled all over it.

The man stands across from me. "Often we find that people such as yourself have lasting injuries they don't find out about until years later. For instance you could have lingering back issues years from now that could cost you thousands of dollars to treat, not to mention the cost of your pain and suffering."

"I'm not going to file a lawsuit," I say, letting him hear the anger in my voice. "I don't care what scare tactics you use, the answer is still no." I go behind the counter and continue to the back room where Alexis is labeling coffee bags.

"What's wrong?" she asks, watching me pace the floor.

"I'm angry and need a break."

"Why? Did something happen?"

"This lawyer was trying to get me to sue Corbin. He acted like he wanted me to make up fake injuries or a fake story so I could get money for pain and suffering." I huff. "I can't stand lawyers, especially ones like him."

"I'll take over out front," she says, setting the labels down. "You stay back here, okay?"

"Okay, thanks."

When I first started working for Alexis she was really mean to me. I'm sure Lauren told her to act that way, and I'm sure it's why she got me the job. She wanted her friend to make me miserable, knowing I was too poor to quit. But within a couple weeks Alexis eased up on me. She saw how hard I worked, and the more time we spent together the more she started to like me. Now I'd say we're almost at the point of being friends, but I'm still cautious with what I say around her, knowing it'll get back to Lauren.

I fill and label the rest of the coffee bean bags, then bring them up front.

"Okay, just calm down," I hear Alexis say.

I look up and see her sitting at one of the tables with Lauren. What's Lauren doing here? She's usually at the hospital this time of day.

Lauren sees me and nudges Alexis.

Alexis looks up at me and smiles. "You done?"

"Yeah. Need me to do anything else?"

"Hold on." She leans over and whispers something to Lauren, who nods, her eyes still on me. What is going on with those two?

Alexis gets up from the table and walks over to me. "Do you think you could fill in for me for an hour or so?"

"Um, yeah, sure. Is something wrong?"

She smiles. "Not at all. Lauren and I just need to talk about some stuff and I don't want to do it here."

"You have to talk *now*? It can't wait?"

She glances back at Lauren, who's checking her phone.

"It'd be better if I talked to her now," Alexis says. "I'll try to hurry."

"Don't worry about it. I can handle it. Afternoons are slow anyway."

"Thanks! Just call if you need anything."

"Is she okay?" I ask, looking at Lauren as she takes a deep breath, her eyes closed.

"Lauren? Yeah. She's fine," Alexis says in a voice that's too chipper to be real. "I'll see you later."

Something's going on. Why would Lauren leave work to talk to Alexis? What could be that important? Is it about Corbin? Is something going on with them?

What am I thinking? Corbin wouldn't do that. He'd never cheat on me with his ex. But he lied to me about seeing her at the hospital, and didn't tell me about that recommendation he's writing for her.

Maybe Lauren got a job in New York and wanted to tell Alexis. But that wouldn't be urgent. Lauren wouldn't have left work for that.

I'm starting to feel sick. Corbin lied to me about Lauren and now Lauren has some urgent need to talk to Alexis. Something's going on and I have a very strong feeling it has to do with Corbin.

Alexis shows up two hours later using that same overly cheerful tone. "Thanks for filling in! You can go home now."

I undo my apron. "So what happened with Lauren?"

186

She shrugs. "She just needed to talk."

"Is something wrong? I mean, it has to be pretty serious if she missed work. She never misses work."

"Don't worry about Lauren," she says with a smile as she refills the cups by the coffee machine. "She'll be fine. Now go ahead and get out of here. You've had a long day. Any plans for tonight?"

"Not that I know of. We'll probably just eat dinner and watch TV."

"Sounds fun! See you tomorrow!" she says before disappearing in the back.

She's acting really strange, like she's covering something up. Something she doesn't want me to know.

Later that night when I'm making dinner, Corbin calls. "Hey, I'm running late at work. I'm not going to make it home for dinner."

"The clinic closes at five. It's after six. What's taking so long?"

He sighs. "Paperwork. I'm way behind on filling it out. I need to take some time to catch up or it'll never get done."

"What time do you think you'll be home?"

"I don't know. I'll text you later with an update."

"Hey, how's your dad? Any news?"

"The tests didn't show anything."

"That's good, right? It means his heart is healthy?"

"Yes, other than the artery that needed the stent."

"It's good it wasn't more than that."

"Yeah. Well, I should get back to work. Before I go, how was your day?"

"Okay. I got to play manager for a couple hours."

"Star, that's great! How'd you end up as manager?"

"Alexis had to leave to talk to Lauren."

"Lauren was there?"

"Yeah. Doesn't she normally work in the afternoons?"

"I don't know her schedule. She could've switched with someone."

187

"Maybe. I just find it odd she had to talk to Alexis like that."

"Like what?"

"Like right that second. Whatever she had to talk about must've been urgent. Has she said anything to you?"

"Lauren?"

"Yeah."

"I never see her."

"But you work at the same hospital. You must run into her sometimes."

"She doesn't come to the clinic."

"You might've seen her in the cafeteria."

"Star, why are you asking all these questions about Lauren? Did she say something to you?"

"No. I just found it odd that she made Alexis leave work so they could talk."

"I'm sure it's nothing. Lauren likes to create drama. Something must've happened to her and she blew it out of proportion and made Alexis think it was an emergency. Did you ask Alexis about it?"

"Yeah and she said Lauren was fine."

"See? False alarm. Lauren used to do that to me all the time. Star, I really need to go or I'll never get out of here."

"Okay. I'll see you later tonight."

He still didn't tell me about Lauren. He said he never sees her but according to Lauren they saw each other at the hospital yesterday. They were together during his dad's procedure. How could he not tell me that? Why is he hiding it?

The more I think about this, the worse I feel. I thought I could trust Corbin. But maybe I can't.

CHAPTER NINETEEN

Corbin

"Star?" I walk in the apartment a little after five and hear Lucky barking from his kennel. If he's in there it means Star isn't home. I go to the kitchen and see a note saying she had to walk the neighbor's dog. I'm surprised she didn't take Lucky with her. He usually tags along on her dog walks.

"I'm coming," I say to Lucky who's crying and whimpering to be let out. When I undo the door to his kennel he bursts out and almost knocks me over.

"Hey, buddy." I rub his head and his tail wags as he jumps on me.

He takes off for his water bowl while I go in the bedroom to change. I'm exhausted and would like to just skip dinner and go to bed but I need to wait for Star to get home to see what she wants to do. I also want to see if she's still mad at me. She turned away from me in bed last night, probably because she didn't like me working late. I'm not sure she bought my excuse. I said I was doing paperwork, which was true, but it wasn't for work. I was writing that recommendation for Lauren. I wanted to get it over with so I stayed until it was done, then dropped it in the mail.

189

Lucky bounds into the room, barking at me, wanting to be pet.

"Let me finish changing," I tell him.

I pull on a t-shirt and gym shorts, then take my work clothes to the hamper. Star's jeans are on the floor of the closet so I pick them up and add them to the dirty clothes.

"Okay, Lucky, let's go." I start to leave but notice something on the floor. A business card. I pick it up and see it's from a law firm downtown specializing in personal injury cases.

"You've gotta be kidding me," I say, not believing what I'm seeing.

There's no way she'd do this. It's been over two months since the accident. And we're a couple. She loves me. She wouldn't sue me. Turning the card over I see a message written, *Looking forward to working with you!*

What the hell? Star hired a lawyer? She wouldn't do that. But then why does she have his card? She obviously met with the guy, but why? Is she seriously going to sue me? I can't imagine her doing that. It's so unlike her. And I can't believe she'd do it behind my back.

Lucky is barking and jumping around like he needs to go out. I hide the card in my dresser and go out to the hall closet to get his leash.

When we get downstairs I see Star coming in from the street. She doesn't have a dog with her. So she lied about that? And lied about meeting with a lawyer? Why is she lying to me?

"Hey," she says when she sees me. She's not smiling or greeting me with a hug, like she normally does. "You just get home?"

"Yeah. Lucky had to go out." I keep hold of his leash as he tries to get to Star. She comes over and pets him, avoiding eye contact with me. She's clearly hiding something, but what? Is it a lawsuit? Is she really planning to sue me?

"I can take him," she says, rubbing his ears.

"I don't mind," I tell her, surprised she's not suggesting we take him together. "I thought you were walking a dog."

"I did. I returned him and then went to talk to Alexis about my schedule for this week."

"You came from outside. You weren't in the coffee shop."

"I was. I just left out the front door because someone was blocking the door to the building." She tilts her head. "Why are you asking so many questions?"

"I'm not. I just saw you without a dog and...never mind. It doesn't matter." I lean down and pet Lucky. "I'm going to take him down the block."

"Okay. I'll need some time to get dinner going. I haven't figured out what we're having."

"Forget it. I'm not hungry."

"You're not?"

"No. I'm really tired from work. I'm just going to go to bed." I go around her. "C'mon, Lucky."

He pulls on the leash, trying to go back to Star. He can't figure out why we're not walking him together like we normally do. I can't either. It's like Star doesn't want to be around me. Is it because she feels guilty about meeting with that lawyer?

Why would she sue me? Her injuries have healed. She's not in pain. She keeps telling me she feels fine. And she knows if she asked, I'd give her money. She doesn't have to sue me to get it. So why is she doing this?

I walk Lucky down the street and as we're passing the deli, Lauren walks out.

She does a double-take when she sees me. Why is she acting surprised to see me? She knows I live a block away.

"Hello, Corbin," she says, hurrying around me.

"Lauren, wait."

She sighs. "What?"

"What are you doing here? I thought you were living downtown."

"I live with my parents now." She adjusts her purse on her shoulder. "I really need to be going."

"Yeah. Go ahead." I watch as she leaves. "Oh! Lauren!"

She turns back. "What is it?"

"I sent in your recommendation."

"Thank you," she quickly says, then continues walking.

She's acting strange. She didn't insult me. Didn't insult Star. Didn't tell me how disgusted she is by Lucky. Maybe she really was in a hurry, although it seemed more like she was avoiding me.

The deli door swings open and Lars walks out. He sees me and gives me his usual laid back smile. "Hey, man, what's up?"

"Just walking the dog." I tug on Lucky's leash as he tries to jump on Lars.

"Hey, boy." Lars leans down and pets Lucky's head. "I wish I could get a dog."

"Why don't you?"

"I'm never home to walk it. And dogs cost too much." He motions to the deli. "I've been picking up extra shifts and it's still not enough to pay the bills." He scratches Lucky's ears. "Good dog."

Lucky lifts his head up to Lars, his tail wagging.

"I think you just made a new friend," I say.

"You ever need a dog sitter, just let me know."

"Star takes care of him. She walks him during her breaks at the coffee shop."

"She was just here."

Lucky drops to the ground and rolls on his back, wanting his belly rubbed.

Lars laughs. "The ears weren't good enough?"

"Star was here?" I ask.

He looks up at me. "What?"

"Did you say Star was here?"

"Yeah." He rubs Lucky's belly. "Like a few minutes ago."

She told me she was at the coffee shop. She lied.

"Why was she here?"

"I don't know. She didn't stay long. Didn't even order anything."

"She just walked in and left?"

"She was talking to Lauren. Sounded like they were fighting."

"About what?"

"Who knows? Chicks are always fighting about something." He stands up. "I better get back in there. My break's almost up. See ya later, man." He goes back inside the deli.

I finish walking Lucky, then go upstairs to the apartment. Star is talking to someone on the phone but quickly ends the conversation when she hears me walking in.

"We'll talk later. Bye!"

"Who was that?" I ask.

"Haley. Why?"

"I was just wondering. You didn't have to end your call."

"She had to get going." Star leans down to Lucky, petting him and ignoring me like she did earlier. "Hey, Lucky. How was your walk?"

"We ran into Lars."

"Oh, yeah?" she asks, her eyes on Lucky.

"He said he just saw you at the deli. But didn't you say you were at the coffee shop?"

She stands up straight, causing Lucky to jump on her, begging for attention.

"Lucky, no," she says in a stern voice. "No jumping. Sit, Lucky."

He sits, but his eyes are still begging her to pet him.

"Star, were you at the deli or not?"

"Yeah." She goes in the kitchen and opens the fridge. "I was thinking of getting something there for dinner but then I changed my mind."

"What changed your mind?"

She sighs and closes the fridge. "Lauren. I saw her when I walked in. I tend to lose my appetite when she's around."

At least she's telling me the truth this time. But why didn't she tell me before? Why would that be a secret?

"Did you talk to her?" I ask.

"She talked to ME. I was hoping to avoid her. As soon as I saw her I was going to leave but then she came up to me and started talking."

"What did she want?"

Star shrugs. "Doesn't matter." She opens the fridge again.

I take the fridge door and close it, my eyes on Star. "Tell me what she said."

"You tell me first." She folds her arms over her chest.

"You saw us on the street just now?"

"No. What do you mean? You talked to Lauren just now?"

"When I was walking Lucky. She was coming out of the deli. She was in a hurry so she said hi and left. Lars said you two were fighting."

She rolls her eyes. "Tell Lars to mind his own business."

"Were you? Fighting with her?"

"We weren't fighting." Star goes around me to the living room.

I follow her. "Then what happened?"

Star looks away from me, her shoulders tense. "She told me she had lunch with you."

"When?"

"What do you mean *when*?" she huffs. "Has this happened more than once?"

"No. Star, I don't know what she's talking about. I didn't have lunch with her."

"She said you did. Today at the hospital."

"We didn't have lunch. She sat down at my table just as I was leaving. She asked how my dad was doing and then I went back to work."

Star looks at me. "Why didn't you tell me?"

"Well, for one, I've barely seen you since I got home. And two, there was nothing to tell. I saw her and then left. I didn't have lunch with her."

Star glares at me. "So you have nothing else to tell me about Lauren?"

"No. Why do I feel like I'm being accused of something?"

Star walks away, then turns back to me. "Lauren told me about the recommendation."

Shit. I should've known Lauren would do that. She's always trying to start trouble. I should've just told Star the truth.

"Okay, yes, I wrote the recommendation, but it was just so she could get a job. I think you and I both agree it'd be good to get Lauren out of Boston. If she gets this job she'll be moving to New York. We'll never have to see her again."

"Why didn't you tell me?"

"Because I knew it'd upset you knowing I was doing something for Lauren."

"So you thought keeping it a secret, lying to me, was a better plan?"

I walk over to her. "Star, I wasn't trying to hide this from you. I should've just told you. I didn't because I didn't want to argue about something that wasn't a big deal."

"But now it IS a big deal. Because you lied to me. For Lauren."

"Yes, and I'm sorry. It won't happen again. I'm not doing Lauren any more favors, and like I said, if she gets this job, she'll be out of our lives." I step up to Star and put my arms around her. "Can we move on now?"

Star looks down. "She wants you back."

"Lauren? Star, no. She doesn't want me back. She's moved on."

"If she'd moved on, she wouldn't have come up to me to tell me she had lunch with you. And she wouldn't have told me about you writing the recommendation for her."

"When did she tell you about the recommendation?"

"At the deli the other day." Her eyes go to mine. "She's trying to break us up. Make me think you want her back. And you're not making me feel better when you do stuff for her behind my back."

"That's not what I was doing. I didn't think it was worth telling you. I'm sorry, okay? Can we just get past this?"

She backs out of my arms and walks away. "I'm going to take a bath. There's leftovers in the fridge if you're hungry."

She leaves and goes down the hall to the guest bathroom instead of the one in our room. She better not be planning to sleep in the guest room tonight.

I'm not letting Lauren do this. She's not breaking Star and me apart. She's obviously trying to but it's not going to work. I'm tempted to talk to Lauren about it but that will just make her think her little plan is working. I'll just have to ignore her and hope she gets the job in New York. Her residency ends in a few weeks. After that, she could move and be out of my life for good.

Star's in the tub for almost an hour. I'm about to go in there and check on her but stop when I hear her talking to someone.

"I don't know," she says. "I haven't decided. I have to talk to him. He came by the coffee shop and we talked about options but I didn't commit to anything yet." There's silence and then, "No, I haven't told Corbin. If I decide to go ahead with it I'll tell him."

It sounds like she's talking about the lawsuit. What else could it be? The lawyer must've come by the coffee shop to meet with her.

Why would she do this? I don't understand. And if she's even considering doing this, why is she still with me? Maybe she's planning to break up with me. Maybe that's why she's avoiding me and won't look me in the eye.

"Yeah, okay," I hear her say. "I'll let you know. For now I just need to fill out some paperwork if I decide to do it. I want to. I'm just not sure if it's the right time." There's more silence and then, "Okay, bye."

I hear water splashing around as she gets up from the tub. I'm not sure what to do. Do I confront her about this or wait and see if she confesses? I want to just ask her about it. If she hasn't decided to do this yet, maybe I could talk her out of it.

A few minutes later she leaves the bathroom and goes in our room. I'm in the living room with Lucky. I give Star a minute to get dressed, then go in the bedroom, deciding I just need to confront her. I can't be around her and not say something. And if she really is doing this behind my back it means I can't trust her and our relationship is over.

"Hey." I step up behind her as she's getting something from the dresser.

She turns around. "Yeah?"

"Can we talk?"

"About what?"

"I need to ask you something."

"Go ahead and ask."

"Let's go sit down." I take her hand and walk toward the bed but she pulls back.

"Corbin, I don't want to do this right now."

"I need to get this out in the open. I can't keep going on without saying anything."

She yanks her hand back. "Is this about Lauren? Is there more you didn't tell me?"

"No! Do you really think I'd cheat on you?" I shake my head, walking away from her. "If you really think I'd do that, then I don't know why you're with me."

"And I don't know why you'd keep secrets from me, especially about Lauren. But you did."

I sigh. "Because I didn't think it was worth telling you. I wrote that recommendation to help her get a job so she'd move away and be out of our lives. I get that I should've just told you and I'm sorry I didn't." I pause, lifting my eyes to hers. "What about you?"

"What do you mean?"

"Is there anything you want to tell me?"

"No. Why?"

"You're not keeping anything from me?"

"What are you getting at? Just say it."

I walk to the dresser and open the drawer. I pull out the lawyer's card and bring it over to her. "This."

She takes the card and looks at it. "What's this?"

"You tell ME. It fell out of your jeans. I found it in the closet."

She looks closer at it. "Oh. Yeah. It's from that guy."

"What guy?"

"This guy came in the coffee shop and was asking about the accident. As soon as I realized he was a lawyer I told him to go away. He shoved his card at me and then left."

"Why'd you keep it? Why didn't you just throw the card away?"

She cocks her head. "Why are you asking me this?"

"I just think it's odd you didn't throw it away."

"What are you implying?" she asks, holding the card up to me. "That I'm going to call up this guy and sue you?"

I don't answer, but she knows that's what I was thinking.

"I can't believe you would think that!" she says, raising her voice. "You seriously think I would sue you?"

"Star, you have to admit it looks suspicious when I find a card for a lawyer who specializes in personal injury cases."

She rips the card up in several pieces, letting them fall to the floor. "There. Happy now?"

She storms off to the bathroom and slams the door.

I walk over and try the door but it's locked. "Star, I'm sorry. I didn't mean to accuse you of anything. I just found the card and didn't know what to think."

"Here's an idea," she yells through the bathroom door. "You see the card and think nothing of it because you love your girlfriend and trust her and know her well enough to know she'd never do something like that."

"I DID think that but then when I got home you were acting strange and I didn't know why. I thought maybe it had something to do with that card."

The bathroom door swings open and she stands in the door frame, her arms folded across her chest. "I wasn't acting strange. You're just saying that to try to explain why you accused me of suing you."

"I'm not accusing you. I was just asking about the card. And you WERE acting strange. You wouldn't look at me. You didn't want to walk Lucky with me. You were acting like something was wrong."

"I wasn't looking at you because I was angry you didn't tell me about Lauren, and angry I had to hear it from her and not you."

"So you admit you were acting differently."

"Yeah, fine. Whatever. It still doesn't excuse the fact that you assumed I was suing you after finding a business card. How could you even think that was a possibility?"

"I didn't but—I don't know. I saw it and panicked."

She looks down. "You don't trust me."

"You don't trust me either if you thought I'd cheat on you."

The room is silent a moment, then Star looks up. "What does this mean?"

"It means we both screwed up. We made assumptions we shouldn't have made."

"It means we don't trust each other," she says softly. "You can't have a relationship without trust."

"Star, don't go turning this into something it's not. We just made a mistake. It doesn't mean we—"

"Yeah, actually it does." She takes a breath. "If we don't trust each other, we shouldn't be together."

CHAPTER TWENTY

Corbin

"I DO trust you," I say.

"Then you wouldn't have thought I was suing you behind your back. All it took was that one little card for you to not trust me. You assumed the worst of me. That means something, Corbin. It means this relationship isn't as strong as we thought it was."

"Star, that's not what it means."

"Then how do you explain it?"

I don't know how to answer her. She's right. I should've trusted her, and she should have trusted me with Lauren. So why didn't we?

"Maybe it was all too fast," Star says, turning away from me.

"What was too fast?"

"This relationship. Maybe we rushed into it before we were ready. Right after we met I moved in with you. You barely knew me. You'd just broken up with Lauren and I'd just lost everything I had. We were both in a bad place. Maybe we rushed into this to make ourselves feel better."

"Star, that's not what happened. I felt something for you right away. Something I never felt for Lauren."

She turns to face me. "You felt sorry for me. And guilty for what you'd done. That could've been the reason you had feelings for me. Combine that with our attraction to each other and it could've felt like love when it wasn't."

"You're wrong." I put my hands on her shoulders and look in her eyes. "I love you, Star, and it wasn't caused by guilt or feeling sorry for you. I fell in love with you because of who you are. How you make me feel." I swallow. "Are you saying all this because it's how YOU feel? Do you think you rushed into this and now you're having second thoughts?"

She looks down. "I don't know. I didn't think that before, but now? I'm not sure." Her eyes lift back to mine. "We didn't trust each other. We assumed the worst. You can't tell me that doesn't concern you."

I sigh. "It does. But that doesn't mean I don't love you." I pause. "What about you? Do you still love me?"

"Of course I do." She takes my hand off her shoulder and holds it. "I love you more than anything. But I don't want to have doubts about us."

"So what does that mean?" I ask, my heart pounding. She has this sad look on her face that's making me nervous. I can't lose her. I love her and I can't lose her.

She lets go of my hand. "I think we need some time apart."

"Time apart? Meaning what?"

"When I was talking to Haley earlier, she said she knows of a girl who's looking for a roommate. She's a grad student at Harvard and lives just a few blocks from here. I could stay with her and still be able to work at the coffee shop."

"Star, no. Don't do this. We can work this out."

She gives me a sad smile. "I want to, Corbin. And I think we can. But in order to get there I think we need some time away from each other. Maybe if we're not together all the time we'll learn to trust each other. We'll have to. We'll have no choice."

"We don't need to live apart in order to do that."

"Maybe you don't but I do. I've been worried about you going back to Lauren ever since we started dating. You two

201

make sense together. You and I don't. And she was a huge part of your life for years."

"None of that matters. And you and I DO make sense, just not in the way Lauren and I did."

"I know you say that, and I think you really do believe it, but I'm not there yet. I still feel like there's this part of you that sees me as the girl from the wrong side of the tracks. And when you accused me of hiring a lawyer to sue you, that just confirmed it. It tells me there really is a part of you that doesn't see me as someone you can trust. I'm just some girl who's desperate for money and will do anything to get it."

"Star, that is NOT true," I say, getting angry. "I've never thought that about you. The only reason I even considered you might have hired that lawyer is because I saw that business card and—I don't know. I guess you not telling me about it made me suspicious. It was wrong and I'm sorry but it doesn't mean I don't trust you."

"Corbin, it DOES mean that. You're not being honest with yourself. The fact that your mind even went there says you don't trust me." She looks down. "I don't want to move out but I think I have to. I think it'd be good for us. We need time apart. I don't want to lose you, Corbin, but I feel like if we don't work this out now, eventually this will end."

Maybe she's right. To have a future together we have to trust each other, and clearly we're both having issues with that. I really believed I trusted her but the evidence shows I didn't. I really thought she'd hired that lawyer.

"For how long?" I ask, accepting her decision to leave even though it's not what I want.

"I'm not sure. I was thinking maybe I'd start with a month and go from there."

"A month?" I ask, sounding surprised. A month seems like forever when I'm used to seeing her every day. "A month is too long."

"It's only a few weeks. And I think we need that long. Why don't we just see how it goes? We don't have to commit to a time."

"Who's this girl you'd be living with? What do you know about her?"

"She's the niece of this woman Haley works with. She said she's really quiet and studies all the time. Her last roommate had to move for a job. She has someone lined up to live there this summer but until then, she could use a roommate to help pay the rent. And if I needed a place longer than that, she knows people looking for summer roommates."

"We're not living apart for more than a month," I say. "That's long enough."

"We need to do this for as long as it takes to get us where we need to be." She wraps her hand around mine. "I want us to have a future, Corbin, and I know you want that too. So whatever it takes for us to get to that point, I'll do it."

She wants a future with me? Relief washes over me as I realize this isn't the first step of a breakup. It's her trying to strengthen our relationship. She wants to work on our issues. To resolve them before they get worse. It's what I always wished Lauren would do but she never would. She just kept pushing our issues aside, which only pushed us farther apart.

Star's committed to this. Committed to *us*. I am too. I want her more than anything, and if being apart a few weeks will help us have the kind of relationship that will last, then I'm in.

"I love you," I say, pulling her into my arms.

"I love you too." She sniffles and I hear her quietly crying as I hold her.

I kiss her head. "We're going to get through this."

"I know we will. I'll just miss you."

"I'll miss you too." I pull back and look at her. "So what are the rules here? Will I still get to see you?"

She nods. "I was thinking we'd date, like we would have if I hadn't moved in with you right after we met."

I smile. "Do I call and ask you out? Text you? What do you prefer?"

"Call. Definitely." She smiles. "And you have to give me notice. I'm very busy."

"I'll keep that in mind. What about our fur-child?"

She laughs. "Lucky will have to stay here with you. Hannah's apartment doesn't allow dogs. That's my new roommate. Hannah."

"Does Hannah allow boyfriends to come over?"

"I don't know. I'll have to ask."

"I'm guessing sleepovers aren't allowed in this arrangement?"

"Probably not. It'd be too much like living together."

"But we could still use the bed. For things other than sleeping?"

"Yes." She smiles. "I don't think I could go a whole month without that. And we ARE dating. It's not like we're just being friends for a month."

"You really think this will help?"

"I don't know but I think we should try it. Just talking about this, getting everything out in the open, is making me feel better about us. I want us to keep doing that. Keep talking about stuff instead of hiding it. And just so you know, I wasn't trying to hide the thing about the lawyer. I just forgot to tell you. I wasn't even thinking about it."

"And you already know why I didn't tell you about Lauren. But that was a mistake. I should've told you."

"So from now on, we'll tell each other stuff, right?"

"Yes. Definitely."

"Oh! Speaking of that, I talked to a recruiter today."

"A job recruiter?"

"No. College. Well, community college. He said my classes would probably transfer so I'd only have a year left for my degree."

That must've been what she was talking about when she was in the tub. And here I assumed she was talking about hiring a lawyer. I didn't trust her. It's more proof that she's right. We need to work on this. We need to trust each other.

"That's great!" I say. "You think you'll do it?"

"I think so, but it won't be until fall. That'll give me all summer to save up money. Oh, I got a couple new dogs to walk. Some customers at the coffee shop saw me walking dogs and asked if I'd walk theirs too."

"Will you still walk Lucky? I'll pay you double what everyone else is paying."

"You're not paying me. He's OUR dog. I'll still walk him during the day and make sure he's fed."

Just then, Lucky walks in, looking groggy, like he just woke from a nap. He perks up when he sees us, running over to Star.

"There's my boy." She leans down to rub his ears. "Lucky, I have to go away for a few weeks but I'll still come see you during the day."

He has no clue what she's saying, his tail wagging as she pets him.

"He's going to miss you," I say. "But I'll miss you more."

She looks up at me, her smile turning to a frown. "I'll miss you too."

"You're not leaving tonight, are you?"

"No. I need to confirm everything with Hannah. If she's okay with it I'll move in tomorrow."

"Meaning you won't be here when I get home?"

"Probably not." She stands up and Lucky sits down beside her, leaning against her leg.

"Can I ask you out for tomorrow? Or is that too soon?"

"I think it's too soon. But maybe this weekend?"

I nod. "I'll call you."

"I know this is going to seem weird at first but I really think it might help. And if it doesn't, we'll do something else."

She's really committed to making this work, which makes me feel a little less anxious about her leaving. I still don't want her to go but I understand why she's doing it.

"So what happens tonight?" I ask.

"What do you mean?"

"Will you stay with me? In my room? OUR room?"

She smiles. "I'll stay with you."

It's still early but we decide to go to bed. I want to hold her in my arms as long as possible before she's gone. I know it's only temporary but it feels like it isn't. It feels like she's leaving for good. I don't know how I'm going to do this. I'm going to miss her so much.

The next day when I get home from work, she's gone. She texted me during the day telling me she'd moved out but it didn't sink in until I walked in my apartment and she wasn't there. No welcome home kisses. No hugs. No smell of dinner cooking on the stove. No one asking about my day.

It's just an empty apartment like it was before I met her. Even when Lauren lived here it felt empty. There was no warmth. No love. And Lauren didn't like noise so it was always quiet. I had to turn the volume on the TV to almost zero in order to watch it, which is why I usually didn't.

Lucky hears me and barks. At least I still have Lucky. He livens up the place.

I go over to his kennel and let him out.

"Hey, boy, I missed you." He jumps around, barking, wanting to go outside.

After I change clothes I take him down to the street and run into Alexis coming out of the coffee shop.

"Hey, Corbin," she says, getting her phone out and walking beside me.

"Hey, are you done for the day?"

"I'm not supposed to be but my dad wasn't feeling well so I'm going to go see him."

"What's wrong?"

"We're not sure. He's going to the doctor tomorrow." She stops at her car.

"I hope he feels better."

"Yeah, me too. Hey, what's up with you and Star?"

"What do you mean?"

"I saw her moving her stuff out. I was going to ask her about it but she was gone before I could."

"She's staying with a friend. Just for a few weeks."

"Why? Are you guys breaking up?"

"I'd rather not get into it. And hey, don't tell Lauren. I don't want to deal with her questioning me about it."

"Yeah, okay." She opens her car door. "See ya later."

Even though I told her not to, I'm sure she'll tell Lauren. They're best friends and she tells Lauren everything. That's why I wish Star would stop working at the coffee shop but she won't because she's making good money, especially now that she works the register and gets tips.

Lucky and I take a long walk, then we go back to the apartment and I call Star. She never said I couldn't call and I've gone all day without talking to her and miss hearing her voice. She doesn't answer the call and it makes me wonder if she doesn't want me calling this soon. But if we're dating I should be able to call her.

Moments later I get a text. *I'm out running errands, then going to bed. Really tired. Talk tomorrow?*

Yeah, okay, I text back. *I love you.*

I love you too! Goodnight!

Lucky comes over and sits by my feet as I lean back on the couch, turning the TV on.

"It's just you and me tonight, Lucky."

He lifts his head and rests it against my leg, wanting to be pet. I rub his ears as I flip through the channels. Even with Lucky here I still feel alone. It's just not the same without Star. I miss her. I already want these four weeks to be over so I have her back.

CHAPTER TWENTY-ONE

Corbin

On Thursday I call Star and ask her out for Friday night.

"I think that'll work," she says.

"You need to check your calendar?" I kid.

She laughs. "My calendar says I'm free so I'll see you tomorrow night. What are we doing?"

"Dinner and a movie. I'm going with a traditional date. Nothing too crazy."

"Funny that we've never done that."

"Dinner and a movie?" I stop to think. "We've done that before."

"Only one time. And it was when we first met, before we were dating."

"Huh. I guess you're right."

By living together right away we skipped the usual dating rituals and went straight to being a live-in couple. This dating thing is all new for us. When we lived together we'd go out to dinner because we didn't want to cook. It didn't feel like anything special. Now it feels like I'm taking her on an actual date. I like that.

We've been living apart for less than a week but I'm already feeling closer to her. Our separation is showing me how much I miss her when she's gone. How much I want her in my life. I can see a future with her now more than ever. And I DO trust her. I always did, but finding that lawyer's card made me question it. That ended up being a good thing because it woke me up to the fact I was letting other people affect my relationship with Star. It was my dad that didn't trust her and I was letting *his* opinion sway *mine*. Now that I know that, it's not going to happen again.

"What time are you picking me up?" she asks.

"As soon as you'll let me. Does noon work?"

She laughs. "You work until five. And then you need to go home, change clothes and walk Lucky."

"So five-fifteen?"

She laughs again. "Let's say six. I'll see you then."

"Okay. Bye."

"Wait! Corbin?"

"Yeah?"

"I can't wait to see you. I really miss you."

"I miss you too. I love you, Star. See you tomorrow."

Tomorrow can't come soon enough, and when it does I'm practically counting the minutes until I can see her. I show up at her apartment, flowers in hand, at exactly six o'clock and knock on the door.

Her roommate answers, or at least I think it's her roommate. She's short and thin, wearing sweats and big red glasses, her black hair twisted up in a bun.

"Hi, I'm Corbin," I say to her. "Are you Hannah?"

"Yeah." She steps aside. "You can come inside. She's still getting ready."

I go in and she shuts the door, then walks down the hall to her room. She's not very friendly. Star hasn't said much about her other than that she's really quiet and studies a lot.

I go in the apartment and look around. It's a small, older apartment but it's clean and seems to be in decent shape. The living room has a brown couch with different colored pillows and blankets on it. There's a coffee table across from it but no TV anywhere.

"I'm ready." I hear her voice and turn around and see her coming toward me, a huge smile on her face. I've missed that smile.

I go up and grab her, hugging her so tight I lift her off the ground. "I've missed you."

She laughs. "I've missed you too."

I set her down and kiss her and keep kissing her until I hear her roommate's door open.

"We should go," Star whispers, taking my hand and pulling me to the door. "Bye, Hannah," she calls out.

Hannah doesn't answer.

"You weren't kidding when you said she's quiet," I say as we're leaving.

"I know, right? She's barely talked to me since I moved in. She just sits in her room and studies all day."

"And no TV? Everyone has a TV."

"I know. It's driving me crazy not having a TV."

"Take ours. We'll go get it tonight and bring it over."

"Then you won't have one to watch."

"I have three. I'll watch the one in our room."

"Maybe I could take the one in the guest room."

We're at my car and I open the door and let her in, then get in on the other side.

"Star, I know you wanted to do this for a month but I think a week is enough. I miss you like crazy. Would you consider moving back?"

"Not yet. We need more time. It's only been a few days."

"Yes, but in those few days I've done a lot of thinking. I don't need more time. Just move back. We'll keep working on this but we'll do it together."

"Let me think about it, okay?" She smiles. "Can we go on our date now?"

I start the car. "You're really excited about this."

"Because it's an actual date."

"When you move back I promise to take you on dates from now on. I'll even call and ask you out. And I'll wait downstairs with flowers like I'm picking you up."

She laughs. "You'd really do that?"

"Definitely. I know we kind of skipped the dating part of our relationship but it's not too late to go back and do it again. I should've been taking you out more. We got so used to hanging out at home, taking care of Lucky, that we didn't go out. That's going to change."

"I'd like that but I still think it's too soon to move back."

"I'm going to keep trying to change your mind. A month is too long."

"How's Lucky? Does he miss me?"

"He's completely lost without you. Just like me."

"He sees me every day when I walk him."

"Yeah, but at night you're not there. He runs through the apartment looking for you, and when he can't find you, he comes to me, barking at me like he's angry you're not there. Like it's my fault."

"You're making that up."

"No, seriously. He's pissed at me. Like I made you go away."

"I'll have a talk with him."

I smile at her. "You're a good dog mom."

"You're a good dog dad."

"We'd be good parents."

She looks at me, surprised. "Parents? It's a little soon to be talking about kids."

"Not according to our new agreement. We said we'd talk about stuff."

"Yeah, but having kids is way off in the future. We don't need to talk about that yet."

"But you do want kids someday, right?"

"Yeah, definitely."

"How many?"

"Two, maybe three."

"Same here. I think three would be the max."

"You're going to have to have them soon," she says with a smile. "You're getting old."

"I'm not old. And I'm dating someone much younger so I don't need to be in a hurry."

"Oh, so you're having kids with me?" She laughs.

"Could happen."

She looks out the side window. "Did you want kids with Lauren?"

"No. I never did, which should've been a sign I didn't see a future with her, but I kept ignoring the signs."

"What about *her*? Did she want kids?"

"She wanted one, maybe two, but not until she was established in her career, which means 35 at the earliest. I'm guessing she'll freeze her eggs, then try to have a kid when she's in her forties. Or it wouldn't surprise me if she never has them at all. She wants a career more than she wants kids." I reach over and take Star's hand. "Let's not talk about Lauren. We're on a date."

She smiles. "You're right. Let's talk about our dog child. He did the funniest thing today."

The date continues and it's perfect. We go to the movie, then have a long relaxing dinner. When I take her back to her apartment I don't want to leave. If she won't come home with me I want to stay here with her, but she won't let me.

"Give it another week," she says as we stand at the door.

"Okay, but Lucky's not going to be happy about this."

She reaches up and gives me a kiss. "I love you, and I'm going to live with you again. Just now right now. Doing this is already making a difference. I feel like it's making our relationship stronger."

"I hate to admit it but you're right. It IS making a difference. It's made me realize how much you mean to me. How much I want you in my life. How happy you make me."

"I feel the same way. As strange as it sounds, living apart has made me love you even more. I was worried we rushed into our relationship and maybe didn't know each other as well as we should have but I don't think that's true anymore. I think that was just me reacting to people's comments telling me it was too soon to be in love."

"So we were both listening to other people when we should've just trusted what we felt for each other."

"Yeah, but sometimes I still worry I'm not right for you and you'll want someone like Lauren again."

"Star, you need to stop thinking that way. I don't want another Lauren. Believe me, one was enough."

She glances at the door. "I should go. Tell Lucky goodnight for me."

"I will." I kiss her. "Goodnight. I love you."

"I love you too."

I leave, still missing her but feeling like everything's going to be fine. We'll spend another week apart, then hopefully, she'll move back in. But it'll be different this time. Even better than before.

Monday at work I'm finishing up with a patient when my nurse walks in.

"Oh, sorry," she says. "I thought you were done."

"We are." I motion to my patient, a guy in his forties who appears to have a broken wrist. "Mr. Alcott needs to go to X-ray. Can you take him there?"

"Sure." Amy, my nurse, smiles at him before looking back at me. "Dr. Sterling, can I speak with you a moment?"

"Certainly," I say, assuming this is about a patient. I follow her out into the hall. "What is it?"

"Lauren," she says in a hushed tone.

"Lauren?" I ask, surprised. "My ex?"

"Yes. She wants to see you."

"Right now?"

"She's waiting in your office."

Why is she bothering me in the middle of the day? What could she possibly want?

"Tell her I'll call her later." I open the door to the exam room and peek my head inside. "Mr. Alcott, Amy will take you for your x-ray now."

He nods and gets off the exam table.

"She won't leave," Amy whispers to me. "She's been in there a half hour."

I sigh. "Fine. Take care of Mr. Alcott."

Walking back to my office I try to imagine what this could be about. Maybe she's telling me she got the job in New York. If so, that's great but not something I need to know about right this minute.

"What is it, Lauren?" I ask as I walk in the door. She's standing with her back to me, looking out the window.

She turns to me and I notice she looks more tired than usual, her layers of makeup unable to hide the dark circles under her eyes.

Maybe she's sick. Maybe it's serious. Maybe that's why she's here.

"Corbin," she says in a solemn tone.

"Lauren, why are you here?" I ask, shutting the door. "Is something wrong?"

She steps closer to me. "I need to talk to you. But not here. Could we go somewhere?"

"It's the middle of the day. I have patients to see. Just tell me what's wrong. Are you sick?"

"Sick?" Her brows together. "No. Why would you think that?"

"Well, for one, you wouldn't show up here in the middle of a workday unless it was serious, and two, you don't look so good."

She huffs. "You never tell a woman she doesn't look good. Did I teach you nothing during our time together?"

"I didn't mean it as a put down. I said it out of concern. You look tired. Have they increased your hours again?"

"No, actually they've cut them. I'm not even working today."

As she says it I notice she's not wearing her lab coat or hospital badge.

"Did something happen?" I ask cautiously. "With a patient?"

She narrows her eyes at me. "What exactly are you implying? That I made an error with a patient? You think that's why I was given time off?" She turns away from me, her arms crossed. "I can't believe you'd think that. You know I'm better than any other resident at this hospital."

"Then what is it?" I ask, stepping up behind her. "I don't have time to play guessing games. I need to get back to work."

She whips back to face me. "Just forget it. We'll talk later." She goes around me to the door.

"Lauren, wait. Just tell me now."

"We'll meet later." She pushes her shoulders back and sticks her chin out, making her look more like the Lauren I know, who thinks she's superior to everyone else.

"I don't have time to meet later."

"Why? Does your little girlfriend not let you go out at night?"

"Would you just tell me what's going on?"

"Tonight at seven," she says, getting the keys from her purse. "At the coffee shop by my parents' house."

I sigh. "Fine, but this better be important."

"It is," she says with a hint of a smile. I'm not sure what that means and I'm not sure I want to know. "See you tonight."

She leaves, and for the rest of the afternoon I'm left wondering what the hell is so important that we have to meet up later for her to tell me. Is it the job in New York? I can't imagine what else it would be. Then again, Lauren loves to overdramatize things so it could be something small that she's making into something big.

At five I go back to my office and text Star. *I love you.*

I love you too, she texts back.

I've been texting her all day, telling her how much I love her and miss her. I can't stop thinking about her. Whenever I have a free moment I get out my phone and text her. I never did that

215

with Lauren. If I didn't see her I could go all day without thinking about her. I told myself it was because I was busy with work but it was really because I didn't love her like I thought I did. It's so clear to me now that I can't believe I didn't realize it when I was with her.

Another text pops up from Star. *Want to have dinner tonight? Maybe around 7?*

Shit. What do I say? Do I tell her I'm meeting Lauren at 7? But if I do, Star will think there's something going on there. I've told her numerous times Lauren and I are never getting back together but Star still worries it could happen. She doesn't trust Lauren. She thinks she'd do anything to get me back. I used to think so too but enough time has passed that I think Lauren's moved on. In fact, maybe that's why she wants to meet. To tell me she's found someone new. If so, I wouldn't care. She could've just told me without having to meet later.

I can't tonight, I text back, but then realize I just turned down my girlfriend for my ex. I should cancel on Lauren and go out with Star but I really want Lauren to leave me alone and she won't unless I meet with her.

When we talk tonight I'm going to tell her this is it. No more texts. No more phone calls. I don't want Lauren having any contact with me anymore. I don't even want to be friends with her. Our families are friends but that doesn't mean she and I have to be.

Tonight I'm going to end things with her once and for all. Whatever friendship we had is over. I'm done with her. For good this time.

CHAPTER TWENTY-TWO

Corbin

You have plans? Star texts, followed by a sad face emoji.

Yes. Sorry, I text, but before I send it I consider meeting her later tonight, like maybe at eight. There's no way I'm talking to Lauren for more than an hour. I'm hoping to be out of there in fifteen minutes. But knowing Lauren, she'll drag it out, making me late to meet up with Star. It's too risky so I just send the text, then send another one that says, *Dinner tomorrow instead?*

A few minutes pass and I start to get worried she hasn't texted back. Is she mad at me for turning her down? Or mad because I didn't tell her what I'm doing tonight? The whole point of us living separately is to learn to trust each other so this is her chance to trust me. I tell her all the time how much I love her and would never cheat on her. If she believes that, she'll trust me and not ask questions.

Okay, she finally texts back. *I love you.*

I love you too. And I miss you. Have you reconsidered the timing? I can't make it three more weeks without you.

I miss you too, she texts back. *Let's talk this weekend. I think Lucky might need his parents back together sooner rather than later.*

I send her a picture of him I took last night. His head is on my knee and he's looking up at me with his sad face.

Another week may be too long, I text.

No sad dog pics! she texts.

Whatever it takes to get you back.

Not fair, she texts.

I just love you and want you back. I miss you so much, Star.

It won't be much longer. I promise.

Can I call you tonight? I text. We haven't been talking at night. Only texting. It's part of our agreement to give each other space but it's driving me crazy. I need to talk to her. Texting isn't enough.

I won't be home. Alexis invited me to go to a club with her and we might be out late.

Star's going to a club? Guys will be asking her out. Wanting to dance with her. Touch her. What if she goes along with it?

I need to stop thinking that way. I have to trust her. That's the whole point of this little experiment of ours and I'm failing if I don't trust her to go to a club without me. She's going there to have fun, not meet a guy. She'd never cheat on me. I know she wouldn't. She loves me. She wants a future with me.

We'll talk tomorrow, I text. *Have fun tonight!*

I will! You too!

Fun with Lauren? Yeah, that's not going to happen. Lauren doesn't even know how to have fun.

At seven I arrive at the coffee shop and see Lauren sitting down at a table near the back. She's wearing black yoga pants and an oversized white sweater. I'm surprised she's dressing so casual. I was expecting her to show up in her usual dress slacks and a blouse or one of her many dresses.

"Corbin," she says, waving me over when she spots me walking in.

"I'm just going to get something," I say as I head to the counter.

"I already did," she calls out.

I sigh as I walk over to her. She hasn't changed. Not letting me order? She always did that when we were dating. It was another way to control me.

"I got you a latte," she says. "With skim milk."

I sit down across from her. "I like it with whole milk, not skim."

"Skim is better for your heart." She sets her purse down on the chair next to her. "You're not a young man anymore. You need to take care of your heart."

I take a deep breath, fighting the urge to argue with her.

A young woman carrying a tray comes over to our table. "Latte?"

"That's me," I say, glancing at Lauren. She gives me a smug smile, like she's happy with herself for making my drink choice. I'm not even going to drink it. I wanted a plain coffee, not a latte, and definitely not a latte with skim milk.

"Herbal tea," the waitress says as she sets the cup down in front of Lauren. "Can I get you two anything else?"

"That'll be it," I tell her before Lauren can. The waitress leaves and I point to Lauren's tea. "Since when do you drink tea?"

"I've had tea before," she says, picking up her cup.

"I've only seen you drink tea once, and that was only because the waiter messed up your order."

It happened last year right before Christmas. We were at a restaurant and the place was packed. The waiter could barely keep up and he was new so it was even harder for him. He gave Lauren tea instead of coffee and she threw such a fit that we ended up getting our meals for free. After dinner, when Lauren got up to leave, I slipped a huge tip under my napkin for the poor guy. He was doing his best. The tea thing was his only slip-up, and he apologized multiple times.

"Things have changed," Lauren says. "I prefer tea now."

"That's a big change," I say, pushing my latte cup to the side. "Are you cutting back on caffeine?"

She really should. She drinks way too much coffee. I did too when I was working long shifts as a resident. It was the only way to stay awake, but Lauren drinks even more coffee than I did.

219

"I've cut out caffeine entirely," she says, "along with alcohol."

I nod, not really caring about her diet. I'm not here to make small talk. I just want her to say what she needs to say so I can go.

"So why are we here?" I ask, leaning back in my chair, my arms crossed.

She sets her cup down. "I have some news."

"And? What is it?"

"Well, first, about my job."

"Yes?"

"The hospital I applied at in New York called last week and offered me a position. The one I wanted."

"That's great!" I smile, not just because she got the job but because of what it means for Star and me. With Lauren in another city, another state, we'll finally have her out of our lives. No more seeing her at work, or the coffee shop in my building, or the deli down the street. She'll have a whole new life, and so will Star and I.

"You're not sad that I'm leaving?" she asks in a disappointed tone.

"I'm happy you got the job," I say, not addressing her question. "I know how much you wanted it and I know you wanted to get out of Boston. This is exactly what you wanted so I'm happy for you."

"I read the letter you wrote," she says, her eyes going to mine. "You had so many nice things to say about me."

"You read the letter of recommendation?" I ask, surprised. "That was supposed to be confidential."

She shrugs. "It was, but I saw it during the interview. It was sitting on the desk and when the man interviewing me went to get some water, I picked it up and glanced over it."

I'm angry she read it. I didn't want her to see it. It was far too nice and over the top, like the part about her kind and caring bedside manner. It's not at all true but I wrote it because I really wanted her to get the job. I wanted her out of Boston.

"That's great news about the job, Lauren. Congratulations. When do you move?"

"The week after my residency ends."

"Have you told the hospital yet?"

"I told them today. They were very impressed I was able to get a position there. Not many people do straight out of their residency." She pauses, looking down, then back up at me. "I was able to get you an opportunity there as well."

"Me?" I let out a laugh. "What are you talking about?"

"I spoke with the people who hired me and they agreed to meet with you about a position."

"A position? Lauren, I'm not looking for a job. I already have one."

"Corbin, you're better than some urgent care doctor. You're wasting your talents there. You could do so much more."

"I like what I'm doing. I like the work. The hours. You never understood this, but it's not always about the money. It's about what you want to get up and do everyday, and for me, that's urgent care. Maybe that'll change someday, but for now this is what I want to do."

"You could at least speak with them," she snaps. "I've already set it up. All you need to do is call and tell them when."

"You set it up?" I shake my head. "Lauren, you can't keep doing this."

"Doing what?"

"Trying to control me. Making decisions for me. We're not dating anymore, and even when we were, you shouldn't have been trying to control me. I never wanted what you wanted for me. I went along with it to make you happy but then it never did. It was never enough. And I was miserable. I was trying to be someone I wasn't. I'm finally doing what I want to do and I'm happy." I lean forward, resting my arms on the table, my eyes on hers. "I want you to be happy, too. I sincerely mean that, Lauren. I want you to be happy. But I also want you to stop interfering with my life. It's time to move on. Find someone new, or just be happy being single. You have so much going for you. Just live your life, and let me live mine."

"You don't understand."

"Understand what?"

"You and I are connected. We always will be. And because of that, we need to make decisions that are best for both of us, like this job in New York. I'm certain they'd give it to you. You're definitely qualified and you've always done well on interviews."

"Lauren, you're not listening to me. I'm not moving to New York. My life is here. I have a job. A girlfriend. A dog. My family's here. I have no interest in leaving."

"But you have to. It's the right decision."

My brows draw together. "Right decision? Lauren, what's going on here?"

She looks down at her cup, running her finger along the rim. "It isn't just about you anymore."

"Meaning what?"

"Meaning..." She slowly lifts her eyes back to mine. "I'm pregnant."

"Pregnant?" I rear back. "You're pregnant? Seriously?"

"I took the test a week ago and had it confirmed last Friday. I was going to tell you then but you didn't—"

"Wait!" I put my hands up, stopping her. "It isn't mine. We haven't been together in months."

"Ten weeks to be exact." She keeps her eyes on mine. "I'm ten weeks pregnant, Corbin."

"No," I say, shaking my head. "That's not possible. And it was longer than ten weeks. We broke up ten weeks ago but the last time we had sex? It had to have been three months, maybe four."

She puts her hand on my arm, her eyes on mine. "Don't you remember? It was right before we broke up. We went out to dinner and we both had a little too much to drink. When we got home we were getting undressed and you kissed me, and one thing led to another."

Shit, she's right. We *did* have sex that night. It was my last attempt to feel some type of connection with her. I'd been thinking about breaking up with her for months and that week I was testing myself. Trying to do anything possible to actually feel what I told myself I felt for her. But it just wasn't there.

That night I took her to dinner was when I decided it was over. Like she said, we went out, had a meal and a few too many drinks, then came home. It wasn't a good night. We hardly spoke during dinner but I still felt an attraction to her. She looked beautiful, and I took that attraction to mean we might still have a chance at making it work.

When we got home I kissed her and it led to sex. I can't believe I didn't remember that. Now it's all coming back to me. We had sex, and when it was over I regretted it. It felt wrong, because by then I'd realized I didn't love her. I didn't even like her. It confirmed my decision to break up with her. After that night I had no doubts.

Lauren's looking at me, waiting for me to respond but I'm too shocked. This can't be true. She was on the pill. She can't be pregnant.

"I know what you're thinking," she says.

I look at her but keep quiet, waiting for her to continue.

"I was trying a new pill," she says. "Remember how the old one was giving me headaches? I tried a new pill that week. As you know, they're not effective right away. You have to use a backup method." She pauses. "And we didn't."

I do remember her saying something about switching birth control pills but I don't remember when she started the new ones. I wasn't keeping track. Even if I had, I wouldn't have thought about it that night. I was too out of it. I'd had too many drinks.

"Corbin, say something."

I inhale a breath and let it out. "Are you absolutely sure? You had a blood test?"

"Yes. It was confirmed. I can show you the results if you don't believe me." She takes her purse from the chair and pulls out a piece of paper. "Here."

Taking it from her I see the lab results. She's not lying. She's definitely pregnant.

This explains why she looks so tired. She's pregnant. Nine weeks pregnant. With my baby!

My heart's racing as I stare down at the lab results. How am I going to explain this to Star? What am I going to tell her? And what the hell am I going to do? Lauren's having my baby and moving to New York. Will I ever see him? Or her? Who's going to care for the baby when Lauren's working all those hours?

"I know it's not what either of us thought would happen," she says, "but I'm actually kind of excited. I didn't think I wanted to be a mother until I got the news. And now? I can't wait." Her hand is still on my arm and she gives it a squeeze. "You're happy too, right? You're going to have a child."

I swallow, my eyes lifting to hers. "I don't know. I need some time."

"Corbin, how could you not be happy about this? You love children. You always said you wanted them."

"Yes, but with the person I—" I stop before saying it.

"The person you love," she says, taking her hand off my arm and sitting back. "I know we've had our problems, Corbin, but maybe this will be a fresh start for us."

"Lauren, no." I set the lab results down. "I'm not trying to hurt you but you have to know this doesn't mean we're getting back together. I'm with Star now, and I know you may not want to hear this but I really do love her. She makes me happy."

She huffs. "Then why are you living apart?"

"Who told you that?"

"Alexis. She said Star moved out of your apartment. Things can't be that great if she moved out. In fact, I'd say that's a sign things are over between you two."

"They're not over. She moved out so we could try living apart. We've lived together for as long as we've known each other and we thought it might be a good test of our relationship to see what it'd be like to live apart. It's only temporary. She's moving back soon."

"You're living apart to test your relationship?" she asks with a smirk. "If your relationship is as strong as you make it sound, why would that even be necessary?"

Why am I telling her this? It's none of her business. And I shouldn't be trying to justify my relationship with Star. I love her, and know she's the girl for me. She's my future. The only girl I want.

"My relationship with Star isn't your concern. We're here to talk about the baby. But honestly, I need some time to let this sink in before we do."

"Will you at least call and set up an interview for the hospital in New York?" She takes a business card from her purse and shoves it at me. "Just call that number and tell him what times would work best for you."

"I'm not calling him. I'm not moving to New York."

"So you're just going to abandon your child?" She frowns. "That's so unlike you, Corbin. I always thought you were a family man."

"I am, but we're not a family. You're my ex-girlfriend who happened to get pregnant. It wasn't planned, and now I'm not sure what to do. I need time to think about this."

She shrugs. "Fine. Think about it." She stands up, grabbing her purse. "Call me next week. We'll set up a time to meet again." She swings her purse over her shoulder. "Goodbye, Corbin."

She leaves and I remain at the table, staring down at the lab results.

Lauren's pregnant.

I'm going to have a child. A child whose mother is moving to New York. I was thrilled she was leaving. I helped her get the job. But now she's taking my baby with her which is not what I want. But I don't want to leave Boston. I love my life here. I love my life with Star.

But I also love this baby. I don't even know him, just found out about him, but I already love him. Or her. I want to be there for my child, not just on weekends or holidays but all the time. For every moment.

So what does that mean? I'm moving to New York?

What about Star? She wanted Lauren out of our lives and I told her she would be. But now? Lauren will be in our lives forever.

CHAPTER TWENTY-THREE

Star

"Last night was so much fun," Alexis says as she hands me the bag of coffee beans. "We should do it again sometime."

"Definitely! Maybe this weekend." I pour the beans in the grinder.

"You're not going out with Corbin?"

"I am, but we haven't picked a night yet. He's usually really tired on Fridays so we'll probably go out Saturday."

"You could still see him. You don't have to go out. You could just have a quiet night at home."

"I know, and I'd love that, but that would defeat the purpose of this whole time apart thing. If we keep seeing each other all the time we might as well go back to living together."

"Isn't that what you want?" She takes the empty coffee bag from me and tosses it out. "Maybe it's time you end this experiment, or whatever it is you're doing. It's obvious you love him. You don't need time apart to prove it."

"That's not why I'm doing it. I know I love him. I love him more than anything."

"Then why are you doing this?"

"Because I felt like—" I pick up a rag. "Never mind. I have to go clean tables."

"No, wait." She holds my arm. "Tell me what you were going to say."

I shake my head. "I really shouldn't."

"Why not?" she asks, cocking her head. "Is it because I'm your boss? You don't want to tell me personal stuff?"

"It's not that."

"Then what is it?"

I look at her. "Lauren."

"What about her?"

"You're her best friend and I know you tell her everything I tell you about Corbin."

"I don't tell her that stuff."

I roll my eyes. "Yeah, right."

"No, really. I used to, but I don't now."

"I'm not sure I believe that." I go around her to clean tables.

She appears beside me. "I admit I was telling stuff to Lauren about you in the beginning. But that's changed now. You and I got to be friends and it didn't feel right telling Lauren that stuff anymore."

I move to the next table and wipe it down. "I want to believe that but you and Lauren have been friends forever. I know if she asked you about Corbin and me, you'd tell her."

"Not if you told me not to."

"I shouldn't have to. You know I don't want Lauren knowing that stuff."

"Okay, so next time she asks, my lips are sealed."

I stop cleaning tables and look at her. "Has she asked about me recently?"

"Last Saturday. She was driving here to get a coffee and saw you going in your apartment. She thought she'd caught you cheating on Corbin but I told her you lived there. I wasn't even thinking when I said it. I just didn't want her going to Corbin and telling him you were cheating when it wasn't true."

I sigh. "So she knows I moved out. Which means she'll be trying to get him back."

"She won't. She's moving."

"Lauren's moving?

"She got the job in New York."

"When does it start?"

"In a few weeks, I think. I didn't talk to her long. We were really busy that morning."

"Have you talked to her since?"

"No. She hasn't even texted me. I think she's busy getting ready for the move."

"Huh." A smile creeps up my face. "I'm happy for her. I'm glad she got the job."

"I figured you would be." Alexis smiles and walks off.

Even though we've become friends I'm still not sure I can trust Alexis, mainly because of her friendship with Lauren. But I think their friendship is starting to change. Alexis doesn't hang out with Lauren as much as she used to and sometimes she seems mad at her. I'd be mad at her too. Lauren's a horrible friend. She insults Alexis all the time, then laughs it off like she's just kidding. Just last week she told Alexis she'll never find a decent man working in a coffee shop, and by decent, she meant rich. Then she told her she needed to lose weight to get a guy, even though Alexis is already too thin.

But the thing that soured their friendship the most is how Lauren treated Alexis after her dad had a stroke. It happened a few weeks ago. Instead of showing sympathy and offering her support, Lauren told Alexis the stroke was her dad's fault because he's overweight. And she said it the day it happened, which made Alexis break down in tears. I was working that day and took Alexis in back and calmed her down. From that moment on, we've become better friends. I've been helping her get through this tough time with her dad while Lauren's ignored her.

Speak of the devil. Lauren just walked in. It's a little after nine and she's wearing black yoga pants with a long, white, loosely knit sweater over it. She always looks so fashionable, even after working out. I assume she just came from her spin class. Her hair is up and she has a dewy glow on her face.

"Hello, Star," she says with a smug grin. Why is she giving me that grin? And why is she talking to me? She usually walks right past me without saying anything. "Is Alexis here?"

"She's in the back," I say, walking behind the counter. "Can I get you something?"

"Hmm." She looks up at the menu board. "It's so much harder now."

"What's harder?" I ask.

"Figuring out what to order." She continues to scan the menu, then looks at me. "Decaf green tea with a shot of skim milk."

"No coffee today?" I ask, because she always has coffee. She lives on coffee. She always gets the largest size.

"I can't." Her smug grin appears again. "Just the tea. Oh, and tell Alexis I need to speak with her."

"You could text her," I mutter as I ring up the order.

"Alexis!" Lauren calls out.

I turn around and see Alexis coming through the door from the kitchen.

"Hey, Lauren." Alexis gives her a smile. "Were you at spin class?"

"Yoga. I'm taking a break from spin class." She gives me a five dollar bill. "Keep the change."

I deposit what she owes in the register, then drop the change in the tip jar and go to make Lauren's tea.

"I need to talk to you," Lauren says to Alexis. "Privately."

There's a glimmer in her eye as she says it. She's up to something and I probably don't want to know what. It doesn't matter. She'll be in New York soon and then Corbin and I will never have to deal with her again.

"I don't have time now," Alexis says. "I have to do orders. My supply guy will be here at noon."

"It can't wait," Lauren says with a huff. "What kind of friend are you if you don't make time for me when I need you?"

Looking back at Alexis I see her take a long deep breath so she doesn't explode with anger at Lauren's comment. Since her dad's stroke, Alexis has needed a friend more than ever and Lauren wouldn't even return her calls, saying she was too busy to talk.

"Okay, fine," Alexis says. "Let's go back to my office."

Lauren comes around the counter. I hand her the tea, then watch as the two of them go to the back.

"Whatcha looking at?" I hear a voice ask. I turn and see Lars standing there, his blond hair held back with an orange bandana, wearing workout shorts and a tank. He's giving me his usual wide smile with his sparkly white teeth that look even whiter next to his dark tan.

"Hey, Lars." I meet him at the register. "Sorry, I was spacing out."

He shrugs. "It happens. Sometimes at the deli I don't even notice when a customer's standing right in front of me. And once I made a sandwich and didn't even remember making it." He laughs.

"I'm not at that point yet." I smile. "So what can I get you?"

"Iced mocha latte." He pulls a wad of crumpled-up bills from his pocket and tosses them on the counter. "Is that enough?"

"Should be." I take the bills and count out what I need, then hand him back the change. "Did you come from spin class?"

"Rock climbing. It was one of those fake walls but I still had a blast. A buddy of mine works there and got me some free passes."

"It's kind of early to rock climb."

"I went before they opened. My friend was working today and let me in. Had the place to myself. It was awesome."

I hand him his drink. "Maybe I'll go there and try it sometime."

"Let's go together," he says in a flirty tone. "Then maybe we'll catch a movie."

"Oh, um, thanks but I'll go with Corbin. I'm sure he'd like to try it."

"You're still with Corbin?" he asks, looking confused.

"Yeah. Why?"

"I thought Lauren said—" He shakes his head. "Never mind. Must've heard her wrong." He turns to leave. "See ya around."

"Lars, wait!" I catch up to him at the door. "What did Lauren tell you?"

"About what?"

"Corbin. Did she say we broke up?"

"Not exactly. But she did say you'd moved out."

"Why was she telling you this?"

He puts his hand up. "Hey, I just came to get coffee. I'm not getting involved in this. Too much drama. See ya later." He goes out the door.

"Drama?" I call out as he goes down the street. "What are you talking about?"

He doesn't hear me, now almost a block away. I have no idea what he meant just now. Maybe it was nothing. Lars says a lot of stuff that doesn't make sense so he's not the most reliable person for information.

"Excuse me," I hear Lauren say. "Could you remove yourself from the door?"

I step back. "Done talking already?"

"I need to get to work." She slings her purse up higher on her shoulder and that odd smile of hers appears again. "Perhaps you should consider getting a better job. Or maybe college. You can't always rely on a man to support you."

"What? I'm not relying on—"

"Goodbye, Star." She leaves and I watch as she walks to her expensive black car.

As she drives off I go to the back office where Alexis is working on orders.

"What happened?" I ask. "What'd Lauren say?"

"Just personal stuff," she says as she types on her laptop.

"You're not going to tell me?"

She stops typing and looks at me. "If I'm not telling *her* about *you*, then I shouldn't be telling you about her. Plus, she made me promise not to tell. Not just you, but anyone."

"So she's hiding something. Something she doesn't want people to know."

"They'll know eventually," she says, continuing to type.

"Can you give me a hint?" I ask, sitting on the chair next to her desk. "She was acting really strange and saying all this weird stuff to me."

Alexis looks up from her laptop. "What stuff? What'd she say?"

"How I should get a better job. Not rely on a man. And she ordered tea instead of coffee, saying something about how she can't have coffee."

Alexis opens her mouth to say something, then snaps it shut as her eyes return to her laptop. "I left coffee bean orders in the kitchen. If you have time, can you work on them?"

"Yeah. Sure." I get up, realizing she's not going to tell me anything. I go to the kitchen and grab the order sheets and take them out front. As I'm filling the coffee bags my mind keeps going back to Lauren and the comments she made. It's like she was trying to tell me something, but what?

A woman walks up to the counter holding a toddler.

"Hi," I say, smiling at her and her little girl. "What can I get you?"

"Chocolate!" the little girl answers, clapping her hands.

Her mom laughs. "She means chocolate milk. Small, please."

"Sure." I punch it in the register. "And for you?"

She scans the menu board. "Do you have herbal tea?"

"Yes. The flavors are right there." I point to them on the board.

"I'll take the ginger peach," she says. "On ice."

She pays for the drinks and as I'm making them, she says, "I really miss coffee."

"You can't have it?" I ask, handing her the chocolate milk for her daughter.

"Not now that I'm pregnant," she says with a smile. "No caffeine for five more months."

I hand her the tea. "I think you'll like this. The peach is really good."

"Thanks!" She leaves and her daughter waves at me from the door.

I wave back, smiling at her. She's cute.

"Who are you waving at?" Alexis asks from behind me.

"A little girl. She and her mom just left." I turn to Alexis. "Done with the orders?"

"Yes. Can you give them to the supply guy when he gets here? I have to run to my parents' house."

"Is something wrong?"

"My dad tripped and fell. He's fine but my mom's freaking out."

She races around behind the counter. She always does that when she's worried.

"Alexis." I hold her arm, stopping her. "Go. Take as much time as you need. I'll take care of everything here."

She gives me a weak smile. "Thanks. I'm sure he's fine but when something like this happens, I panic."

"I know." I give her hug. "If you need anything, just call." I let her go.

"You're such a great friend." She grabs her purse from under the counter. "I'll try not to be too long."

"Don't worry about it. Take the rest of the day if you want. I can stay late if you need me to."

"Thanks, Star," she says. "You're the best." She goes to leave, then turns back. "My phone! It's in my office." She runs to the back.

Grabbing a rag I wipe down the counter and notice a tea bag on the floor. I must've dropped one when I went to make that woman's tea. Or maybe when I made Lauren's.

Why would Lauren order tea? She never has tea. She always gets coffee. But not today. And when I asked her why, she said she can't, as in she can't have it. Just like the customer who was just here. She can't have coffee. Because she's pregnant.

I suck in a breath as it hits me.

Lauren's pregnant! That's her secret! That's why she was wearing that baggy sweater and not drinking coffee.

"Okay, I'm going," Alexis says, stuffing her phone in her purse on her way to the door. "Call if you need me."

"Alexis, wait." I run up to her. "Is Lauren pregnant?"

She bites her lip and looks to the side.

"Just tell me," I say. "You don't have to hide it. I already know she is."

Her eyes return to mine. "How'd you find out?"

"I guessed. And you just confirmed it."

"Star!" She swats my arm. "I wasn't supposed to tell!"

"She made it pretty obvious with her comments and then ordering tea instead of coffee."

"Yeah, the coffee was a dead giveaway. It used to be Lauren couldn't go an hour without coffee and now she can't have it."

"So who's the father?" I ask, surprised Lauren's been hiding her mystery man from Corbin. I would've thought she'd want to show him off to try to make Corbin jealous.

Alexis looks down. "Um, I'm not sure."

"Not sure? Meaning she didn't tell you?"

"Star, I really need to go." She turns to leave but I grab her coat, stopping her.

"You know."

She looks at me. She seems sad, almost pained.

I let her go. "Why are you looking at me like that?"

She sighs. "I'm really sorry."

"About what?"

"It doesn't mean things have to change. I mean, they will, but it doesn't mean you can't still be with him."

"Who? What are you talking about?"

She doesn't answer but that sad look is still on her face.

My stomach knots and an uneasy feeling comes over me. "No. It can't be."

"I'm really sorry," she says.

"Corbin?" I say, raising my voice. "You're telling me the father is Corbin?"

"Maybe I should stay. You're not going to be able to work now." She gets her phone out. "I'll call my mom and explain."

"No." I take her by the arm and lead her to the door. "Go take care of your dad. I'll be fine."

She frowns. "Star, I know you're not fine."

"I'm not, but I'll deal with it." I take a breath. "Just tell me how long it's been."

"What?"

"How long have they been seeing each other?"

"Oh! No, they haven't been together since he started seeing you. This happened before he met you."

"And she's just telling you this now?"

"She said she just found out. I don't know how that's possible, given she's a doctor. You think she'd know before now."

"She probably did," I say, my voice trailing off as I try to absorb the news.

Lauren's pregnant. With Corbin's baby.

"I'm just as shocked as you," Alexis says. "I didn't even think she wanted kids, although this wasn't planned, but still. I'm surprised she isn't giving it up. I can't imagine her as a mom."

"Does he know?" I blurt out. "Did she tell Corbin?"

"Last night. They met somewhere and she told him. I don't know what he said. She didn't tell me. I'm just wondering what he plans to do. Will he move to New York with her? But that would mean you'd have to move and—" She stops, her hand resting on my arm. "Sorry, I shouldn't be talking about this. I'm sure you and Corbin will figure out a solution. Star, I really do need to go. I told my mom I'd be there five minutes ago."

"Yeah. Go ahead. I'll check in with you later."

She hurries off and I walk back behind the counter in a daze, not wanting to believe this is true. I thought my luck had changed. That finally, my streak of bad luck was over. But I should've known better.

I found the man of my dreams. The man I want to be with forever. Lauren was his past. She was moving to New York. She was finally going to be out of our lives and we'd never have to see her again.

But now? Corbin's having a child with her.

Everything will change.

My streak of good luck has ended.

CHAPTER TWENTY-FOUR

Corbin

"Hey," I say when she answers. I called Star as soon as I got home from work. I've felt sick to my stomach all day knowing I had to tell her the news and now the time has come. I can't wait any longer.

"Hi, Corbin," she says, a hint of anger in her voice. I don't know why she's angry but it's going to get a lot worse when she finds out the news.

"Can you come over tonight?" I ask.

"What time?"

"Right now?"

"Yeah. I'm just getting off work so I'll just come upstairs. See you in a minute." She hangs up before saying goodbye. She's definitely angry. This is going to go even worse than I imagined.

Taking deep breaths I try to calm down as I quickly change into jeans and a t-shirt. I hear her come in the door, her keys dropping on the counter, then Lucky's paws clinking on the wood floor as he runs to greet her.

"Hey," I say, going up to her. I give her a hug. "I miss you."

"I miss you too," she says softly.

I let her go. "Can we sit down?"

She nods and we walk to the couch. Once we're seated, she turns to me and says, "I already know."

"Know what?" I ask, my heart pounding.

"About Lauren. She was in the coffee shop today."

"And she told you?" I ask, both shocked and angry Lauren would do that. She knows I wanted to be the one to tell Star the news.

"I figured it out. She was acting weird and then she ordered herbal tea instead of coffee." Star's eyes lift to mine. "Why didn't you tell me?"

"I was going to. Right now. I swear, I was just about to tell you but you beat me to it."

"Why'd you wait? Why didn't you tell me last night?"

"I don't know," I say, shaking my head. "I guess I just needed some time to let it sink in. When she told me I was so shocked I'm not even sure what I said. I couldn't believe it. I wasn't even sure it was possible. I mean, obviously it was but we hadn't—never mind." I look down at my hands, which I'm wringing together as my nerves get the best of me. I'm so afraid this will change things between Star and me and I can't let that happen. Everything was going so well. This time apart made me love her even more and showed me I can't live without her. That I want her in my life forever.

"I thought you two weren't getting along at the end," Star says.

"We hadn't been getting along for months."

"Then how? Why?" She struggles to find the right words but I know what she's asking.

"We did it right before we broke up. We hadn't for weeks, but that night we'd been drinking and one thing led to another."

"And you didn't use protection?"

"She was on the pill but she had just changed to a new one. It needed more time to take effect." I take her hand. "Star, I know this complicates things but I promise I'll do all I can to keep Lauren out of our lives. Obviously I'll be involved with the baby but that doesn't mean I have to be involved with Lauren."

"Are you kidding?" Star bursts up from the couch. "This is Lauren we're talking about. The woman who's been trying to get you back the whole time we've been together! And now she's done it! She has you back! You're tied to her forever now!"

I follow Star to the window. Her back's to me as she looks down at the gardens below.

"Star, it's not like I planned this. Lauren didn't either. I'm not sticking up for her. I'm just saying this wasn't planned. Neither one of us was trying to have a baby that night."

"What if she was?" Star turns to face me. "How do you know she wasn't trying to get pregnant those last months she was with you, hoping a baby would make you stay?"

"She wouldn't have done that. She had no reason to. She thought I'd stay with her forever, even if she treated me like shit. When I broke up with her she didn't believe me. You know this, Star. You were there when Lauren kept showing up, acting like she and I were still together."

"Fine, so maybe she didn't plan it but now she's using this to get you back."

"I'm not going back to her. Ever." I take Star's hand. "I love YOU. You're the one I want to be with. Even if I was single I wouldn't take her back."

"She's going to use this baby to manipulate you." Star rips her hand from mine. "She's already doing it."

"How? What do you mean?"

"You're moving to New York."

"What?" I look at her, confused. "Who told you I'm moving to New York? Lauren?"

"Nobody told me, but I know she'll make you move there. You want to be with your baby, and in order to do that, you'll have to follow Lauren wherever she goes. And she's going to New York."

"That doesn't mean I'm going with her," I say.

"So you're just not going to see your kid?" She rolls her eyes. "You and I both know that's a lie. You're going to love that kid more than anything. There's no way you're not going to be around to see him or her grow up. And you SHOULD be there. It's the right thing to do."

I sigh. "I know it is, and you're right. I already love this baby and I haven't even met him. And when he's born I'm not going to want to go a day without seeing him. But there's gotta be a way to fight this. Lauren can't be the one controlling everything. She and I both have rights. I can talk to my lawyer tomorrow and see what my options are."

"He?" Star asks, looking up at me. She has a slight smile but her eyes are sad. "You're having a boy?"

"I don't know yet. It's too early to tell. It could be a girl, although for some reason I have a feeling it's a boy."

"Either way, it's great," she says, trying to sound happy. She turns and walks away, wiping her eyes.

"Star, wait." I hurry over to her and pull her into my arms. "I'm so sorry this is happening."

She sniffles. "It's a baby. It's a good thing. And I'm really trying to be happy for you. I just..." She doesn't finish the thought.

"You wish it was ours," I say quietly as I hold her.

She nods against my chest.

"I know. I do too. Not that now would be a good time for that but if it was going to happen, I'd rather it be with you."

"I don't know what to do now." She sniffles.

"I think you should move back in. And not next month or next week, but now." I pull away from her. "Let's go get your things."

She shakes her head. "I don't know if I want to."

"I know you wanted more time but things have changed. We need each other, Star. We need to be with each other to get through this."

She looks down. "What I mean is I don't know if I can do this."

"Do what?"

She swallows and her eyes lift to mine. "I don't know if I can be with you with Lauren in your life."

"Star, I told you, she's not going to be in our lives. Yes, I'll see her when I pick up the baby but I'll make sure she—"

"It won't work. She manipulates you, Corbin. You don't even realize when she's doing it, and when I try to tell you, you don't believe me. And now you and her will have to make decisions together. Decisions that'll affect me but that I won't get a say in because Lauren will take over and decide everything and convince you to go along with it."

"Star, you're making assumptions that aren't true. None of that is going to happen."

Star walks over to the window. "Just wait. She'll make sure you move to New York. I bet she's even got a job lined up for you."

I don't respond.

Star turns to me. "She does, doesn't she? She got you a job."

"I'm not taking it," I say, walking up to her. "And it's not a job. It's a lead. There's a guy she wants me to talk to. I told her I wouldn't. I wouldn't even take his card."

"She won't give up. She'll keep pushing you until you agree to it. Or she'll find some way to force you to do it."

"Okay, stop." I place my hands on her shoulders. "Stop trying to predict the future. I don't know what's going to happen but we're not going to make decisions about our relationship based on worst case scenarios. We'll take it a day at a time."

"I don't want her in our lives, Corbin."

"I know you don't. We'll figure this out. I promise you, we will." I hug her to my chest. "I love you." I kiss her head. "I love you so much."

"I love you too," she whispers.

We stay there a moment, then she pulls away and tells me she has to go. Before I can stop her, she's on the elevator and I watch as the doors close. I could run after her but I don't. She needs time to think about this. We both do. I send her a text later, telling her how much I love her and that we'll talk tomorrow. She doesn't text back.

The next day at work I'm having lunch in my office when my phone rings. It's my father.

"Hey, dad," I say.

"I hear congratulations are in order."

Lauren told my father? What the hell? She told me we'd each tell our families separately and wouldn't do so for at least another week.

"Yes, it was quite a surprise," I say. "Who told you?"

"Lauren's mother called last night. Apparently she wasn't supposed to tell us but she was so excited she wasn't able to hold back the news. I'm curious why you didn't tell me yourself."

"I wasn't ready to. I wanted to let it sink in a little before I started telling people."

"Eve said Lauren is nearly three months along."

"More like two and half."

"But it was when you two were together," he confirms.

"Yes. And nothing has happened since, if that's what you're wondering."

"So what happens now?"

"What do you mean?"

"With you and Lauren? I assume this means you'll be getting married."

"Married?" I laugh. "Uh, no, we are definitely not getting married."

"But you're having a child together."

"Dad, I know you're old-fashioned but you can't seriously believe we'd get married just because we're having a kid. It doesn't work that way anymore."

"It's the right decision for your child."

"I'm not going to argue with you about this. I'm not getting back with Lauren."

"But you're moving to New York with her."

I hesitate. "I don't know yet."

"You don't want to be with your child?"

"Of course I want to be with him," I say, getting angry. "That's not the issue."

"Then what is it? Is it that girl you're seeing? Does she not want you to move?"

"Her name is Star, and no, she's not the reason. This is about Lauren. I don't want her making this decision for me. She knows I don't want to live in New York and now she's trying to force me to, using our child to guilt me into it."

"A child needs his father. Put your petty differences with Lauren aside and do what's right for your child."

"Dad, I'm not talking about this with you. I'm going to make my own decision and you're just going to have to be okay with it."

"If you two had just stayed together."

"But we didn't. It wasn't working and never will. I don't love Lauren, and I don't want my child growing up in a house with parents who don't love each other." I get up from my desk. "I have to get back to work."

"We'll talk later," he says, then ends the call.

I whip open my office door and walk down the hall to the door that goes outside. I can't see patients when I'm this angry. I need to walk around and get some fresh air to calm down.

My father really expects me to get back with Lauren? And marry her? He doesn't care about my happiness and never has.

Following the path that goes around the clinic I take long strides and deep breaths, already feeling a little better. After a few minutes I stop at a bench and get out my phone to call Star. She doesn't answer so I text her.

Thinking about you. I love you.

She doesn't text back. I haven't heard from her since last night. I'm starting to get worried. Even if she's angry with me she still responds to my texts so I know she's okay. After her bike accident I always worry something might happen to her so not hearing from her for this long is concerning.

I text her again. *Star, please let me know you're okay.*

I'm fine, she texts back. *I just need some time.*

She's worried. She thinks Lauren will use this baby to break us apart. I've told Star a million times I'm not getting back with Lauren but she still sees Lauren as a threat and I don't know how to convince her otherwise.

This isn't what Star wants. She's finally getting her life on track. She has a job she likes. She's planning to go back to school. She doesn't want to move to New York and have to deal with Lauren and all her demands. I don't want that either but I may not have a choice. Star *does*. She could choose to end things between us, but I hope she doesn't. I love her and can't imagine my life without her. I know we can work this out. I just need to convince her of that.

When I get home from work I walk in my apartment and Lucky runs up to me.

"Did I leave you out all day?" I say, rubbing his head. "I thought for sure I put you in your kennel. You didn't destroy the couch, did you?"

"It's fine," I hear Star say. "I let him out when I got here."

I look up and see Star walking toward me. She's wearing the dress I bought her a few weeks ago when we were at the mall. It's a casual knit dress, something Lauren would only wear to the beach, but Star wears it out to dinner. She loves it because it's comfortable and doesn't wrinkle. And I love it because it clings to her body and the hot pink color looks great against her tan skin. When I saw it in the store window I knew I had to get it for her.

"I didn't know you were coming over." I go to kiss her but she backs away.

"We need to talk."

Shit. Those aren't the words I wanted to hear. Those are the words you use before breaking up with someone.

"Can we sit down?" she asks.

"Yeah. Of course." I drop my keys in the bowl and walk over to the couch. Lucky goes to his bed that's next to the TV and lays down, looking at us like he knows something bad is coming. Did Star tell him she's leaving me? God, I hope not. She can't do this. She hasn't given it enough time. Neither one of us knows what's going to happen. We just found out. We've barely even talked about it.

"You look really nice," I say, trying to put off this talk as long as possible.

"Thanks," she says, glancing down at herself.

"Are you going somewhere tonight?"

"Yeah. At least I think I am. I have to ask him first."

HIM? What's she talking about? Is she going on a date tonight? With some other guy? She hasn't even broken up with me and she's already making plans with someone new?

"Corbin, I've been thinking about this a lot. The baby. Lauren. Us. Our future. In fact, I took today off from work just to think about what to do." She takes a breath. "This isn't how I saw my life going. Not that I had any real plans but I didn't think I'd end up dating a guy with a kid. I'm only 23. I'm not ready for all the stuff that comes with having a kid."

She's breaking up with me. She doesn't want this. It's not what she signed up for and I totally understand. This baby will change everything and it's not fair for me to expect her to accept something that she doesn't want. But that doesn't mean I'm just letting her go.

"Star, please," I say, taking her hand. "Before you go on, please hear me out." I pause. "I know this isn't what you wanted. It's not what I wanted either, but it happened and I can't stop it. This baby is coming and I'm going to love it and take care of it and be the best dad I can be. And maybe I'm being selfish when I say this but I'm saying it anyway. I want you beside me, Star. I know this'll be a huge change to our lives and maybe you'll decide you want to leave and get away from it all, but I'm asking you not to. I'm asking you to give this a chance. I love you more than anything, and someday I want to marry you and have kids of our own. But right now, I need you beside me, helping me through this. It's a lot to ask and I'll understand if you decide it's too much, but please...please give it more time."

A tear runs down her cheek. Dammit. My speech didn't work. She's still breaking up with me. And my heart's already aching at the thought of not having her in my life.

"Corbin," she says, smiling through her tears. "I'm not leaving you."

"You're not?" I ask, my heart picking up speed.

She shakes her head. "No. That's what I came here to tell you." Her eyes go to mine. "I spent all last night and all of today imagining every bad thing that could happen if I stayed with you. Lauren being mean to me. The baby not liking me. Having to leave here and move to New York." She looks down. "I came up with a whole list of things. The worst possible outcomes I could think of." Her eyes rise back to mine. "But even knowing any or all of those things could happen, I still wanted to be with you." Another tear slips down her cheek. "Because I can't imagine my life without you. We haven't even lived apart for two weeks and I miss you like crazy." She takes a breath. "Whatever happens with Lauren and the baby and New York and whatever else, I want you to know I'll be beside you. I love you and I want to support you."

I bring her into my arms. "God, I love you. How did I ever get so lucky to find you?"

Lucky jumps up and appears by our feet. We both laugh.

"I wasn't talking about you," I tell him. "Go lay down."

He looks at us both, then returns to his bed.

"You have to be careful when you use that word," Star kids.

"Then I won't say it but it's still true. How did I ever find such an amazing woman?"

"You hit me with your car," she says with a smile.

"Yes, well, I wish I could've avoided that and still met you."

"It was meant to be. The accident was bad but something good came out of it. Same with this thing with Lauren. It was a bad relationship but this baby will be good." She smiles. "It has to be. Babies can't be bad. They're too cute."

247

"But it's going to change things. It's going to change a lot."

"I know, but like you said, we'll figure it out."

I hug her again. "Thank you. Thank you for not giving up on me. Or *us*."

"So now that we've talked, will you go out with me?"

I let her go and sit back. "You're asking me out?"

"Yeah. I'll even pay."

"You don't have to pay, and the answer is yes. Of course I'll go out with you. Is that why you wore the dress?"

"The dress is because we're celebrating." She stands up, a big smile on her face. "I've officially moved back in. I did it earlier today. I hope you don't mind."

I jump up from the couch and kiss her. "Mind? Are you kidding? I've been begging you to move back since you left." I grab her hand. "Let's go so we can come back here and celebrate you moving back in."

We go to her favorite restaurant, then come back and make love. In our room. Our bed. And I've never been happier. We have a difficult road ahead but we'll make it work. Together we can get through this.

CHAPTER TWENTY-FIVE

Star

It's been three weeks since I moved back in with Corbin and in those three weeks, we've done a lot of talking about the future. As of now, we've decided to stay in Boston, at least until the baby arrives, then maybe move to New York. Corbin is working with a lawyer to figure out his parental rights but so far, it's not looking good. Lauren can move wherever she wants unless Corbin takes her to court, which he's considering.

"What's going on?" I ask as I come in the apartment. Corbin's in the kitchen, his head down, gripping the phone in his hand.

"My lawyer said I can't do anything until I have a paternity test to prove the baby is mine."

I've been wanting him to do a paternity test since the moment I found out Lauren was pregnant. When I brought it up he got angry, insisting the baby was his, so I haven't brought it up again. He's really excited about this baby so even the suggestion it might not be his upsets him. But he needs to find out for sure.

"Are you going to do it?" I ask cautiously.

"I don't have a choice."

I walk up to him. "Corbin, this isn't a bad thing. You need to know it's yours."

"Of course it's mine. Lauren wasn't cheating on me. She didn't have time to. She worked constantly, and when she wasn't working she was asleep or at spin class."

"Maybe she was with someone right after you broke up."

"How would she meet someone that fast? Lauren's not the type to go pick up a guy at a bar."

"It could've been someone she already knew."

He shakes his head. "She wasn't with anyone. I talked to Alexis. She confirmed it."

So he HAS been questioning the paternity. This whole time he's insisted he's the father but he couldn't have been that sure if he asked Alexis if Lauren had been with someone else.

"Have you said anything to Lauren?" I ask. "About a paternity test?"

"Not yet." He walks to the living room and sits on the couch, picking up the remote and turning on the TV.

"Corbin." I sit beside him. "If you don't get that test you can't move forward with the lawyer. You're putting your parental rights at risk. The sooner you do this the better."

He lets out a harsh laugh. "You seriously think Lauren would agree to that? She'll refuse, saying I'm insulting her by even asking."

"But she can't refuse, can she?"

"I don't want to talk about this," he says as he flips through channels.

"Corbin, we need to talk about it. We're planning our future around a baby that may not be yours."

"It's mine, dammit!" He tosses the remote on the coffee table, making a noise so loud it startles Lucky, making him look up and bark.

I go over to his dog bed and pet him. "It's okay, Lucky,"

"I'm sorry," Corbin says with a sigh. "I shouldn't have reacted that way. I didn't mean to yell at you. I'm just really on edge right now." He gets up. "I need some fresh air. I'll be back in a few minutes."

He leaves and I stay behind with Lucky, wishing there was something I could do to make Corbin feel better. He's angry and frustrated with Lauren because she keeps avoiding him at the hospital and won't talk to him when he calls, saying she's busy. I'm sure he's right that she'd refuse the paternity test but there's got to be a way to force her to do it. Corbin needs to ask his lawyer about that.

A half hour later Corbin comes home and goes straight to bed. He didn't even eat dinner. He's so stressed out, and so am I. I'm trying to be strong for him and support him but I'm starting to wear down. Everything right now feels so uncertain and that's mostly because of Lauren. Because she refuses to talk to Corbin. As usual, she holds all the cards. She's the one with all the power while Corbin and I sit here waiting for her next move. Will she demand he move to New York to be with the baby? Or will she try to take away his parental rights and raise the baby on her own? I'm guessing she'll wait until the baby's born and then try to get Corbin back. She'll use the baby to lure him back into her life and try to convince him they should all be one big happy family.

The next morning I'm working at the coffee shop in a total daze, my mind still on Corbin. He tossed and turned all night, then around two in the morning he got up and watched TV in the living room until it was time to leave for work.

"You awake over there?" I hear Alexis say.

I look over at her. "What?"

She points to the counter which is covered in coffee grounds. I was pouring them in the coffee filter and was too out of it to stop when it was full.

"Oh, shit," I say, setting the coffee bag down. "Sorry about that. I'll pay for what I spilled."

"Don't worry about it," she says, coming over to me. "Why don't you go take your break?"

"But it's only nine."

"Yeah, but the rush is over and I think you could use a break."

"Are you sure?" I glance around at all the dirty tables. "Why don't I wipe tables before I go?"

"I can do it." She points to the door. "Go. Get some sun and fresh air. It'll help you wake up."

"Okay," I say, taking off my apron. "Be back in ten."

When I get outside the brightness and warmth of the sun does make me feel better. It's a beautiful day. If I had more time, I'd run upstairs and get Lucky and take him on a walk.

"Excuse me," a woman says as she rushes past me, holding her yoga mat and a water bottle. The woman behind her is also holding a yoga mat.

There's a new yoga studio down the street. Class must've just got out.

As I continue down the street I spot Lauren. She's coming out of the yoga studio.

This is my chance. I'll run up to her and demand she talk to Corbin. This avoidance game she's been playing has to end. She's moving next week and then it'll be nearly impossible to get in touch with her.

"Lauren!" I call out, waving at her.

She doesn't hear me. She's looking back and smiling at someone coming out of the yoga studio. I stop and watch as Lars walks out. He goes up to Lauren and leans down to her ear to say something. She smiles and they turn and walk down the street, the opposite direction of me. They get in Lauren's car and she drives off.

What is Lars doing with Lauren? I know they're friends but they seemed to be acting like more than that. But Lauren would never date a guy like Lars. She's serious and high-strung and he's laid-back and always joking around. And he has no money. He has a low-paying job, lives in an apartment with three roommates, and takes the bus everywhere because he doesn't have a car. He's definitely not Lauren's type.

When I get back to the coffee shop I go up to Alexis who's restocking things behind the counter.

"How well do you know Lars?" I ask.

"The guy who works at the deli?" she asks as she refills the cups.

"Yeah. What do you know about him?"

"Not much. Why?" She takes out a box of napkins and refills the stack.

"I saw him just now coming out of that yoga studio down the street."

"Yoga? I thought he did spin class. He's always telling me about it. He even tried to get me to sign up." She rolls her eyes. "I'm pretty sure he was asking me out."

"What'd you tell him?"

"That I'm not interested. In that class. Or a date. He hasn't bothered me since. But he went out with Missy."

"The Missy who works here?"

"Yeah. It was a few months ago. They only went out one time."

Missy works the afternoon shift. She's in college and on the swim team. She's really pretty.

"Did Missy say anything about him?"

"Yes, but I shouldn't say."

"Why? What happened?"

"If I tell you, you need to keep it quiet."

"I will. What is it?"

Alexis looks around to make sure no one's listening. "They had sex on the first date. She said it was the best sex of her life."

"Then why didn't they go out again?"

"Because she found out he sleeps around and dates multiple women at a time."

"Has he ever been with Lauren?" I ask.

"Lauren?" She bursts out laughing. "Are you kidding? The guy works at a deli and doesn't even own a car. Lauren wouldn't be caught dead with a loser like Lars."

"You sure about that?"

Her brow ticks up. "What do you mean?"

"I just saw them together outside the yoga studio. Lars leaned down to whisper something in Lauren's ear and she smiled. Then they left together."

Alexis shakes her head. "Must've been someone else. A lot of women look like Lauren, especially the ones at that yoga studio."

"No, it was definitely her. And definitely Lars. And it looked like they were more than just casual friends."

She pauses a moment. "That would explain why she suddenly liked the deli."

"What do you mean?"

"The deli where Lars works. Whenever I'd suggest we go there she'd refuse, saying she didn't like the menu. But then all of a sudden she started going there. She said she'd decided it wasn't that bad after all, but now that I think about it, she started going there right after Lars started working there."

"Which was when?"

"Maybe five or six months ago? I can't remember. I just remember thinking it was odd that she hated the place, then suddenly liked it. At one point she was going there almost every day."

"And they did spin class together."

"Lars was in her spin class?"

"They went to the same class at the same time. And now he's going to her yoga class. Don't you think that's odd?"

She shrugs. "I don't really care. If she wants to risk getting some disease being with Lars, that's her business. I think my friendship with Lauren is over. I don't even like being around her anymore. I really don't care who she dates."

"I don't either but what if..." I lower my voice. "What if he's the father?"

"Father?"

"Of Lauren's baby."

She laughs. "No way. Lauren's too cautious to let that happen. She would've used a condom with Lars, especially knowing how many women he's been with."

"Maybe she didn't know. Or maybe she got caught up in the moment and forgot to use one."

"I guess it's possible."

"Do you think you could ask her?"

"About Lars? I could, but Lauren would never admit to being with him. Not even to me."

"But you're her best friend."

"Who she knows is now friends with you. She's not going to tell me anything that might get back to Corbin."

"What if you just casually asked her some questions about Lars? Nothing direct. Just questions that might get her talking."

"I can try, but she's not going to tell me anything. You'd have better luck talking to Lars. That guy's an open book. You wouldn't believe the things he told Missy. She didn't even have to ask."

"Then I'll talk to Lars and you talk to Lauren. Just see if you can get anything out of her."

"I guess I could try. I'm going over there tonight to help her pack. But I really don't think he's the father."

"I don't either but I have to know for sure."

After my shift ends at three I hurry upstairs to change clothes. I walk Lucky, take him back to the apartment, then race down to the street to the deli. It's Thursday, which is when Lars usually works but I don't know how late.

When I walk in I don't see him working the counter. Neal, a college student who works part-time, is there instead.

"Hey, Neal," I say. "Is Lars here?"

"No, he switched days with me. He took today off to go rock climbing with his friend. I think they were driving up to New Hampshire. He's off tomorrow too."

"Oh," I say, disappointed he's not there.

"What can I get you?" Neal asks.

"Um, nothing. I'm not really hungry," I say but then my stomach growls. I took Lucky for a long walk during my lunch break and didn't get time to eat.

"Actually," I say, "I'll take a turkey club."

"Sure." He smiles. "Anything else?"

"No, that's it."

He makes the sandwich and I take it to a table by the window. Getting out my phone I check messages while I eat. There are several texts from my mom, all about the wedding. My brother finally proposed to his girlfriend after years of dating. They're getting married in August, just three months from now. My mom's doing most of the planning and keeps asking me for advice, as if I would know. I keep telling her to ask the bride but apparently the bride has no interest in the wedding. She wanted to elope but both her parents and mine insisted on a traditional wedding.

"Hey, bro, what's up?" I hear Lars' voice and look up. He's standing at the counter, talking to Neal.

"Hey, what happened to the trip?"

"My buddy broke his hand so we couldn't go." He shrugs. "Shit happens."

"So what are you doing here?"

"I need to eat. Give me the usual."

Neal makes the sandwich and hands it to Lars.

"Thanks, man." Lars takes his sandwich and looks for a table.

"Lars!" I call out.

He looks over and smiles. "Hey, Star." He joins me at the table. "Where's Corbin?"

"At work."

He laughs. "Yeah, I forgot what day it was. I don't usually have Thursday off." He takes a bite of his sandwich. "So what's new?"

"Not much. I missed lunch today so I stopped in to get a sandwich."

He just nods and continues eating.

"So I saw you this morning on my break," I say, casually.

"Where?" he asks, gulping down water from the bottle he brought in.

"Coming out of the yoga studio." I take a sip of my drink. "You were with Lauren."

"Yeah, she's in my class," he says, like it's no big deal. He doesn't seem nervous or like he's trying to hide something. Maybe I was wrong. Maybe they really are just friends.

"Did she give you a ride home? I thought I saw you get in her car but I could be wrong."

What a dumb thing to say. I either saw him get in the car or I didn't. I'm getting nervous, worried he'll clue in to what I'm trying to figure out and not tell me anything. Then again, Lars isn't too smart.

"She always gives me a ride," he says, and then smiles, "and not always in her car."

I let out a laugh. "What do you mean?"

"You know what I mean." His knee brushes mine under the table and I quickly move it away.

"So you and Lauren are...seeing each other?"

Lars shrugs. "It's just casual. The girl is wound up tight. She needs to let loose, you know?"

"And you help her...unwind?"

He smiles. "Oh, yeah. It's why she keeps coming back."

So he's had sex with her, but when? When did it start? How do I find out? He seems open to telling me stuff but I don't want him figuring out why I'm asking.

"It's good she has you," I say. "Even if it's just for, you know, letting loose. Sounds like her job is really stressful, although it's getting better now that her residency is ending. I'm sure last spring it was a lot worse, having to work all those long shifts at the hospital."

"Yeah, she was a mess. I had to spend hours..." he smiles, "loosening her up."

"Hours?" I ask, sounding surprised, hoping to appeal to his ego so he'll tell me more. "You have a lot of stamina."

"I like to think so," he says with a laugh. "The ladies sure seem to like it."

"So you two have been doing this for awhile now, huh?" I ask casually as I pick up my water to take a drink.

He stuffs some of his sandwich in his mouth and chews while he talks. "Lauren and me? We've been doing this for almost a year now. It started out being just every now and then, but then she got demanding." He smiles. "Not that I'm complaining."

Demanding, how? Is he talking about her demands in the bedroom or how often she wanted it? I don't really want to know. I just want to know if they were doing it when she got pregnant.

"That must've been why she was here so much," I say. "When I moved here last March it seemed like she was always here at the deli when I'd stop by."

"Yeah, we'd do it in the back room. Just a quickie." He grins. "The girl's horny as shit. You'd never guess it from how she dresses, all prim and proper, her hair up. But get her alone and, well, I probably shouldn't say. Point is, the girl doesn't hold back."

"Too bad she's moving," I say. "She's going to be really uptight without you."

"I'll still see her. I got friends in New York."

"But she won't want to do those things as much now that she's pregnant."

He rears back. "She's WHAT?"

"Pregnant."

From his reaction it's clear he didn't know. How could he not know? She's not really showing yet but still, I would've assumed she told him.

"Lauren is pregnant?" He runs his hands through his hair. "Fuck!"

"She said it's Corbin's."

He looks at me moment, then exhales a breath. "Corbin. Yeah, that makes sense. Shit, for a minute there I thought you were going to say it was mine."

He goes back to eating his sandwich, seeming to no longer care about the pregnancy news now that he knows it's not his baby.

But it might be.

Now we really need that paternity test. Corbin may still turn out to be the father but there's a good chance he's not. From what Lars said about his numerous encounters with Lauren I'm putting the odds on Lars being the father. Or at least I'm hoping that's the outcome.

CHAPTER TWENTY-SIX

Corbin

"I have to tell you something," Star says as we're sitting on the couch. It's after eight and we just finished dinner.

"What is it?"

"Can I turn this off?" she asks, picking up the TV remote.

"Go ahead."

She shuts off the TV. "I was having a late lunch at the deli today and ran into Lars. He had the day off. He was there to get a sandwich and when he saw me he came over to talk."

Knowing Lars he wanted to do more than talk.

I turn to Star. "Did that asshole hit on you?"

"Asshole? I thought you liked Lars."

"I put up with him. I wouldn't say I like him. He's a player and sleeps around. You're hot so it wouldn't surprise me if he hit on you."

"But he knows I'm dating you."

"Doesn't matter. Guys like him don't care if a girl has a boyfriend."

"Well, he didn't hit on me but he did hit on someone else. Actually, I don't know who started it but he slept with her."

Corbin's brows draw together. "Who are we talking about here?"

"Lauren."

He cocks his head. "Lauren was with Lars? When?"

"For the past year."

He laughs. "Yeah, I don't think so. Lauren would never be with a guy like Lars. One time she told me he looked like a homeless guy. She joked that he probably hadn't showered in days."

"Apparently that didn't matter because according to Lars they've been doing this for a year, and not just now and then, but a lot."

I pause a moment, letting this sink in. Lauren cheated on me? With Lars? It doesn't make sense. Maybe Lars was making it up.

"If that really happened, why would Lars tell you?" I ask. "He knows we're dating. He knows you would tell me."

"Maybe he thinks it doesn't need to be a secret now that you and Lauren aren't dating anymore."

"How did the topic even come up?"

"I mentioned that I'd seen him earlier with Lauren. When I was on break this morning I saw them coming out of the yoga studio and leaving together."

"So they're dating now. That doesn't prove they were together last year."

"Corbin, think about it. Lauren was always going to that deli. And she and Lars went to the same spin class. Remember how you'd say she'd go straight from work to spin class without coming home? It was probably because she was going to Lars' apartment."

I think back to last year. Lauren worked a lot of overnight shifts and had mornings off while I was at work. She could've easily done things with Lars without me finding out.

"I guess it's possible," I say. "I just can't imagine her being with him. They're complete opposites. And I can't imagine her cheating. It's so unlike her."

"But maybe it wasn't. You're always saying you felt like you really didn't know her. So it's possible she was doing all this and you didn't know."

I shake my head, my anger building. "If she really did that..." I don't finish the thought, my mind now picturing her with Lars.

"I know it's hard to believe," Star says, "but I don't think Lars would lie about this. Why would he? He has no reason to."

All last year Lauren lied to me. Cheated on me. Why didn't she just break up with me? She knew I wasn't happy, and she obviously wasn't either if she was with another man so why did she stay with me? And why did I stay with HER? I should've ended things with her a year ago when I wanted to, but instead I stayed, blaming work on our relationship issues when it was so much more than that.

"You know what this means, right?" Star asks.

How could Lauren do this? How could she be with another man in the morning, then be with me at night? Did she not feel even the slightest amount of guilt or shame?

"Corbin," Star says. "Do you know what this means?"

I look up. "It means she cheated."

"More than that." Star grips my hand. "It means this baby may not be yours."

I consider that a moment, then get up and walk around. I'm too anxious to sit. "She would've used a condom with him."

"Maybe. Or maybe not." Star walks over to me. "Corbin, you have to get that paternity test. You have to know if you're really the father. It can't wait. We're making decisions based on something that may not be true."

I was pacing the floor but I stop. "You're sure about this? You really think Lars was telling the truth?"

"Yes. But just to be sure, I'm having Alexis ask Lauren about it."

"Wait—Alexis knows?"

"She didn't until this morning. I told her my theory and she said she'd ask Lauren about it tonight. She's over there right now, helping Lauren pack."

"Lauren's not going to admit to it."

"She might not, but it's worth asking." Star's phone rings. "It's Alexis."

"Put her on speaker but don't tell her I'm here."

Star nods as she answers. "Hey, Alexis."

"Hey, I just left Lauren's place."

"And?"

"She wouldn't tell me anything."

Star's shoulders slump as she looks at me. "Nothing? I thought she'd at least give you some clues."

"She said Lars is just a friend. What'd *you* find out? Did you talk to Lars?"

Star repeats what Lars told her as I pace the floor, shaking my head. I can't believe Lauren cheated. That's not something I ever thought she'd do.

"It's gotta be Lars' baby," Alexis says.

"Not if she used a condom," Star says.

"I'm sure she did sometimes but not always. She's not as perfect as you'd think. She can be careless sometimes, especially when she's tired, and she's always tired. The girl never sleeps."

It's true. Lauren got careless when she was tired. It's why I used to tell her to sleep after her shift instead of going to spin class. But now I know she was going to that class because Lars was there. Maybe they didn't even go to class. Maybe they just went straight to his apartment. Or maybe they went to mine. They better not have done it here. Just thinking they might have makes me even angrier.

I go over to Star and grab the phone from her. "Where is she?"

"Who's this?" Alexis says.

"What are you doing?" Star whispers, trying to take the phone from me.

"It's Corbin," I say to Alexis, pacing the floor again. "Star told me about Lars. Did you really not know about this?"

"No. I swear. Lauren never said a word to me about it."

"And you asked her about it tonight? You asked her if she'd been with Lars?"

"I wasn't that direct. You know how Lauren gets if you accuse her of something."

"So what did you say?"

"I told her I thought Lars was really hot. Then I said I always see him looking at her when we go to the deli and how he totally wants her."

"And what'd she say?"

She laughed and said he's not her type. I told her he doesn't have to be her type to fool around. It's just sex. She brushed me off and said they're just friends, then changed the subject."

"She's really trying to cover this up if she doesn't even tell her best friend."

"I know, which is why I think Lars might be the father."

"Just because she didn't tell you doesn't mean he's the father. She didn't tell you about Lars because she thinks you'll tell Star which will get back to me."

"That might be it, but it also might be that she's trying to cover up the fact that Lars is the father. Star said Lars didn't even know Lauren was pregnant. I'm telling you, Corbin, she's trying to make you the father because that's what she wants. Having a guy like Lars be the father is her worst nightmare. He may be good for a fling but he's not who you want to father your child."

"But that isn't something she can hide. She knows I want a paternity test. I need one in order to move forward in getting legal rights as the father."

"Maybe she thinks she can fake the report. Who knows? When Lauren's desperate, she's capable of anything."

"Where is she right now?" I ask as I walk to the elevator.

"At her parents' house. Why?"

"I'm going over there. If you find out anything else, let me know." I end the call and put Star's phone on the table.

Star races up to me as the elevator opens. "You're really going over there?"

"I need to talk to Lauren. It can't wait."

She nods. "Okay."

I lean down and kiss her. "I love you."

"I love you too."

When I get to Lauren's parents' house I'm greeted by Eve, Lauren's mother. I've never liked her. She feels the same way about me, even though she pretended to be thrilled at the idea of me marrying her daughter. It wasn't me she liked, but my family's money.

"Corbin." Her brows draw together. "What are you doing here? And at such a late hour?"

"I need to talk to Lauren."

"She's asleep." She shoos me away. "Go. You can speak with her tomorrow."

"I need to speak with her now." I go around Eve, walking into the house and straight to Lauren's room.

"Corbin!" Eve calls out, but when I look back she's not following after me. She knows she can't stop me.

I knock on Lauren's door.

"Mother, I'm busy," Lauren yells.

"It's not your mother," I say. "It's Corbin. Open the door."

She does, but just barely. She's in her pajamas, her hair in a ponytail and no makeup on. She actually looks better that way than when she's all done up. I used to tell her that but she never believed me.

"What the hell are you doing here?" Lauren asks. "It's almost nine. I'm going to bed."

"Doesn't look like it," I say, pushing the door open as I go in her room. Her bed is covered in clothes and there are suitcases all over the floor.

"I was going to move them," she says, folding her arms over her chest. "As you can see I'm in the middle of packing. I don't have time for visitors."

"I'm more than a visitor. I'm the father of your child. Isn't that right, Lauren?'"

She stares at me a moment like she's not sure what to say next. Then she narrows her eyes at me. "Just tell me what you want. I have things to do."

I stand in front of her. "I want to know who the father is. The REAL father."

"YOU'RE the father." She walks around me to the bed and starts folding sweaters. "Why are you even asking such a ridiculous question?"

Coming up beside her I say, "I know about you and Lars. I know you were with him when we were together."

"Lars?" She laughs. "Please. You seriously think I'd be with someone like Lars? He works a minimum wage job and doesn't even own a car, not to mention he's been with practically every woman in Boston."

"And yet you were sleeping with him for a year. Probably still are."

"We're not—" She clears her throat as she picks up another sweater. "I'm not even going to address such ludicrous accusations."

"They're not accusations. Lars told Star all about your relationship with him. In detail."

"You got this information from Star?" She turns to me, her hand on her hip. "The girl who stole you from me and would do anything to keep you?" She huffs. "Even you can't be stupid enough to not see her motive here. She's jealous I'm pregnant with your child, and threatened by it. She's afraid you'll leave her to be with me and our baby, not even considering it's the right thing to do."

"Star didn't steal me from you. I broke up with you before I even met Star. And she doesn't have a motive. She doesn't need one. I'm not leaving her, even if this baby IS mine. But I don't

266

think it is. I think you're just saying it's mine because you don't want it to be Lars'."

She says nothing as she picks up another sweater and folds it.

I grab it from her. "Lauren, stop lying to me. And stop lying to yourself. You know this baby isn't mine. Just admit it. You can't hide it forever. I'm getting that paternity test even if I have to take legal action to get it."

She whips her head up and glares at me. "Why are you doing this? Can't you see I'm already under enough stress with the baby and the move and a new job?"

"Yes, and trying to cover up who the father is only adds to your stress. So just end this, Lauren. Get the test and find out who the father is."

"It's you!" Her lips quiver and she collapses down on the bed. "It has to be you," she whispers.

For the first time ever I'm finally seeing her walls crumble. The walls she puts up to hide all her insecurities, like the one that says she's not good enough. That's something I've always known about her but she'd never admit it to me. She wouldn't share anything personal with me, which is another reason our relationship failed.

Shoving her clothes aside I sit beside her. "Lauren, I know this is hard and I know you're panicking right now because this baby wasn't part of your plan. But the plan changed and you need to accept that, just like you need to accept the fact that Lars might be the father."

"It can't be Lars," she says, wiping a tear from her eye. "It just can't. What will people think? My mother? My friends? People at work?"

"That's always been your problem, Lauren. You care too much about what people think instead of doing what makes you happy. Like us. Our relationship. You never really loved me. You were with me because it made sense. Because people approved of us. To everyone else we were the perfect couple and that's what you wanted. Perfection. Even if meant not being happy."

She looks down. "I wanted to love you."

"But you didn't. The two of us just were meant to be. And you can't keep chasing that dream by trying to break up my relationship with Star. Or making me move to New York. Or saying I'm the father of your child."

Her eyes go to mine. "I can't do this on my own."

"You can. And you will. And if it's mine I'll help raise him. It won't just be you."

"And if it's Lars'?" She sighs. "I'm screwed. He can't even take care of himself, let alone a child."

"You don't know that. Maybe he'll step up and be a man when he finds out. Having a child can change a person. Lars might surprise you."

She shakes her head. "Maybe someday but not now. Right now, he's too young. Too immature." Her eyes lift back to mine. "I need it to be yours. You're mature and responsible and you'll be a good father. And if it's yours, people will never know I was with Lars. I can't have anyone knowing that. My mother..." She rolls her eyes. "She'll kill me. I'll never hear the end of it."

"She'll just have to accept it. Lauren, you can't keep worrying about stuff like that. Your focus needs to be on the baby now. Nothing else matters."

She gets up, her back to me. "Could you leave now?"

"Not before you agree to the test."

She sighs. "Fine. I'll call tomorrow and set it up. Now go. Please."

I get up and leave and she shuts the door behind me. On my way out I pass Eve in the living room but keep walking, not saying anything to her and she says nothing to me.

Back at my apartment Star is waiting for me on the couch with Lucky at her side. They both jump up when they see me walk in.

"What happened?" Star asks, running up to me.

"She admitted Lars might be the father."

"She actually told you?"

"Not really," I say, dropping my keys in the bowl. I put my arm around her. "Let's go sit down." When we're on the couch I say, "She didn't come out and tell me she'd slept with Lars but she said enough to confirm it was true."

"And what did you say?"

"Not much. When I got there I was ready to blow up at her for cheating on me and lying about it, but then I just felt sorry for her."

"You felt sorry for her?" Star huffs. "So she's manipulating you again."

"It's not that. I felt sorry for her because she's so focused on what other people expect of her that she can't let herself be happy. I told her that but I don't think it sunk in. Maybe once she has this baby she'll finally realize what's important in life."

"Did she tell you anything about Lars? About their relationship?"

"No, and I didn't ask. I didn't want to know. Knowing she cheated is bad enough. I don't want details."

"What about the test? Did she agree to it?"

"She said she'd set it up tomorrow."

Star leans over and hugs me. "I'm sorry you're having to go through this. Hopefully, we'll have answers soon so we can figure out what to do next."

I pull back and look at her. "You've been amazing through all this. I'd be even more of a mess if it weren't for you."

"I love you. You know I'll always support you." She smiles. "And I owe you. You gave me a place to stay when I lost my apartment. You even bought me clothes."

"You keep forgetting I'm the reason all that stuff happened to you. If it hadn't been for me you'd be——"

"Living in some crappy apartment with crazy roommates, working that horrible job with the mean boss, and dating losers I met on the internet."

I laugh. "You were going to try online dating?"

"Maybe. Who knows? The point is, you saved me from all that."

"By almost killing you," I remind her.

She shrugs. "It all worked out."

I pull her into my arms and kiss her. "Let's go to bed."

"It's only nine."

"I said bed, not sleep."

She gives me that smile I love and we go to our room.

That night I actually sleep, which I haven't done since finding out about the pregnancy. But I'm feeling better about it now. Seeing Lauren tonight, seeing her show actual emotion, made me think maybe she's starting to change. If so, maybe dealing with her won't be such a nightmare going forward. Or maybe that's just wishful thinking.

The next morning Lauren calls to tell me she arranged for the paternity test for both Lars and me. She says she called Lars after I left last night and told him he might be the father. I was shocked she called him that fast, and even more shocked she actually set up the test. Part of me was sure she was just agreeing to it to get rid of me last night, but maybe she, too, is tired of wondering who the father is and just wants to find out.

Over the weekend Star and I are a nervous wreck as we wait for the results. They aren't due to come in until the middle of next week. Friday was Lauren's last day at the hospital and she'll have a week off to move before starting her new job. Lars actually offered to help her move, which isn't like him at all, according to Star. I really don't know him that well but Star does and said he'd rather be playing video games or skateboarding than doing actual work. So maybe he really will step up and be a man if this baby turns out to be his.

By Monday my nervousness has eased and I'm back to telling myself everything will work out, even if I end up being the father. Worrying about it isn't productive and I need to focus on my patients.

"Dr. Sterling," my nurse says as I'm leaving an exam room. "You have a phone call."

"It'll have to wait. I have a patient in room four."

"Dr. Kellins took room four. She was done early with her previous patient so she took room four so they wouldn't have to wait. The call is on line two."

"I'll take it in my office." I go to my desk and pick up the phone. "Hello, this is Dr. Sterling."

"Corbin, it's Lauren."

"Lauren? Why did you call the office phone?"

"I didn't want you answering your phone with a patient there, especially given why I'm calling."

"This is about the test," I say, sitting down.

"Yes. The results arrived early."

"And?" I ask, my heart beating out of my chest.

There's a long pause and then I hear her sigh. "It's not yours."

I collapse back in my chair, letting out the breath I was holding.

"I haven't told Lars yet," she says.

"Isn't he in New York with you?"

"Yes. He's staying with me. Some things in the apartment needed to be fixed and the landlord said it'd be weeks before he could send the handyman over so Lars is taking care of it."

"Lars knows how to fix things?"

"Surprisingly, he can fix most anything. He said his stepfather taught him when he was younger. Anyway, he's fixing the sink right now."

"Lauren, you need to tell him. I'm sure he's as anxious as I was about the results."

"Yes, but not in the same way."

"Meaning what?"

"He wants this. He wants it to be his."

"He does?"

"He's so excited he even bought a book with baby names. He's been listing off possible names for days. He's driving me crazy."

I smile. "Lauren, that's great. It means he really wants this. He wants to be a dad. And the fact that he helped you move and is fixing up your place shows he's ready for this. He's not as immature and irresponsible as you thought."

"He really has changed since I told him he might be the father. I didn't even know he had this side of him. But I still don't know if there's a future for us. We're so completely different. He didn't even go to college."

"That doesn't mean he won't be a good father. Or a good husband someday."

She laughs. "Husband? My parents would kill me if I married Lars. They'd definitely disown me."

"Stop worrying about them. If you love him, marry him. Star and I are nothing alike but I'm still marrying her."

"You and Star are getting married?" Lauren asks.

"Not yet. I haven't even asked. But I plan to, and if she says yes, I'll marry her without an ounce of hesitation, despite my parents' objections. I don't even care if they come to the wedding. It isn't about them. Same with your parents. You need to do what's right for you, not them, and if Lars is the guy, then go for it."

"I'm really not sure how I feel about him. It's always been casual between us but now...now it feels different. More serious. I'm not used to that."

"Give it some time. Get to know each other. See how things go."

"I guess I could." She pauses. "It's really strange having my ex encourage me to be with the man I was cheating on him with."

"It's all in the past. And right now, the last thing you need is someone telling you what you did wrong. I'm sure your mother's doing plenty of that."

"She is, along with my father."

"I'm just trying to be a friend, Lauren. We were friends long before we dated and probably should have kept it that way."

"Probably," she mutters.

"As your friend, I want you to be happy, and maybe Lars is the guy who'll make you happy."

"Lauren?" I hear a guy say.

"That's Lars. I should go."

"Tell him the results. Don't put it off. Just tell him."

"I will. Goodbye, Corbin."

"Bye."

That might have been the most mature, civilized conversation the two of us have ever had. Maybe she's starting to change because of this baby. A baby she never expected to come into her life but who I have a feeling will change her for the better.

It makes me think of Star and how she came into my life, unexpectedly, and made my life better. I'm so much happier with her. I'm not so serious. I have a more open mind. I'm more positive. I'm just a better person with her.

Leaving my office I see Maya, or Dr. Kellins as she's known around here, going down the hall.

"Hey, Maya."

She turns. "Yes?"

I walk up to her. "Would you mind covering for me for a half hour or so?"

"Sure. Is everything okay?"

I smile. "Better than okay. Everything's great. I'll be back soon. I promise."

I race outside to my car and drive to the coffee shop where Star is working. Walking in, I see her behind the counter. Alexis is there too.

"Hey!" Star goes around the counter and hugs me. "What are you doing here?"

"I wanted to talk to you."

Star looks back at Alexis. "Can I take a minute?"

"Go ahead," she says with a smile, almost like she already knows the news. Maybe Lauren told her.

"Let's go over here," I say, taking Star to a table near the back. But I don't sit down. I'm too excited about the news.

"What is it?" Star asks. "You're making me nervous."

I smile. "It's not mine."

"The baby?" she asks, hesitantly. "It's not yours? Are you sure?"

"Positive. The test results came back early and it is definitely not mine."

She hugs me. "Corbin, that's great!"

"I wanted to tell you in person. I knew you'd be happy."

She lets me go. "What about you? Are you happy? I know part of you was excited about having a baby."

"But not with Lauren. I'd love to have a baby someday but only with the right person. Hopefully, that person will be you."

She smiles. "I'm hoping that too."

I bring her into my arms. "It's over, and we can finally move forward. Lauren is gone. The baby isn't mine. We can live our lives, just the two of us."

"Don't forget Lucky."

"Yes." I laugh. "And Lucky, our dog-child."

Feelings of relief and happiness wash over me as I hold Star in my arms. Just like our time living apart, this whole thing with Lauren was just another test to see if my relationship with Star was real or just something we both rushed into during a bad time in our lives. And it proved, once again, that it's real. If we made it through this, we can make it through anything.

CHAPTER TWENTY-SEVEN

One Year Later

Star

"So we'll meet tomorrow at ten?" Brielle asks. She's my lab partner in biology and we have to meet tomorrow to finish up our report.

"Yeah," I tell her. "At the coffee shop."

"See you then!" She walks off as I continue along the path that winds through campus.

I'm back in school now at a four year college. I haven't decided on a major. For now I'm just taking the general requirements. It's summer and I'm only taking one class. In the fall I'll take more. I kept my job at the coffee shop but cut back on my hours now that I'm going to school.

Corbin is still working at the clinic but he's thinking about opening his own practice or maybe partnering with another doctor. He's in no hurry to decide. He likes what he's doing and likes the regular hours, so for now he'll stay where he's at.

We're both really happy, not just with our jobs and school but with each other. Every day together seems better than the last. And every day I wake up wondering if this is real. I used to have the absolute worst luck and now here I am, living with a hot doctor who is also my best friend and the man of my dreams. How is that possible?

My head is so far in the clouds thinking about Corbin that I run into some guy.

"Sorry, I wasn't—" I stop when I look up and see that the guy I slammed into is Corbin. "What are you doing here?"

"I came to see you." He rubs his wrist. "I think you broke it."

"Seriously?" I ask, reaching for it. "Let me see it."

"I'm kidding." He laughs. "Didn't you see me coming?"

"No. I wasn't paying attention."

"You need to be careful. If you're not paying attention you might run someone over. Believe me, I know this firsthand."

I smile. "But running someone over could lead to love."

He smiles back. "Only if you're lucky."

"Which I'm usually not."

He takes my hand and starts walking. "How was class?"

"Good. Corbin, why are you here?"

"Because I couldn't wait any longer."

"For what?"

He keeps walking, heading toward a park that's next to the campus. It's a gorgeous day. Warm and sunny and not too windy.

"Corbin, are you going to explain what's going on here?" I ask as we cross the road that takes us to the park.

"I was sitting in my office thinking about you, and about us, and I just couldn't wait."

"Couldn't wait for what? I don't get it."

I hear a dog barking, a familiar bark. I turn to my right and see Lucky running toward me, along with Alexis. She's got his leash but he's pulling on her, making her run to catch up.

"Lucky!" I lean down and rub his head as he licks my cheek, his version of hello. "What are you doing with Alexis?"

"I'm the dog walker today," she says with a laugh. "More like runner with this one."

"Sorry about that," Corbin says. "He takes off when he's excited."

"Here you go." She hands him the leash and smiles. "See ya later."

"You're leaving?" I ask, standing up.

"Have to get back to work." She waves as she walks off. "Have fun!"

I turn to Corbin. "What's going on here? Not that I don't love seeing you but I don't get why you left work in the middle of the day."

"I told you, I couldn't wait."

"Wait for what? You're not making sense."

He looks down at Lucky. "Should we tell her?"

He sneezes, which almost sounds like 'yes' in dog language.

"I agree," he says to Lucky. "Lucky, sit."

He sits and looks up at Corbin.

"Check his collar," Corbin says to me.

"Why? What's wrong with his collar?"

"Just check it. See if there's something on it."

I kneel down and move Lucky's fur aside to get to his collar.

"I don't see anything," I say, laughing as Lucky licks my face. "Lucky, that's enough kisses." And then I notice it. The little pouch hanging from Lucky's collar. I take it off and stand up. "Is this what you mean?"

Corbin nods. "Open it."

I reach into the pouch and pull out a ring. A ring with a huge sparkling diamond. "Oh my God, is this..." I can't even say it. I'm too shocked.

"A gift from Lucky?" Corbin jokes. "He did help pick it out but it's actually from me." He takes it from me as he gets down on one knee. "Star, I love you more than anything, and although I know you've told me you want to wait, I just couldn't do it anymore. I want to marry you and I don't want to wait. So even if you say no, I'm still going to ask." He holds out the ring. "Star, will you marry me?"

"Yes!" I nod really fast. "Yes, I'll marry you!"

He looks at Lucky. "She said yes, right?"

Lucky barks.

"I thought so too." He puts the ring on my finger, then stands up and kisses me. "I love you."

"I love you too." Then I hug him. "We're getting married!"

Lucky starts barking and jumping on us, trying to be part of the hug.

"We should go celebrate," I say.

"That's where we're going next." He takes my hand and tugs on Lucky's leash. "Let's go, Lucky."

"Where are we going?" I ask as we walk.

"To our engagement party."

"Engagement party?" I stop. "You planned an engagement party not knowing if I'd say yes?"

"I called it a summer cookout until I knew for sure. Now it's an engagement party. Alexis did all the planning."

"Where's it at?"

"Our apartment building. Around the flower gardens out back. George is running the grills. It's nothing too fancy but I think you'll like it."

George is Alexis' boyfriend. They've dated for six months. He's tall with thick dark hair and black-rimmed glasses. He dresses really preppy with polo shirts and khaki pants or dress shirts with plaid ties. Alexis loves that look. It's what got her attention when they met. George is getting his PhD and seems really serious until you get to know him and find out he's really fun and likes to joke around.

"Who's going to be there?" I ask as we're driving.

"Let's see. Alexis and George. A few friends from work. My parents. Your parents."

"My parents are here? They came all this way for what they thought was a cookout?"

"I might've mentioned the proposal part but I had to. I had to ask for their daughter's hand."

"You didn't have to do that. They're glad to get rid of me."

"Actually, your dad choked up. I don't think he was ready for his little girl to get married. And your mom made me promise to take you back there to visit."

"Really? Huh. Maybe they really do miss me."

"Oh, and your friend, Haley, will be there too."

"Seriously? I get to see Haley?" I practically jump out of my seat with excitement. I haven't seen Haley in over a year.

When the car is parked, Corbin turns to me. "Lauren and Lars are there too."

"At the party?"

"Yes, but I can tell them to leave if it makes you uncomfortable. They're in town visiting Lauren's parents. Alexis was over there and accidentally mentioned the party. Lauren called me and asked if she and Lars could be there. I told her yes but now I'm thinking maybe it was a bad idea."

"It's fine. Really. I don't mind. Will the baby be there?"

Corbin smiles. "Yes. Charlie will be there."

"Then they definitely should be there. I want to meet Charlie."

Alexis is still friends with Lauren and she's been showing me baby pictures of Charlie since he was born. He's adorable with his thick blond hair and chubby cheeks. The blond hair alone would've been proof he was Lars' kid but he also has his smile.

Lars and Lauren got married right before Charlie was born. Lars found a sales job in New York that Alexis says pays almost as much as Lauren makes as a doctor. I can totally see Lars working in sales. With his smile and outgoing personality, he's a total sales guy.

Corbin takes my hand as we walk out the doors that lead to the garden.

"Congratulations!" everyone yells when they see us.

Alexis runs up to me and gives me a hug. "Hope you like the party!"

"It's great," I say, noticing all the balloons and the tables set up with food and drinks. The garden is in full bloom, making it the perfect place for a party.

279

Alexis takes Lucky as Haley runs up and hugs me.

"Congrats! You snagged a doctor!" Haley lowers her voice. "And he's really hot!"

I laugh. "It's so good to see you! How'd you get off work?"

"I'm actually working here this week. There's a convention downtown and they're making me work the booth. But I don't have to be there until tomorrow so if I'm free all night."

"That's great!"

"Honey, congratulations," my mom says, appearing behind Haley. My mom's single again. So is my dad, who's right beside her. They're divorced now but they still live in the same house and do stuff together. It's strange. I don't get it.

"Your brother couldn't be here," my dad says. "Had to stay with the wife."

"That's fine. How she's doing?"

"She's good," my mom says, "but tired of being on bed rest."

My brother is married now and his wife is eight months pregnant. They're having a girl.

Corbin's parents come up to me next, and although they pretend to be happy for us, I know they're not thrilled I'm marrying Corbin. But maybe with time they'll accept it.

Music starts playing and Alexis tells everyone to help themselves to the food. People fill their plates, then mingle throughout the garden. It's such a perfect day and a perfect party.

As Corbin goes to talk to one of his friends, I go to the beverage table to grab a water.

"Star, can I talk to you?"

It's Lauren. She snuck up beside me. She looks the same but seems more relaxed than when I knew her before. Maybe motherhood has mellowed her.

"Sure." I take my water and we walk off to the side.

"Congratulations," she says.

"Thanks. To you too. Lars is a great guy."

"He really is." She glances at him and I see him in the distance, holding Charlie. "He's matured a lot the past year. He's a great dad." She looks back at me. "I just wanted to say I'm sorry for the way I acted back when I was living here. I was hung up on this dream of being with Corbin and I would've done just about anything to break you guys apart."

I'm surprised she's being so honest. I didn't think she'd ever admit to that.

"It's all in the past," I say.

She smiles. "I've been seeing a therapist and she said I have to deal with the past before I can truly move forward. I actually do feel better now that I said that."

I just nod, wishing we could end this. Even when she's being nice to me she still makes me uncomfortable. "Could I go meet Charlie?"

Her face lights up. "Yes, of course! I forgot you'd never met him."

We walk over to Lars. Charlie sees his mom and holds his arms out to her.

"Charlie, this is Star," she says as she takes him.

He smiles at me as he hugs his mom.

"He's adorable."

"Hey, Star," Lars says. "Congrats on the engagement."

"Thanks."

"There you are," Corbin says, coming up beside me, his arm going around me.

"Corbin." Lauren smiles at him. "Good to see you."

"You too." He looks over at Lars. "I hear you've got a new job."

Lars shrugs. "Not so new anymore. Been about a year now."

"You like it?"

"Yeah, it's been good."

Charlie reaches for Lars and he takes him from Lauren.

"Cute kid," Corbin says.

Lauren tickles Charlie's tummy and he laughs. "He's growing up way too fast."

"How about you two?" Lars asks. "Planning on kids anytime soon?"

Corbin looks at me. "I'm not sure Star's ready for that."

"I wasn't ready either," Lauren says, looking at Charlie. "Not even close. But it turned out better than I could've imagined."

Lars puts his arm around her. "We should get him down for his nap."

Lauren smiles at Corbin and me. "It was good seeing you both."

"Good seeing you too," Corbin says. He waits for them to leave, then says, "That wasn't so bad, was it?"

"No. She was actually nice to me. She even apologized for how she acted."

"Huh. I guess motherhood has changed her."

"You think it'll change *me*?"

"I hope not." He kisses me. "I love you just the way you are."

"I love you too." I kiss him back.

He looks at me. "Wait, you weren't asking me that because you're—"

"Pregnant?" I smile. "No." I pause. "But I might want that sooner than I told you."

"Really? Like when?"

"Like maybe next year. I mean, you're not getting any younger. You'll be thirty soon. That's really old."

He laughs. "It's not old. But I'm all for starting a family sooner rather than later."

"Then I say we go for it. But first we have to get married. And finish our engagement party." I take his hand. "Let's go."

"Wait. Before you go I want to give you something."

"What?"

"It's not much. Just something I saw at a store and immediately thought of you." He takes it from his pocket but keeps it in his hand. "You know how you always say you have bad luck?"

"Yeah."

"It's not true. Or maybe it used to be but it's not now. It changed the moment I hit you with my car. It may not have seemed lucky at the time but it got us to the place we're at now. I never would've met you if that hadn't happened. And you've had good luck ever since."

"I have, haven't I?" I say, thinking about it.

"So no more saying you have bad luck. Believe it'll be good and it will." He hands me a necklace. "This is so you won't forget."

It's a silver necklace that has the words 'Lucky Star' in silver script letters hanging from the chain.

I smile as I put it on. "I love it! It's perfect!"

"I thought so too." He takes my hand. "Let's go join the party."

As we mingle with our guests I keep looking down at the necklace. Those two little words are exactly how I feel right now. How I've felt since meeting Corbin. And how I'll feel forever, having Corbin at my side.

I have everything I could ever want. I'm happier than I've ever been. My bad luck is gone. Now I'm lucky.

Lucky Star.

www.ingramcontent.com/pod-product-compliance
Lightning Source LLC
Chambersburg PA
CBHW050715180626
46814CB00002B/446